Finding the Way Back to Me

Finding the Way Back to Me

TALISHA RENEE

Finding the Way Back to Me.

"The only way to master love is to practice love."

— DON MIGUEL RUIZ

1

I AM AT a restaurant in the middle of Dallas, sitting across from my fiancé and the woman who claims to have stolen him from me. I was lured here under the pretense that I was meeting Ziggy for dinner so that we could talk and hopefully salvage what is left of our broken engagement, or at least leave this situation with our friendship intact, but when I walked through the restaurant doors, I was accosted by the sight of him with another woman. Part of me wants to laugh loudly in her face as she basks in a glow of superiority, but the other parts of me are sympathetic, and I mourn for her. I mourn for the pieces of her soul that will get lost in loving a man like Ziggy. I wish that I could tell her the real reason why he gives his attention. I could explain that he has this incessant need to feel loved, and as soon as he feels that she has no more to give, he will replace her with another, more eager woman. For a second, I consider grabbing her by the hand and guiding her away from him, but I don't move. Instead, I sit back in my chair, mindfully taking deep breaths because this is the only way to keep my ego in check.

I was not always this calm. In fact, if this confrontation occurred six months ago, I would have jumped across this table and fought for what was mine, but Ziggy is not mine, and I was never his. Now, I know what you may be thinking. How can you not belong to one another if you almost said "I do" in front of God and all of your family and friends? I have asked myself that same question many times over the past five years, but I can't seem to find the answer. So, here I am, sitting with my hands folded in my lap, listening to this woman explain how sorry she is that Ziggy fell in love with her.

The waiter comes to take our order, and Ziggy and his mistress beam with pride as if this is one big happy family gathering. He orders the prime rib steak while she orders a thirty-dollar appetizer, lobster, and champagne for the table. I assume that this is her way of letting me know how far their pockets stretch, but her efforts are childish and unnecessary because I was the one in the trenches with Ziggy as he built his company from the ground up the past three years, and I am fully aware of how much money sits in his account. To be fair, the idea for his app was all his doing, and I must admit that it was a brilliant one, one app that allows you to keep track of your physical health, check in on your mental health, set life goals, listen to over a thousand meditations, and receive a text with daily affirmations. He had a great product, but not enough people knew about it, so I told anyone that I came in contact with to give his app a try.

I even enlisted our friends, coworkers, and family members to help spread the word about his app, and after a few months, he had about seven-hundred active users. You would think that these changes would have impressed Ziggy, but he was still dissatisfied with his lack of popularity and was ready to give up. That's when I got the idea to visit local yoga shops, coffee shops, and any store that would let us post flyers for free. When the app gained 3,000 more followers, I suggested that Ziggy pay for advertising which led to his app being highlighted on several popular social media platforms. It was Ziggy's app, but I believed in it as if it was my own dream. I knew his vision and felt like it was my responsibility as his woman to help build him up, so after an eight hour-work day, I came home and put in four more hours in the home office with Ziggy. His app now has over a million users, and six months ago, he sold it for two million dollars.

During our time together he seemed grateful for all my hard work. After a long day of work, he would run bubble baths, rub my feet, and order takeout from my favorite restaurant since spaghetti is the only thing he knows how to cook. He was always sure to let me know how much he appreciated me, so I thought that meant he really did. Maybe on some level he did truly care for me, but if a person really loves you, can they lie to your face for months and bring another person into the relationship before letting you know that things with you have ended?

"Excuse me, ma'am. Are you quite alright?" The waiter leans over me with a concerned expression. Ziggy also looks concerned, but his mistress looks amused.

"I'm fine." I push my seat away from the table abruptly.

To clarify, I am not fine. My hands are shaking, and my breathing is erratic, and by the time I reach the restroom, my face is covered in tears. I may be out of sorts right now, but I cannot let Ziggy or that woman see me cry. What I really want to do is fight. My mother taught me early on not to be a person who starts drama, but she gave me permission to end drama if it was ever brought to me. I can't say that she would approve of me fighting over a man, but, technically, I wouldn't be fighting for Ziggy. I would be defending my honor.

"Be strong." I say, staring into the mirror. "God, please help me to be strong because if I go out there and slap her in this expensive restaurant, I know I'm going straight to jail."

Flashes of heat begin to take over my body, which is a common symptom for me in stressful situations. I place my hands under the faucet to trigger the sensor, and once the water reaches my hands, I lean over to splash water onto my face. Lifting my head slowly, I open my eyes and look at myself in the mirror. *You can be calm tomorrow, but today you should definitely slap the disrespect out of her.* My anger attempts to convince my conscience to disappear for a while, but, once again, I manage to hold it together.

I walk out of the restroom and head straight to the valet booth to retrieve my car because Ziggy would only win if I act crazy in a restaurant full of rich white people. The "angry black woman" is what he has tried to make me out to be the past few months. He even reached out to several of my family and friends hoping to convince them of his innocence, but they saw through his façade. They were all there to witness me help build his company from the ground up, and with the first signs of success, he changed and behaved as if everything was all his doing. To make matters worse, he cheated on me the last six months of our relationship, but the fault rests solely on me. I had signs of his true character way before I agreed to marry him. So, my question to myself is why did I waste so much time trying to make him my husband?

I get to the valet booth to turn in my ticket and retrieve my car, but the worker is so occupied with his phone that he doesn't seem to notice me. I clear my throat hoping to get his attention, but he continues to ignore me, obviously consumed by the video playing on his cell phone. If this was any other night, I would be patient, but I've had enough of being calm, so I reach over to where the keys are stored and snatch mine off of the hook and shake them in his face relentlessly.

"Lady, what is your problem?" He jumps angrily from his seat, but his scowl is quickly replaced with a huge grin. He looks over my head, ignoring me once again, and begins to speak to the person behind me.

"Hey, aren't you the guy who sings that *make love to me song?*" He walks from behind his booth to greet one of the many pompous customers who dine at this overpriced establishment. I take another deep breath, desperate to hold it together a little while longer, but my efforts are short-lived when a tear slips from my eyes and a wail escapes my lips.

"Yeah man, that's me, but I think this lady is waiting on you to finish helping her." The man's tone is laced with concern.

Returning his attention to me, the valet driver quickly apologizes and asks for my keys. Rather than letting the stranger see me cry, I mumble a quick thank you and walk to the curb to wait for my car. My back is turned to him, but I can feel his eyes boring a hole into me. I am tempted to ditch my attitude and offer a formal thank you, but I probably have mascara running down my face, and I do not need anyone to witness me looking like this especially not someone who apparently has a popular song about making love. After what I have just been through, I am staying away from all forms of love which includes saying I love you, making love, or hearing songs about love because love is for suckers.

"Babe, I've missed you so much!" I hear a woman squeal loudly.

I adjust my body, curious to see if she is talking to my mystery guy. *Well not my mystery guy per se but the kind stranger.* If I turn at the right angle, he will only be able to see the side of my face, and because I am nosey, I am willing to risk being seen. I turn slowly and see a tall thin woman wearing a sparkly pink dress wrapping her arms around mystery guy's neck. She is so concerned with the gift in his hand that she doesn't notice that throughout their entire interaction his attention is focused solely on me. His hazel colored eyes are filled with concern, and he looks as though he is about to say something when the valet pulls up with my car, and I jump in.

"That was Noah freaking Daniels." I whisper in astonishment before driving away.

2

THE PAST TWO weeks were sort of a blur. I went to work, came home, ordered takeout, and laid on my couch until it was time to do it all over again the next day. The only people I have stayed in constant communication with are my parents who happen to be vacationing in Jamaica, so most of our conversations have been brief, and they are none the wiser as to my current predicament. My sister Justice on the other hand, has left me several angry and concerned voicemails all of which I responded to through text. She threatened to show up at my house, but with a newborn baby, I know that she doesn't have the time to fly in from Atlanta. She did, however, have time to assign my best friend and coworker, Janae, to keep tabs on me. In their defense, they are the two people that I would typically go to for support in times like this, but they both warned me about Ziggy, and rather than hearing them say *I told you so*, I decided that it would be best to keep my feelings to myself.

My doorbell rings, and I hop off of the couch, grabbing my wallet along the way to pay the delivery guy. Tonight's takeout is pineapple fried rice from a Thai restaurant down the street from my condo. I realize that I could have used this as an opportunity to get out of the house, but why do that when I can have someone bring food to me? I look out of the peephole only to be disappointed. Janae and three of our friends from our monthly book club group are standing in my doorway, and it looks like they intercepted my food.

"Shit," I say in a hushed tone.

"Go ahead and open the door, Willow. We hear you in there cursing." She is peering into the peephole.

"Sorry ladies but I can't host book club today. I'm not feeling well, and the doctor says that I'm contagious." I fake cough a few times, hoping to send them on their way.

"Listen, I gave you your space for two weeks, but I have strict orders from Justice to make you shower and spend time with your friends, and before you say no, please understand that we intercepted the food you had delivered. Plus, we brought snacks, drinks, and a book that I know you're going to love." She is holding up a bottle of wine and the Queen Afua book that I've been dying to read titled *Sacred Woman*.

"Come on now, sacred woman. Let your sisters in," she mocks.

I step back, opening the door wide enough for everyone to enter, and they zoom past me, knowing that I could change my mind at any moment. Lonnie, Renee, and Brandy make a beeline for the kitchen and start pulling out plates while Janae disappears into my room. I roll my eyes and slam the door before plopping back down on the couch, which has been used as more of a bed lately. I know that I shouldn't mope for as long as I have been, but the house doesn't feel as lonely when I am lounging in front of a 65" inch TV with tons of romantic movies to watch.

"What are you doing in my room, Janae?" I call out, not wanting to move from my spot. She ignores my question, and after about five minutes, she comes out of the room, sits on the couch across from me, and shakes her head in a disapproving manner.

"Your bathtub awaits you. I already started the water and added lavender oil." Her tone is soft but stern.

She knows that I consider bubble baths with lavender oil to be one of life's greatest treasures, so despite my anger, I hop off of the couch and stomp into my room, sure to slam the door behind me. Janae and I have been friends since we were ten years old, so naturally, we have nursed each other through heartbreak, but I have never allowed myself to wallow for more than four days. In fact, I have always been the one to take care of others, and I hate when people try to take care of me. As much as I hate to admit it, her and Justice are right. I've had two weeks to process things, and now it is time to move on even if it hurts, so I decide to use my time in the bathtub to figure out what my next moves in life will be.

I currently work as an assistant at one of the biggest fashion companies in the country. As much as I wish that I could say that I love my job, I must admit that I have outgrown my role as assistant, and every day that I go back there I become more unhappy. My role as assistant was only supposed to be temporary, but after three years, I am still stuck working at the same company. I studied Sociology in college, and I easily graduated at the top of my class, but I was never as passionate about school as I was art. Society made it clear that my generation was expected to go to school and find a job, so that's exactly what I did. As a child, I used art to release emotion. I wrote poetry, danced, and painted whenever I felt inspired, but after working eight hours a day as an assistant and putting so much energy into my relationship, I started to ignore the things that made me happy. Now that Ziggy's junk is no longer crowding the spare room, I might as well put it to good use and tap back into my creative side. As cheesy as it sounds, I think I am going to call it my *healing room*.

◆ ◆ ◆

I walk back into the living room to find the ladies drinking wine and listening to music. Having them here makes me realize just how much I needed to be around genuine people who care about me. If they hadn't forced their way into my home, I am not sure if I would have gotten off of the couch long enough to realize that it was time to get back to a routine. I planned to wallow for at least three more days before I kicked myself into gear, but seeing them here and happy instantly lifts my spirits, so I strut into the center of the room to get their attention.

"She looks good. She feels good. What more could you ask for?" I say, jokingly.

"Good because we were ready to have an intervention." Renee throws a chip at me.

"Whatever! I know you only came over just so you can be nosey and find out what happened with Ziggy and me."

"We did not!" Lonnie says sincerely.

"I believe you Lonnie, but nobody else said anything."

"I'll be honest; I came over to find out what happened between you and Ziggy but mostly to make sure that you were okay," Brandy confesses.

"Thank you for honesty." I roll my eyes jokingly before continuing, "I'll make a deal with you. Today we can relax and talk about my failed relationship, but next month, we are officially starting our book club. We always talk about sisterhood, so let's put our money where our mouths are. Deal?"

"Deal." They all agree.

"Speaking of sisterhood," Lonnie stands and reaches into her bag pulling out a tan envelope, "we decided to send you on a trip next week. You'll get to spend a few days in California doing yoga, meditation, and all that hippie shit you're into."

"And the coolest part is that it's hosted by that famous yoga chick you like," Renee happily adds.

"Who? Zane?" I say in disbelief.

"Yes, ma'am. Zane is the host of the retreat, and before you come up with a thousand reasons why you can't go, please know that I already cleared it with Carter. He will be out of town with his family those days, so I made up a story about needing your help on one of my projects. You will have four days to relax like you deserve to," Janae adds.

"Really?" I am surprised by their generosity. I knew my friends loved me, but I didn't know they loved me enough to plan a surprise like this.

"Girl, you pour into everyone all the time, so let us return the favor," Janae says, sincerely.

"Yeah because self-love is the best love!" Brandy quotes the lyrics from my favorite song, which causes us all to erupt in laughter.

We spend the next few hours talking about relationships, our dreams, things we need to let go of and things we hope to manifest. I filled them in on what happened at the restaurant, but I left out the part about Noah Daniels. He is a new R&B artist who is becoming quite popular. His songs are constantly played on the radio, and he has an album coming out this year. I don't feel comfortable gossiping about a man that has women making up stories about him on a daily basis, and technically, nothing happened between us. No words were exchanged; he simply saw a woman in distress and showed concern. I plan to tell Janae the full story once the other ladies leave, but I know that she is going to hassle me for not introducing myself. She doesn't understand that I am not interested in meeting anyone new, even if the guy is Noah Daniels.

"Hello. Earth to Willow!" Janae waves her hands at me.

"Oh, sorry. I was daydreaming. What were you saying?" I cover up the fact that I was actually replaying the events of that night.

"I said that you needed to get out of the house for a while. Let's go out tonight." She has a mischievous grin.

"Or, we can get dinner and then go to the store to get some materials for me to paint? You know it's been years since I've picked up a brush, but I think it's time for me to start creating again." I flash a huge grin.

"Ugh. You used to be so fun. I want my best friend back!" she complains.

"Okay, fine. If you go with me to get materials now, then I promise to go out with you tonight." I reach my hand out for her to shake.

"Deal. But we have to try that new reggae spot. I heard they have amazing food, and we are going to find you a beautiful man to dance on," she says, confidently.

"Wow. It is way too soon for me to be thinking about men. At least let me attend my healing retreat before you start trying to find me a new boyfriend," I state firmly.

"Uh. We know when an argument is brewing, so we're going to leave, so you two can talk. Make sure you call us and let us know how your trip went." Lonnie Brandy, and Renee walk over to give us both a hug.

"I'm actually headed out too," I lie. I didn't have plans to leave without Janae, but I do not want to argue. My spirit has been lifted for the first time in weeks, and I don't want to ruin it with an argument between my best friend and me, so I grab my keys and wait for her to follow me out. I know that she didn't mean any harm by her suggestion, but I just got out of a five-year relationship, and she's acting as if it meant nothing.

Pouting, she says, "Willow, I apologize for upsetting you, but you take things too literal. It's okay to live. You don't always have to have every single part of your life figured out right this second. When my last relationship ended, you didn't just walk away and let me sulk. You were with me every step of the way, and you also gave me tons of fun distractions until it no longer hurt to think about what he did to me."

"Fine!" I throw my hands up in surrender. "Let's have an epic night tonight because tomorrow I'm spending the entire day packing for my trip and creating in my healing room."

3

I WAKE UP to a pounding head, which is the first sign that I might have partied a little too hard last night. The second sign comes when I walk out of the room to find Janae who is laid out on my kitchen floor with a blanket and a half-eaten sandwich in her hand. "What the heck did we do last night?" I step over her. The last thing I remember is several people in the bar chanting for me to take a shot. I rarely drink, and when I do, it's wine or mimosas, so after a few shots, my alter ego was in full effect. We danced the entire night until my dance partner mistook my dance moves as an invitation to come home with me. He leaned in for a kiss, and that was my cue to go home.

"Please, stop talking so loud." Janae reaches out to grab my ankle.

"So, I guess those shots caught up with you after all?" I grab a bottle of water and a bottle of aspirin from out of the kitchen drawer.

"Spare me the lecture, please? All I want is to eat my sandwich in peace." She reaches up to grab the items from me.

"There will be no lecture. I went out and drank just like you did, and I imagine that my head feels just as bad as yours does. If I hadn't made a commitment to myself, I would be laid out on the floor next to you, but I made a promise, so I am about to sit here and struggle through this headache. I need to work on some new sketches because I am tired of being an assistant and I need to start designing more of my own pieces."

"It's about time! I've been telling you to invest in yourself for years now. You see me working a full-time job, but I also teach yoga and make jewelry on the side. I'm just glad that you're finally listening to me."

"I'm listening, and I hear you loud and clear. I may not always like your approach, but I know that you always have my best interest in mind, so thank you for taking me out last night and for always being here to lecture and listen to me."

"You've always been there for me, so I will always be there for you." She folds her hands to make a heart sign. This is the part where we would usually hug, but she seems pretty adamant about staying on the floor, so I accept her gesture by making the same symbol with my hands.

"Once you finish your sandwich, you should go lay in my bed for a while and then join me in my healing room." I remove the blanket from over her face and toss it in my room.

"Okay, let me take a quick nap, and I'll be there."

◆ ◆ ◆

Three hours go by before Janae finally joins me. Her hair is disheveled, but she looks well rested.

"Hey, sleepy head." I pat the seat next to me, signaling her to sit.

"Willow, what have you been doing?" She looks around the room in shock.

"I'm not really sure. I tried to paint, but I don't like how it turned out." I shrug.

"Yeah, the painting definitely has room for improvement, but what are all these papers doing on the floor? Are you writing poetry again?" she says, enthusiastically.

"I wrote *a* poem, as in *one*. The rest of this is scribble. I guess some of it could be used as song lyrics, but I'm not really feeling any of it except for this poem."

"Okay, so do I get to hear you read this one poem, or do you plan to keep me in suspense?" she says, sarcastically.

I return her sarcasm with an eye roll then I grab the journal where the poem is written. Usually I would give a dramatic speech about how it's been a while since I've shared one of my poems, but each time I did that

I was operating out of fear. I feel this poem deep down in my core, and it deserves to be shared without trepidation, so I toss the journal back where it was and close my eyes. I had it memorized as soon as I wrote it.

I dared him to touch the deepest parts of me.
To become intimate with my soul
Before he entered me and without hesitation —
He accepted willingly.
Exploring my mind
And
quickly gaining access to my body.
Access
To
My
Body
Which is my temple.
Did I forget to mention that I am royalty?
So naturally he gifted me with beautiful things and reminded me that I
carried the same strength and beauty as Nefertiti.
Speaking in poetic soliloquy...
Saying "we"
His I's became WE
So, I assumed that he loved me —
Unselfishly.
Then another woman tossed a challenge his way
And his ego answered just as quickly as it did for me.

I open my eyes and find Janae staring at me with a blank expression. She looks as if she is unimpressed, and for a split second, I worry that she hated the poem. I stand up and begin to clean the papers that are sprawled across the room.

"That is some deep shit!" She finally speaks and stands to applaud me. "Do you know how many times I've wanted a man to become intimate with my soul before he entered me? Sheesh girl. I felt every word of that poem."

"Dammit, Janae. You had me worried!" I ball up one of the pieces of paper and toss it at her.

"Worried for what? You don't need me to tell you how amazing you are, Willow. You have to stop looking for other people's approval," she says firmly.

"You're right, but I guess that means I shouldn't ask for your opinion on a situation that happened the night I met Ziggy and his minion at the restaurant." I shrug my shoulders and walk out of the room, and she follows me just as I expected her to.

"Spill it!" she says, eagerly, and I do. I tell her the entire story, and this time, I don't omit any of the details. Her first reaction is to be mad at me for not telling her sooner, but she quickly agrees with my decision not to share it with the other ladies.

"Wait, so you mean to tell me that Ziggy was in the restaurant feeling like he was on top of the world while you were outside getting ogled by THE Noah Daniels?" She falls to the floor, unable to contain her laughter.

"That's the thing. I don't think he was trying to come onto me. It seemed like he was genuinely concerned with my well-being, but it doesn't matter now anyways because neither of us said a word."

"Uh, hello. That's what social media is for. Send him a message and let him know that you're okay. I bet he will remember you!" She reaches for my phone.

"No, I am not contacting him, and this is exactly why I didn't want to tell you. I need to pack for my trip, so I'll catch up with you later." I give her a quick hug and walk to my door, holding it open for her to leave.

"You might feel like you're kicking me out, but I actually needed to leave and go run errands, so enjoy your trip and call me soon." She smirks before walking out of the door.

4

I AM WALKING off of the plane second guessing my decision to attend this trip. I did some research on the healing retreat and though it sounds like an amazing opportunity; I have never been to an event like it before. I never even attended camp as a kid, yet here I am preparing to spend the next four days with total strangers like some sort of girl scout. I grab my suitcase from baggage claim and head towards the exit to find my ride. My younger brother, Omari, works in Los Angeles a couple months out of the year, so I am spending a few hours with him before we make the hour drive to the house where I will be staying this weekend.

Omari is two years younger than me, and though he claims that I am his role model, he has lived a life that is the total opposite of mine. In high school, he bought a camera and started saving for a trip to Africa. He wanted to start his career by capturing beauty in the motherland, so while most of his friends were leaving for college, he was starting his own photography business. After a few years, his work gained popularity, and he is now a full-time artist. We haven't seen one another in a while, so I am glad to be spending time with him, but I must admit that I am also using him as a distraction to calm my nerves before I head to the retreat.

I scan the row of cars in the arrival section of the airport, but he is nowhere in sight, so I reach into my bag to grab my cellphone, deciding that it would be easier to call him. I smile when a text comes through, instructing me to turn around. I look behind me to find him standing with a group of drivers that are wearing black suits and holding signs with passengers' names on them. Their signs have first and last names, but Omari is holding a sign that says: **Looking for a wannabe Erykah Badu mixed with a little India Arie.**

"Are you sure you want to start with your jokes? Remember what happened the last time?" I remind him of the time when Justice and I put salt in his water every day for a week straight because he wouldn't stop pranking us.

"Willow, I'm a grown man now, and your childish threats no longer work on me," he replies, confidently.

"Whatever. Just take this bag or else I'll call mama and tell her you aren't being the gentleman she raised you to be."

"You've always been a snitch." He takes the suitcase from me.

"I've never actually snitched on you, but it's fun to threaten you. Now, where are we going?" I ask excitedly.

"I know you don't have a lot of time, but I'd like to show you a new project that I'm working on. Then, maybe we can go to the beach and grab lunch before I drop you off." He tosses my suitcase into the trunk.

"That's cool with me." I pull him in for a hug.

We drive down the Pacific Coast Highway in comfortable silence. Omari is sitting in the driver's seat with the windows down as he nods his head to the music playing loudly over the car speakers. My hand is rested out of the window as the breeze softly makes contact with my skin. My hair is blowing all over my head which in normal circumstances would annoy me, but in this moment, it feels like absolute freedom. It's interesting how you can either choose to recognize the little things that matter the most during tough times or completely overlook it all.

"You good over there?" Omari puts on his blinker to exit the highway.

"Yeah. Why are you asking me that?" I am confused by his question.

"Because I switched the music to Bobby Brown's "Rock Wit'cha" song like five minutes ago, and you didn't sing all loud and off key like you usually do. I hope you're not over there thinking about Ziggy." He scoffs.

"No Omari, I was most definitely not thinking about Ziggy." I punch him in his right arm.

"Ouch," he squeals, "I'm telling ma you hit me."

"And I'm telling mama that you're being a jerk." I cross my arms, annoyed by his accusation.

"Seriously Willow, how are you feeling?" He pulls the car into park and turns to face me.

"Honestly, I didn't realize just how much I needed this vacation until I got off the plane."

"Well, you know that you're welcome here anytime, and I'll be back in Dallas in a couple of months for a few gigs. Just do me a favor and promise that you won't let him back into your space because I will catch a flight to kick his ass, and if I run into him in Dallas, it's a done deal." He hops out of the car, ending our conversation just as quickly as it began.

"I don't need you to fight my battles, Omari." I follow him into the studio.

"Then make smarter choices Willow," he responds firmly. His tone reminds me of our father which annoys me. He is my little brother, and he has no right to lecture me about my life.

As much as I want to come back with a rebuttal, I am too distracted when he turns on the light in the studio. There are pictures all over the walls and paintings spread across the room. It looks hectic, but I can tell that there is also a sense of order to the chaos. He follows me proudly as I make my way around the room, studying each piece of art. His collection consists of black and white images of people from all walks of life, and each one demands that you pay attention. After I finish checking out the collection, he leads me to a covered easel sitting near the back of the room. He nods in approval as I carefully remove the sheet, and I am taken aback when I find a giant painting of me as a kid running freely in a field of sunflowers.

"What made you paint me?" I say after a minute or so of studying the painting. I was a wild child growing up, but I never ran in a field full of flowers. Though now I wish I had.

"I dreamt it, and I swear I saw it clear as day. At first, I wasn't going to paint it because I know you hate taking pictures and would most likely hate having a self-portrait made, but I figured you would like to hang this in your house someday."

"Wow," is all I manage to say.

"Is that a good wow or a bad wow? Ma is the one who told me to paint it after I showed her the sketch."

"It's a good wow, but I'm jealous of the little girl in this picture. She seems so free. I bet she never expected a confused version of herself to be staring back at her."

"Maybe she couldn't imagine it. Maybe this is nothing more than dried paint on a canvas. Either way this version of you still exists somewhere. Even if it is buried deep inside of you." His words cause a lump to form in my throat, but I swallow it, choosing to focus on his talent instead of my emotions.

"One thing I do know is that mama was right when she used to say that one day your name would be blown in the wind."

"Don't forget she said that one day yours would be too." He pushes my shoulder softly.

"Dang, right!" I laugh.

◆ ◆ ◆

We spend the next two hours sitting in Omari's studio catching up on each other's lives. We didn't get to go to the beach or sit down for a meal. Instead, we ordered takeout and started the hour drive to the healing retreat in the hills. He listened attentively as I explained everything that happened between Ziggy and me. He tried to hide his anger, but I could see it in the tensing of his jaw. He also filled me in on his dating life, which is full of noncommittal acquaintances. It's interesting how a man can be protective over his sister but have little regard for other women. Hearing about his escapades was so entertaining that the time flew by, and I am surprised when the GPS announces our arrival.

"You nervous?" Omari smirks at me.

"Not at all." I roll my eyes in response.

"Yes, you are, but it's okay. People love you everywhere you go. Remember when mama use to tell you that favor isn't fair? Just have fun this weekend and try to relax," he says supportively.

"First, I get a lecture from Janae and now you? What is the world coming to?" I respond, sarcastically.

"Whatever." He unlocks the door. "I love you. Have fun. Now get out."

"I love you too and thanks for the ride, baby brother."

"You're welcome, and hey … have fun sis."

5

T HE BROCHURE FOR the retreat described the location as a beautiful California home, but they failed to mention that this place is more like a mansion. It has tons of windows and a beautiful green lawn with wind chimes and lights strewn across the yard. I wouldn't be surprised to learn that this house belongs to some snooty rich person who only comes out here once a year for vacation. There have to be at least ten rooms in a place like this, and I bet there is a basketball court or a giant movie room. I expected to stay somewhere nice, but my girls definitely rolled out the red carpet for me with this gift.

"Nice isn't it?" A woman walks up from behind me. I try to hide my surprise, but my body definitely shifted in defense.

"Yes ma'am. If this is what the outside looks like, I can only imagine how beautiful the inside is." I relax after getting a good look at the older woman with grey locs that fall past her waist.

"Shall we check it out together then?" She rings the doorbell.

"Sure." I nod my head in agreement. "I'm Willow, by the way."

"Nice to meet you Willow, I'm Lotus. And hey, ignore anything you hear about me this weekend. I'm not as bad as they say." She winks playfully and walks ahead of me into the house, leaving me clueless as to what she means.

We are greeted by a tall high-spirited woman named Zora who is in charge of guiding the guests to their rooms. I overhear her tell Lotus that she will be staying in the guesthouse on the opposite side of the property, and by the woman's reaction to her being here, I can tell that Lotus is someone she holds in high regard. She doesn't look familiar, and her name doesn't ring a bell, but Zora is definitely a fan of whatever it is that Lotus does for a living. I make a mental note to research her name later tonight.

"I hope to see you later, Willow." Lotus waves to me.

"Yes, ma'am. See you later." I walk in the opposite direction towards my room.

"I see you've already met Lotus," Zora says, excitedly.

"Yeah, she seems nice," I reply casually.

"You mean you don't know who she is?" Shock is written all over her face.

"No, but I get the feeling that I should. Who is she?"

"You're young, so that may be why you haven't heard of her. She's a well-known therapist, holistic healer, and author. She's also Zane's grandmother and our chef for the weekend."

"Wow, so I just met an elder, and I addressed her nonchalantly." I am slightly embarrassed.

"Lotus actually prefers to blend in, so I bet you made a great first impression." Zora tries to reassure me. "Well, here we are. This is where you will be staying for the next few days." She points to a room on the left side of the hallway.

"Also, the meet and greet dinner starts in an hour, and all guests are encouraged to attend. It will help you meet the other ladies and get an idea of what activities we have planned for the weekend," she smiles assuredly.

"Sounds good and thank you, Zora." I accept the key from her.

"It was my pleasure." She leaves me to check out my room.

I unlock the door and walk straight towards the Queen sized bed, collapsing onto it face-forward. I still cannot believe that I agreed to stay here all weekend, but now that I am here, I might as well stay and see how things go. I roll onto my back and reach for my phone to let my friends know that I made it safely. Janae responds right away, reminding me to have fun and use this time to focus on self. I reply with a thumbs up emoji and exit out of our messages. A silver flash in the corner of the room catches my eye, and I walk over to inspect the basket with silver ribbon tied across it. I bypass the notecard that has my name written in fancy writing and head straight for the goodies. To my surprise, the basket is filled with sticky notes, essential oils, and pens which I immediately turn my nose up to because what sane person would consider sticky notes and pens to be a gift? I pick up the card to gain a better understanding of this gift basket, and after reading the instructions, I feel like a brat because this isn't some random thoughtless gift.

> *We often speak life into everyone and everything*
> *And forget to nourish ourselves.*
> *This weekend we are disrupting that pattern and*
> *actively choosing to go within.*
> *So, take bubble baths with oils.*
> *Leave love notes around the room*
> *And romance yourself.*
> *Remind YOU of how YOU deserve to be cherished.*

I grab one of the pens and write three intentions for the next three days: I promise to laugh as much as I can, to practice self-care, and to figure out how to let go of the past. I post each of the sticky notes on the mirror in the bathroom so that they will be in my direct view every morning that I am here. Feeling accomplished, I lean against the sink and stare at the goals I just set for myself. If I wasn't short on time, I would run a bubble bath, but a shower will have to do, so I walk into the bathroom and adjust the knob on the shower. A light knock at the door catches my attention. I look over at the nightstand to check the time. I have about forty-five minutes to shower and get dressed for the meet and greet. I would prefer to ignore the knock, but it could be Zora, so I walk over to the door and press my eye against it. I laugh when I realize that there is no peephole for me to look through which serves as proof that I have been actively avoiding social settings way too much over the past few weeks.

"Hi." I offer a smile.

"Sorry, did I catch you at a bad time?" A petite woman with curly hair stares back at me apprehensively.

"I was about to start getting ready for the meet and greet, but it's ok. Can I help you with something?" I reply.

"Well, I'm staying in the room next door and wanted to see if you'd like to walk down for the meet and greet together. I went to ask the woman staying on the other side of me, but she was already heading down there."

"Sure. Let me finish getting dressed, and I'll meet you in the hallway in about twenty minutes?" I am relieved to have an ally.

"Awesome. I'll see you in twenty minutes. Oh, and I'm Nova by the way." She walks backwards and almost passes her room.

"Nice to meet you, Nova. I'm Willow." I try not to laugh at her awkwardness.

◆ ◆ ◆

Twenty-five minutes go by and Nova is nowhere in sight. I do not want to make a bad impression on my first day here, so I knock on her door to see if I should continue to wait for her or head downstairs with the rest of the group. After the third knock, she finally opens the door and is dressed in the same t-shirt and leggings from when I saw her earlier. Though I am frustrated, I force myself to practice patience.

"You ready?" I politely ask, hoping to hide my irritation.

"No, I tried on three different outfits but none of them look right. No point in both of us being late, so you go ahead and go." She falls face forward onto the bed.

I step inside the doorway and peek at the clothes that she has scattered around. Most of the outfits appear to be either too dressy or too casual. Without explaining myself, I turn towards my room to grab an outfit. Zora didn't mention a dress code, so I decided to dress casually in a denim jacket and frayed high waisted jeans. Most of my wardrobe consists of shorts, tank tops, and yoga pants since the majority of our planned activities will be physical and outdoors, but I did throw in two outfits that I upcycled at the last minute in case we went out as a group this weekend.

"Here, try this on." I hold out one of my designs.

"Are you sure you don't mind me borrowing your clothes?" She reaches for the hanger but suddenly pauses to say "because I would definitely understand if you felt weird about it. We did just meet like thirty minutes ago, so my feelings won't be hurt."

"It's no big deal." I hope to hurry her along. "I had the outfit for a while and made a few changes to the design last weekend. It would be good to see it on someone other than myself."

"Wait, you made this?" She holds the design up for inspection.

I release a heavy sigh, no longer willing or able to hide my annoyance. Nova finally catches on and disappears into the bathroom to change. I stand in the doorway, counting the seconds that go by. The meet and greet started five minutes ago so walking down a few minutes early to blend in with everyone else is no longer an option, but at least I won't be alone when I walk down to meet the others.

◆ ◆ ◆

We rush down the stairs only to be met by an empty living room with no sign of the group's whereabouts. The sound of clinking dishes causes us to turn our attention towards the kitchen where Lotus is too busy preparing dinner to notice us. I shake my head in disbelief when Nova takes a seat at the kitchen island and lifts the foil off of one of the food trays without permission. She too seems to be unaware of Lotus' apparent fame, or maybe she isn't awe-struck by it.

"Did we miss the meet and greet?" I look around the empty living room.

"Chile, you better get out of the kitchen unless you want me to put you to work." Lotus moves the tray away from Nova.

"Can I please try some before everybody else comes down here. I'm starving." She pushes her lips forward in a frown.

"You can taste the okra, but you'll have to wait until I serve dinner to have anything else. Willow, you go ahead and grab a few for yourself and then you two should head to the backyard with the rest of the group. They got started a few minutes ago." She hands us each a fork.

"Dang it. I knew we were late! Nova, grab your okra and come on, or I'm leaving you," I say, dramatically.

"So, you're really going to stand there and pretend not to want some of these?" Nova dangles the fork in front of me, and I reluctantly grab a few of the okra fries and stuff my mouth before heading towards the door.

"Don't pretend like that wasn't the best okra you've ever tasted." Lotus winks in my direction.

We join the group, and just as I predicted, all eyes are on Nova and me. Their lively conversation comes to a halt as soon as we step outside which increases the nervousness that I was already feeling. I do a quick count in my head to tally up the number of people present. There are seven of us including Zane, who I quickly recognize seated amongst the women in the circle. While everyone else looks timid, Zane is sitting confidently as though the world is at her feet. The two of us find an empty space to squeeze in and take our seats.

"Welcome, ladies. We were just about to begin introducing ourselves. No one else has offered to go first, so would either of you like to start?" Zane smiles at us brightly.

"I will." I realize that Nova's silence means she doesn't want to speak first which is honestly quite surprising based off of her interaction with Lotus and me thus far.

"Awesome. Start by telling us your name, where you're from, why you decided to attend this retreat, and a fun fact about yourself." Zane folds her hands in her lap and leans in to listen attentively.

"My name is Willow Westbrook. I am twenty-nine years old. I'm from Dallas, Texas, and my friends actually surprised me with this trip. I guess they felt that I was in desperate need of relaxation, and I must admit that I sort of agree with them. I guess something fun is that I work as an assistant at a fashion company, but my dream is to be a stylist and have my own clothing line."

"She styled and designed my outfit even though she says it's not a big deal." Nova stands for the group to see. Her sudden burst of energy causes everyone to laugh which leads to an easing of tension which then leads to questions about the dress.

"Do you have a website?"

"Do you have other designs with you?"

"How much do you charge?"

"Do you have any business cards?"

They bombard me with a list of questions to which I have no answers for. I haven't created a website; I don't have business cards or social media pages to promote, and I didn't bring any pieces to sell out of respect for Zane and what this weekend represents. I didn't want anyone to feel as though I came here to hustle them into supporting me. I came here to relax and start addressing the pain I've been holding onto, but I take note of their interest.

"I don't have any of those things yet, but all of your questions just helped me realize that I have work to do when I get home. I truly appreciate your interest in my designs." I hope to steer the conversation back to introductions.

"We are only a few hours into our four days together, and you sisters are already supporting one another. That truly warms my heart. Willow, you have obvious talent, so don't give up. Leave us your information, so we can keep up with your progress and support your product when it launches," Zane says sincerely.

"Now, let's keep the momentum going. Who's next?" She looks around the circle, and this time, her question results in raised hands from all of the women.

These women's stories are proof that we all come from different backgrounds but have one thing in common; we each seek healing - healing from relationships, from the loss of a loved one, from lack of purpose - and want to address the fear of being alone. These women look so happy and put together just like me, but underneath our exterior, there is pain. I imagine that our stories are similar to millions of other people around the world.

Once introductions are complete, Zane goes over the agenda for the next four days. She informs us that we will wake up at six-thirty every morning to do yoga. Then, we will have breakfast together, which will be prepared by Lotus. After breakfast, we will have two hours to relax and complete the required journal work before meeting up for group meditation. Lunch will be provided around noon and then we will attend a one on one session with either Zane or Lotus. She didn't go into much detail about the one-on-one sessions, but she assured us that we would be given the proper tools to begin our healing process. After our sessions we will attend a session on self-care in which we will learn about the different tools that can be used to spend time with and work on self. Dinner is served from six thirty to eight o'clock each night; afterwards, we are free to go to the beach or explore the local area. However, the door to the house locks at nine o'clock, so she asked that we respect the rules and be in on time. The retreat will end with a hike at night on the third day to honor the full moon followed by a breakfast feast on the fourth day before departure.

◆ ◆ ◆

The conversation around the dinner table flows more smoothly than it did during the introduction session, but things are still awkward. Minutes of conversation are quickly followed by moments of silence. I assumed that Nova would be her usual chatty self, but she is too busy stuffing her face with food to hold even the slightest conversation. Zane has made several attempts to steer the conversation, but I can tell that the other ladies are still wrapping their minds around the fact that they will be spending the next four days with strangers. I admit that I am nervous to open up in front of a group of strangers myself, but I agreed to come, and I plan to be fully present while I'm here.

"I'm going to the beach after dinner if anyone would like to join me." I break the silence.

"I'll go!" Nova quickly agrees.

"We will too." Alicia and Lizzy, who I learned are best friends and live in South Los Angeles, also agree to come. Their energy seems to match Nova and mine's, so I don't mind them tagging along. The other two ladies in the group politely decline my offer because we only have an hour until curfew. I understand their logic, but with the beach being less than a mile away, I can't deny myself the chance to put my feet in the sand.

"Okay, cool. We can leave as soon as Nova finishes her *third* plate and be back just before the doors lock for the night." I put an emphasis on the word third because the girl does nothing but eat.

"Hey, I'm finished now. Thank you very much." Nova points at her empty plate.

"Don't blame Nova for knowing good cooking," Lotus smiles teasingly. "Now be on your way." She shoos us out of the dining room. Taking her advice, we begin our walk to the beach.

"Remind me why we chose to walk instead of catching a ride?" Nova dramatically leans over holding her stomach.

"Because the beach is literally less than a mile away. All that food is catching up with you, isn't it?" I study her. She looks as if she is about to go into a food induced coma.

"Wow," Alicia chuckles. Her and Lizzy seem to snicker each time Nova or me speaks.

"Yes, but while I'm sleeping peacefully in my bed tonight, you will be in the kitchen warming up leftovers because you were too busy thinking about the beach when you should have been eating," Nova retorts.

"Are you two related somehow or just friends?" Alicia finally asks.

"Neither." We reply in unison.

"Today was our first-time meeting," I explain.

"Oh. We just assumed you knew each other since you walked into the meet and greet together."

"And you go back and forth in a way that only family and friends do," Lizzy adds.

"That's because she reminds me of my best friend." I am suddenly aware of my instant connection to her.

"I only have a brother, but I could see someone mistaking us for cousins." Nova nods her head in approval.

"You might end up being close friends after this weekend. I know I'm happy to have my best friend with me," Alicia confesses.

"I don't think I could focus with my best friend being here. We would rely on each other too much, and sometimes, it's best not to have a comfort during situations like this. I am happy that I met you three though. Plus, I need tour guides for when I come back to visit," I say jokingly.

"Same goes for you. I have family in Dallas, so if we don't end up hating each other after this weekend, maybe we can meet up for lunch when I visit, and, in the meantime, we should all exchange information, so we can stay in touch," Nova suggests.

"Deal." I say making a pact with each of them.

"Sounds like a plan," Lizzy and Alicia agree.

I smile when we finally start to see signs guiding us towards the beach. I look over to Nova who seems to be captivated by the sounds of laughter and crashing waves. I guess her mind finally recognized the essence of her surroundings even though her full belly and aching feet wanted to convince her not to make the trip here. Our toes begin to sink into the sand as we walk onto the beach. I find myself starring in awe of the people who are swimming in the ocean with smiles on their faces.

"We only have about thirty minutes before the door to the house locks. Does anyone actually plan to get in the water, or do you want to find somewhere to sit? I am completely fine with staying dry, so this is not a complaint," Lizzy asks.

"I think I want to walk down a little further and at least get my toes wet." I am skeptical of my own admission. I've only been to the beach three times in my entire life, and I have never actually gone in the ocean, but the waves are calling to me, so I inch towards the water but come to a sudden halt when I reach the point where the sand and waves begin to meet. I gasp in excitement as the ice-cold water washes over my toes and then I plant my feet firmly into the earth, preparing for the next wave. I steady myself for the pushback, but the tide comes in smaller this time, causing me to inch forward slowly to greet it.

"Aren't you going to get in?" Nova walks next to me.

"This is as far as I plan to go. I didn't grow up around beaches, and I don't trust the ocean enough to just thrust myself into it," I admit.

"Well, I'm fine with that because I just got my hair done, and I really didn't want to get it wet," she confesses.

"Same." Alicia seconds Nova's notion.

"Why didn't anyone else get in?" I am interested to hear their reasons. If I grew up around the beach like them, I would have learned to trust it by now.

"Honestly, I don't want to get my hair wet tonight, but I'll be by your side over the next four days if you decide to conquer your fear and go in further. I was a lifeguard in high school, so I got you," Nova offers.

"Yeah and Alicia and I will be on guard, ready to jump in if you need us," Lizzy giggles.

"Good because if I do decide to go further, I'll need all the emotional support I can get." I laugh, but underneath the joke there is a serious layer of truth.

6

WE WALK INSIDE the house with three minutes to spare. Nova, Lizzy, and Alicia go straight to their rooms, but the grumbling sounds coming from my stomach lead me to the kitchen. I open the fridge and grab the containers of leftover food from tonight's dinner, scooping a healthy serving of okra, sweet potatoes, and black-eyed peas onto my plate. I am fully aware that there is a microwave less than two feet away, but I dig into the cold plate of food deciding not to waste time warming it up. If my mom saw me right now, she would say that people are going to think that she never fed me home cooked meals as a child, but I am starving, and I could care less what anyone thinks right now.

"Wow, I knew I could cook, but I didn't know it was that good." Lotus' voice startles me, causing me to cough up some of my food.

"Sorry. I didn't mean to scare you. I came for libations." She grabs the teakettle from the stove.

"It's okay." I am trying to catch my breath. "I just didn't expect anyone to walk behind me. The food is amazing by the way. I never like leftovers, but here I am eating *cold leftovers*."

"You do know there's a microwave and a stove a few steps away, right?" she chuckles.

"Yes ma'am, but I wanted to hurry up and eat so that I can shower and rest up for tomorrow. I have a feeling it's going to be a *long* day."

"Maybe." She shrugs. "But I've learned not to fret over tomorrow. It will be whatever kind of day you need it to be."

"Hmm. I hope so." I scoop another bite of food into my mouth.

"While you hold onto hope, I'll have faith and know that it will be." She lifts her cup in salutation and excuses herself from the kitchen.

7

AFTER OUR YOGA session, Nova, Alicia, Lizzy, and I meet in the kitchen to have breakfast. It felt refreshing to do yoga outside in the sun, but we are all now starving and ready to fill our stomachs with food. Before the yoga session, I found out that our one-on-one sessions begin today, and I have been chosen to have Lotus as my mentor while all three of my new friends get to meet with Zane. I considered trying to coax one of them to switch mentors with me, but I figured that wouldn't go over too well with Zane or Lotus. So, I will be following Zane's instructions and finding Lotus after breakfast.

"You look nervous." Nova observes me from the across the table.

"You would be too if Lotus was your mentor." I pout.

"I know I would be!" Alicia admits.

"I don't know", Lizzy says, "Tori and Riley have her as their mentor, and they seem excited to work with her," she shrugs.

"That's because they are fans of her work. I heard that she is some sort of well-known holistic healer, so I don't doubt her ability to help me but I'm not sure that I can open up to a complete stranger. At least with Zane I'm familiar with her work; Lotus is not only a complete stranger, but she's also much older than me. What if she can't relate?"

"Lotus is a family friend, so I know that she isn't as bad as she seems. Just give her a fair try," Nova reassures me.

"You're probably right, but can I at least complain in peace for the next fifteen minutes and twenty-three seconds before I have to meet with her?" I ask, jokingly.

"Sure, but when she smells the negative energy radiating from you, don't blame us," Nova teases.

"You know, I actually heard that is one of her superpowers." Lizzy adds in her two cents.

"Oh, whatever!" I laugh. "I'm about to get a smoothie from the kitchen and then find Lotus, so let's meet up later?"

"Sure, if you survive your session with Lotus then we will see you later." Lizzy sounds serious, but her smirk lets me know that she is only teasing.

"Wouldn't it be funny if your sessions end up being worse than mine?" I quickly leave the table, deciding it best to leave the conversation before they think of a comeback.

I walk over to Lotus' assistant, Mrs. Carla, who is in the kitchen eating breakfast with Zora, one of the staff members helping out for the weekend. They inform me that Lotus is in the garden, picking vegetables for tonight's dinner and is expecting me to join her, so I take a few sips of my smoothie, no longer hungry due to nerves but knowing that I will need to coat my stomach, and head for the backyard.

"Hey, Willow?" Carla calls me back over.

"Yeah?" I ask.

"I just wanted to say that I'm glad your energy picked up. We wouldn't want Lotus to smell the negative energy radiating from you, now would we?" She grins before nodding her head towards the backdoor.

8

*T*HIS HOUSE IS so big that I literally have to follow an outlined path to the garden because if I make one wrong turn, I could end up at the tennis court or at one of the two swimming pools on the property. I hear Lotus humming on my way to the garden and find her with her back turned to me as she kneels onto the soil, inspecting the greens that are growing. Rather than rushing up to her, I stand back, careful not to startle her the way she startled me last night in the kitchen.

"Don't just stand there, Willow. Grab a pair of gloves and join me," she commands, without ever lifting her head.

"Ms. Lotus, that was such a mother thing you just did." I am impressed by her ability to recognize me.

"Well, I've raised five children, so I've gotten good at hearing footsteps when they approach. Also, last night you mentioned that you were anxious, so I knew it could only be you standing there like a *Nervous Nelly*."

"Oh." I feel slightly offended by her choice of words. It's only natural to be nervous, and I am not the only attendee that is nervous to be here.

"So, did you take my advice and trust that today would be whatever kind of day you needed it to be?" She wastes no time jumping into conversation.

"Honestly, I woke up with a positive outlook but then I found out that you were my mentor instead of Zane, and I sort of freaked out. As an elder, I hold you in high regard, and the women here respect and admire you so much. I just don't know if I'm comfortable sharing openly with you."

"So, you think because I'm old I can't relate to you?" she laughs. "You know, my life wasn't always so spiritual and put together. People see me now and forget that I am more than a title, but I won't force you to talk to me."

"So, you really won't force me to talk, and you aren't curious to know my reason for attending the retreat?" I study her.

"I didn't say I wasn't curious; I said I won't force you to speak. It has never been my style to pry things out of people, and I think you will open up to me when you're ready," she says, matter-of-factly.

"Okay?" I am confused by her style of mentorship. It's either reverse psychology, or she really is this mellow?

"Have you ever worked in a garden before?" She eyes the gloves that I am holding in the palm of my hands rather than on my fingers.

"No, but I've always wanted to learn. I have plants all around my condo, but I don't have a yard to grow vegetables."

"I can give you a few tips during our time together if you're interested."

"I would appreciate that, and if you have time, maybe you can share your black-eyed peas recipe with me?"

"Never ask for someone's secret recipes before establishing a trusting relationship with them," she smirks.

"Fine," I huff. "Is this the part where we negotiate a deal?"

"Sure, I'll make a deal with you. I'll teach you how to garden and also show you how to make two dishes of your choosing *if* you let me do my job and help you in healing."

"Fine," I yield to her request. "But I've never had a counseling session or done anything formal like this, so I need you to tell me where to start."

"There are no rules to how this is supposed to go. I want you to start wherever you feel comfortable, but first, let's take a few deep breaths together." She closes her eyes.

Following her lead, I place my left hand on my heart and the other on my belly and take a deep inhale and slow exhale. As if on cue, tears begin to well in my eyes despite my will to keep them in. I haven't shared my true feelings with someone in a while, and I realize that lately my story consists of nothing but sadness and sorrow.

"I guess I should start with my reason for being here this weekend?" I ask, nervously.

"Yes, let's start there." Lotus nods in agreement.

"Well I ended a five-year relationship and allowed myself to wallow on the couch for over two weeks which scared my friends because that is so unlike me. I usually roll with the punches, but this relationship took a lot out of me, and laying on the couch seemed like the easiest way to deal with things. I guess my friends saw that I was in a rut and wanted to do something to help me out of it."

"It sounds like your friends really care about you," she admits.

"They do. Especially my best friend. She was not happy watching me put my all into loving a man who went against his promise to honor me and instead betrayed and disrespected me and everything we built together."

"May I ask what he did to dishonor you? To dishonor the relationship?"

"He lied; he cheated, and the biggest insult was how he treated me once the relationship was coming to an end. He literally behaved as if our five years meant nothing."

"How did you find out he was lying to you and cheating?"

"I had a feeling. I guess you could call it woman's intuition, and like a fool, I ignored that voice inside of my head for weeks because I wasn't ready to face the truth. This probably sounds weak, but I put so much into my relationship, and I wasn't willing to end it simply because I had *a feeling*."

"So, what did you do?"

"For a while, I went on as if everything was okay. Then one day, my best friend called to say that she thought she saw him out at a bar with another woman. She put her head down to grab her phone to take a picture of the two of them, but when she looked up, they were gone. Without proof, I was left with a decision. I could either ask him directly or continue to ignore that feeling."

"Hmm." She makes eye contact with me. "What is it about him that made you want to ignore your intuition?"

"I've known him since I was twenty-four years old, and we had plans to get married. I guess I just wasn't ready to be alone, but he forced my hand."

"How did it feel to walk away from him? From the relationship?"

"It felt amazing to be free of the drama, but it was also one of the hardest things I've ever had to do. Hence, my wallowing for two weeks."

"But you got back up, and now, you're here," she smiles.

"I got back up, and now, I'm here," I affirm.

"I believe that relationships are meant to teach us things. Those things can be both good and bad. Is there anything that you learned from this relationship?"

"I guess you could say that I manifested *what* and *who* I needed at a specific point in time, but our relationship wasn't meant to last longer than I allowed it to."

"Can you explain what you mean?"

"Well, the first few years of our relationship were really good. We were young, and we believed in one another wholeheartedly. He taught me how to be strong and stand firm in what I believed, and I showed him how important it was to dream and create goals. My mistake was confusing his dreams as our shared dreams. I showed him and his dreams way more love than I ever showed myself which in turn resulted in a horrible ending to a five-year relationship. Maybe it was God's way of punishing me for my own lack of self-love. I've thought about it, but I don't know."

"One thing I've learned is that change almost always requires a loss. What do you think about that?"

"Do you mean that I had to lose him to find me?" I nod my head in understanding.

"I do, and if that logic holds true for you then I think you owe it to yourself to spend the next few days starting the process of self-love. I along with the other women at the retreat will support you along the way. *If* you let us."

"I'm willing to try," I say, half-heartedly.

"That's a start. Now, let's finish gardening, so we can have our next session in the kitchen rather than the garden," she winks.

9

"SOMEBODY HAD A great session," Nova peers over the kitchen counter at Lotus and me. Everyone else cleared out to give us privacy, but Nova nominated herself as our taste tester for today's cooking lesson which shouldn't surprise me because all she does is eat. My mentoring sessions with Lotus the past two days have been a step in the right direction. She takes a no-nonsense approach, but she seems sincere in her willingness to help me.

"Do I need to tell Zane to assign me as your mentor too?" Lotus sounds serious, but the smile lines forming around the corners of her mouth give her away.

"If it means I get to spend time with the marvelous holistic healer and chef, Ms. Lotus Hill, then absolutely," Nova quickly responds.

"You know your mother and I go way back, right?" Lotus smiles, daringly.

"Ms. Lotus, are you threatening to tell on me?" Nova asks.

"I'm simply saying that I will call an old friend if necessary."

"Fine. I'll leave." Nova mumbles before exiting the kitchen.

"Her mom must be the real deal if she jumped up that fast." I laugh as Nova disappears from the kitchen.

"Nova is as sweet as pie, but she's greedy. I don't understand how she stays so small the way she eats," Lotus chuckles.

"She's a mess, but this trip wouldn't be the same without her," I admit.

"I'm glad you two are becoming friends. You would both be good influences on each other."

"Have you known her folks for a long time?" I ask, curiously.

"I met her mother thirty years ago at a conference, and we've been good friends ever since."

"Well, remind me to never introduce you to my parents because you don't need that kind of power over me," I say, jokingly.

"You never know. I may have already crossed paths with your parents. Now, stop stalling and grab that apron. You get to help me make lunch for the group today."

"Ms. Lotus, how did a little cooking lesson turn into lunch for the group?" I am confused by the turn of events. She doesn't respond; instead, she hands me an apron and turns on the faucet for me to do as instructed.

◆ ◆ ◆

After about an hour of cooking lessons, I began to understand why Lotus is well respected in her field of work. She managed to cook for a group of twelve while teaching me and continuing our mentoring session from yesterday. Her manner of openness coupled with her sincerity allowed for a natural bond to be created between us, and I feel a new sense of commitment to myself. Throughout the cooking lesson, I could tell that she was asking questions to get a sense of how serious I am about continuing the work required to heal once the retreat is over. She kept casually asking about my fears, my strengths, and my perceived limitations, and though I am afraid to go deeper, I know that I have to. In the past two days, a recollection of painful memories has stirred up emotions that I haven't felt in a long time, and I do not want to continue to hold onto them.

"Ms. Lotus, have you ever felt as though you gave away pieces of your soul that were meant for you and God alone, but you were so naïve and vulnerable that you gave those pieces away willingly and called it love?"

"I did many times until I decided that love shouldn't require me to lose myself just to find another," she admits.

"Some days I find myself being angry for giving my body, time, and energy to someone who wasn't worthy of it. I feel like I'm still carrying his energy around with me, and I'm ready to shake it off, but I don't know how. I thought I healed myself, yet here I am again angry at the past."

"Who told you that healing was a one-time thing?" She challenges my thought.

"Nobody, but in my defense, no one told me that I'd have to keep re-healing the same pain either."

"It sounds like this recent situation with this Ziggy fella has caused old feelings to resurface, but that doesn't give you the right to discredit yourself for all the healing you've done thus far."

"You're right," I admit.

"Yesterday, you shared that you felt as though Ziggy was the manifestation of who you were at a certain point in time. If I remember correctly, you said that you saw the lessons that came from being with him as punishment for a lack of self-love?"

"That's right."

"So, you manifested punishment?"

"I guess I did, but I wasn't conscious of it."

"Who taught you how to love?"

"I learned by example, I guess. From watching my parents and just living in this world in general. It seems like we as humans measure love by how much shit we can tolerate from another person, but that's a lie."

"Are your parents still together?"

"They are, and I wouldn't want it any other way. Their dynamic is one that I admire, and I can tell that they really love one another, but if I'm honest, I have to admit that there were times when it seemed like they were unhappy but stayed together out of comfort."

"And you feel that was the wrong thing to do?"

"I don't think it's wrong, but I also don't feel that it's right."

"Hmm," she says, "I have an idea, but you have to trust me. It may seem silly or feel uncomfortable, but it seems to always work for me."

"Okay." I nod my head in agreement.

"Let's try an exercise. Close your eyes and put your hand over your heart. Now, tell yourself that you love you. Literally think or say the words

I love you and then I want you to sit and listen to what words come to mind. See if your higher self has a message for you."

I lean back against the counter and cautiously close my eyes, afraid that I won't be able to hear myself. Still, I open my mouth, deciding it best to say the words aloud.

"I love you. I love you and I am listening," I inhale deep into my belly, and on the exhale, tears began to flow unreservedly. I've heard my inner wisdom before, but it has never been as clear as this.

"You don't have to tell me what you heard, but you owe it to yourself to listen. I believe that you can have love again; you can run a successful business, and you can have the family that you hope for, but you need to love yourself first because that's where you'll find God and all good things." Lotus reaches for my hand in comfort.

"Ms. Lotus, I heard my higher self, but I think my higher self is confused," I say in a serious tone.

"What did you hear?" She is amused by my reaction.

"This is going to sound weird, but I need to go back to the beach. I know Zane has activities planned for the group, but this important." The words pour from my lips before I even comprehend what it is that I'm actually saying.

"Okay, calm down and explain it to me," she chuckles.

"I'm going to face one of my biggest fears by going into the ocean. It's how I plan to release the things I've been holding onto. It probably sounds cliché, but it's what I need to do."

"Okay."

"That's all you're going to say. No long speech or questions?"

"There's no need for a speech or questions. I'll talk to Zane and explain everything, but there is one condition... Nova and I are coming with you. Now, let's get this lunch served and meet back here in two hours."

"Wow, so I'm really going to do this?"

"If Nova and I have anything to do with it, you're doing it. Now, go wash up for lunch and join your friends. I can get my assistant to help me from here."

10

I GOT A text from Lotus saying that she received an urgent phone call and would need to meet Nova and I at the beach. I considered inviting Lizzy and Alicia to come with us but decided not to make a fuss of things. To everyone else, the beach is simply a pastime where going into the water is expected, but it is also a vast body of water that is unpredictable and has the ability to be both calm and chaotic which terrifies the hell out of me. It may sound crazy, but when I closed my eyes in the kitchen yesterday, I heard myself clear as day, and I was told to use this fear to thrust myself forward into a new chapter of life, and that's exactly what I plan to do. However, I will be bringing a life jacket in case I was confused, and my higher self actually said to thrust myself into motion, as in exercise and activity, not the ocean.

"Do you think Zane is mad that we're both missing the group hike?" I try to spark conversation on our walk to the beach.

"This weekend is about growth, and if this is what it takes for you to grow, I think she'd be supportive of that. Plus, with a stern grandmother like Lotus, I don't think Zane had much of a choice but to let us go," Nova chuckles uncontrollably.

"You're real confident now, but you were quiet when she kicked you out of the kitchen earlier."

"Oh, miss thing, I wasn't scared, I just don't believe in disrespecting my elders," Nova quickly defends herself. She tries to sound serious but erupts with laughter.

"I joke a lot but, in all seriousness, I'm honored to be a part of your journey, Willow. Thank you for including me."

Finding the Way Back to Me

"Truthfully, it was Lotus' idea, but I wouldn't have wanted it any other way."

"Wow, so Lotus really does see the value in me being here?" She stops in her tracks.

"Of course, she does. We all do," I say, sincerely.

"That's good to hear," she relaxes.

"Hey, I've been meaning to ask why you signed up for this retreat? You never told us during introductions." I realize that she probably kept it quiet for a reason.

"It's sort of a long story. I actually didn't sign up. My mom was supposed to be one of the mentors here this weekend, so she invited me to tag along, but something came up, and she had to cancel. When I told her that I wasn't going, she enlisted my older brother, Teddy, to convince me that this weekend was a great opportunity for me. He thought he was selling me on this trip, but truthfully, he scared the shit out of me. The way he described Lotus when she is in her teaching mode sounded intense which is hilarious because now that I'm here, I realize that her intensity is wrapped in layers of care, and I am really glad I came, but don't tell her that!"

"I won't tell her as long as you promise not to tell anyone that I'm terrified to get in this water."

"Oh, that's obvious. We can literally smell your fear from a mile away," she scoffs, covering her nose.

"Sorry girl! It's my nerves. Don't pretend like you've never had bubble guts."

"I'm not judging you. I'm just saying that your nervous farts are sort of a dead giveaway. Now, let's find Lotus. She said to meet her on a part of the beach that's more private."

"Good because I do not need anyone to witness how fast I'm about to dunk my head under the water and come right back up." I follow her lead.

11

HE SOUND OF drums catches our attention, and Nova and I debate
as to whether we should continue our search for Lotus or postpone it
see where the music is coming from. After several minutes of arguing, we
decide to satisfy our curiosity and walk towards the drumming. We trace
the sounds to a secluded part of the beach where a group of women are
laughing and dancing. While it is understood to me that the appropriate
thing to do is watch from afar, Nova decides that she would rather go closer
to see what the hype is about.

"Come on. Let's introduce ourselves." Nova struts towards the group.

"Are you crazy? We don't know those people." I follow her cautiously.

"You forget that I'm an L.A. native, so I know how these things work.
It's completely normal for people to join bonfire parties on the beach." She
walks ahead and leaves me behind once again.

"Nova, I'm curious to see what's going on too, but I do not want to be
kidnapped." I kick sand around, trying to decide what to do.

"Okay, well come find me when you are done being scary." She yells
over her shoulder.

I watch as she joins the group of women and points in my direction.
They all begin to wave their hands, signaling for me to join them, and after
a few seconds, I finally give in. As I get closer, I realize that the group of
strangers are actually the women from the retreat, and they are all smiling
at me in excitement as if they are aware of a secret or a joke that I wasn't in
on. I stop in my tracks, no longer willing or able to keep walking towards
them. This was something that I wanted to do privately with Lotus and
Nova, but now, I have ten pairs of eyes staring back at me.

"I thought you figured the surprise out earlier when I disappeared, but I see I was wrong. You look shocked." Lotus walks towards me.

"I appreciate them being here, but I don't want everybody staring at me all night. They probably think this whole idea is dramatic."

"See, that's where you're wrong. They actually thought the idea sounded like a unique way to let go of things. You aren't the only person here with problems, beloved. I know you had an original idea of how you wanted tonight to go, but Zane and I came up with an alternate plan. The concept is the same though, and we will absolutely still be supporting you as you do what you came here for."

"Ugh." I peek over my shoulder to take another look at the women dancing and laughing together.

"This weekend is all about support and sisterhood, and I take those two things very seriously. With so much of our culture being stolen from our ancestors, it's easy for today's generations to forget how important it was and still is for us to support one another as African people. I hope you don't see the group being here as an intrusion of privacy because that was never my intention. All of these women came here to heal some part of themselves, so I figured if you needed to do something symbolic like this to heal that the others might need to as well."

"I get that, and I don't mean to sound ungrateful, but you did not have to go all out and hire a drummer and set up a bonfire. I have a feeling you did most of this with me in mind."

"Don't be so cocky, Willow." She winks at me playfully. "Now, the drummer will only be here for another fifteen minutes. You aren't going to let us dance and have all the fun, are you?" She offers me her hand.

"I guess I should come show you a few moves." I place my hand in hers.

We make our way into the middle of the circle where the ladies are shaking and moving like they have no care in the world. I immediately spot Nova next to Lizzy and Alicia who appear to be following Nova's guidance. The two women are swaying their hips and throwing their hands up, trying to keep up with her fast pace which in no way matches the beat that the drummer is playing. As I watch them, I remember Omari's warning to have fun this weekend, so I take my place next to the

three women, and we dance until we all fall to the ground in sheer tired-
ness ten minutes later.

"Can I get everyone to form a circle?" Zane yells over the laughter and
loud conversations going on amongst the group.

"Sure." We all say in unison, forming a circle like we did our first day
here except this time we aren't strangers.

"First, I want to say thank you to my dear friend Kofi for playing the
djembe drum for us tonight. Now that everyone has loosened up a bit from
dancing, I hoped that we could spend a few minutes connecting. Is that
cool with you all?" Zane asks. We nod our heads in approval.

"Okay, so because she is the elder of the group, I am going to give the
floor to my grandmother. She is the one who made it possible for us to be
here tonight, so let's give thanks for her."

"You did a good thing Ms. Lotus!" Nova yells out.

"Yeah, thank you for this," I say, sincerely.

"No need to thank me. The reward is in seeing you all be so free and
have fun as a group." Lotus looks around the circle at each of us.

"As you all know we came here to support Willow, so I must thank her
for being the reason for tonight's celebration." She smiles at me before continuing. "When Zane and I spoke earlier today, we realized that we needed
the entire group to be here. Not only to support Willow but to also give us
all the chance to support one another. So, use tonight as an opportunity
to release anything that has been holding you back. It is my hope that
tonight's exercise helps each of you find your voice and to make a memory
that you can always go back to when times get hard."

"What exactly will we be doing?" Lizzy raises her hand.

"I'm glad you asked." Lotus smiles at her. "I am going to lead you
through a meditation where each of you will visualize the things that you
want to let go of, and with each thing you let go of, I want you to in return
think of something that you want to allow in. And once everyone is ready,
we are going to take a dip in the water and cleanse ourselves of the things
that no longer serve us."

◆ ◆ ◆

I close my eyes and follow Lotus' voice as she leads us in meditation. *Inhale. Two. Three. Four. Exhale. Two. Three. Four.* My thoughts automatically jump to Ziggy, but I quickly shake it away. Then I start to wonder if I need to dig deeper to see what role I played in my relationship ending so tragically. I admitted to Lotus that I hadn't been practicing self-care during most of our relationship and that I put more energy into loving him than I put into loving myself, but there has to be more that I can acknowledge. And if I can admit those things, maybe I can finally let go of the disappointment that I have been feeling the past few weeks. An outpour of sadness and regret begins to take over my thoughts, and I immediately try to shove them away.

"There is no such thing as perfect meditation. Thoughts may come and go during this time, and that's okay. Gently acknowledge them and bring your awareness back to your breathing."

I peek open one of my eyes to see if she is referring to me, but she is sitting with her legs crossed and her eyes are closed with the rest of us. I readjust my body so that my spine is straighter, and I bring my attention back to my breathing to give this meditation one more try. The last time she had me try a meditation exercise, I placed one hand on my heart and the other on my belly, so I decide to do that and as expected, it brings me into the present moment, and I hone in on Lotus' voice.

"Imagine that you have a notebook. Now, open the notebook and begin to write down the things that you need to let go of. Write whatever comes to mind. There is no right or wrong answer." Her voice is clear, and once again, I wonder if her words are directed at me, but I keep my eyes closed, not willing to risk losing the connection.

I open the imaginary journal and fill it with things that I am ready to let go of. The inked pages reek of fear, much like my spirit lately, but I follow instructions and write each thing down. For so long, I have feared success which is why I haven't started my own clothing line; I also fear failure which is why I haven't taken advantage of the resources that are available to me at work, and most of all I am terrified to admit that I may not find love again or have a family of my own.

"Now I want you to turn the page and write the things that you need to allow in. Maybe you want to invite love in or make a commitment to self-care. Whatever it is, mentally write it down on that page."

I inhale deep into my belly and mentally write down the things that I need to allow in. I am not giving up on finding love, but first, I have to practice radical self-love which means taking myself on dates, meditating more, praying more, and affirming myself more. I highlight those things in my mind because they can no longer be optional. I also have to learn to flow and live more presently. *And forgive. You can't forget to forgive yourself and go ahead and forgive Ziggy while you're at it.* The words flow across my mind in bold letters, and I want to swipe them away, but Lotus' voice is guiding me to my higher-self, and my consciousness deserves honesty from me if no one else. So, I write forgiveness down on the list of things to let in and take another deep inhale to solidify my affirmations.

Once the meditation ends, we all line up horizontally so that we are facing the ocean, each of us holding the hand of the person next to us for physical and emotional support. As the elder of the group, Lotus is standing at the head of the line with me to her right. As promised, I am standing with her and Nova at my side. Zane decided to stand at the end of the line as co-leader and mentor, and the rest of the women are standing in the middle. I close my eyes as Lotus leads us in prayer, and at the end, we all yell *Asè* which is another way of saying 'Amen' and 'So it is'.

I smile as Lotus leads us in taking the first step towards the ocean. A wave of water grazes my feet before quickly returning back into the sea. We take a few more slow-paced steps until our thighs are covered with water. I grab Nova's hand tighter, and she gently squeezes mine back to reassure me that she is here. Lotus instructs us to stop, and in unison, we dip our heads back and cleanse ourselves of the things that we agreed to let go of, and for the first time in a long time, I am more excited than nervous for what is to come.

12

$\mathcal{M}$Y ALARM CLOCK goes off, forcing me to get out of bed. Today is my last morning here, which means that I have to pack my belongings and join the others downstairs for the farewell breakfast. I stand up, stretching my arms wide and releasing a yawn. I jump when I feel something stuck on the bottom of my foot but relax once I realize that it's only a sticky note. I reach down to grab it from the bottom of my foot and laugh when I realize that it says: *Don't be so serious all the time; say yes more!* Words I casually wrote the first day I came here but will now hold onto with devotion.

My door swings open, and I roll my eyes as Nova plops down onto my bed without permission. I try to feign annoyance, but I am truly going to miss having her around. She watches me with gloomy eyes as I brush my teeth, and I can tell that she is preparing a speech in her head, but I spit the toothpaste out, rinse my mouth with water, and suggest that we hurry up and go downstairs before they start without us. She hesitates for a second but agrees, and I make a mental note to exchange contact information with all of the women at the retreat. In a few weeks, I will have answers to all of the business information they asked about on the first day of the retreat.

The mood amongst the table is bittersweet. The pending goodbyes weigh heavy in the air, and though most of us are happy to have survived this weekend, we are sad to see it end so soon. Four days ago, we sat in awkward silence as strangers, but today, we sit in triumph as allies who share a common bond. Each of us came here afraid and desperate to heal, but, today we leave reassured of our own personal strengths.

"I must say that it has been a pleasure getting to know each of you. Thank you for putting your faith in me and going on this journey." Zane breaks the silence just as she did at our first dinner as a group.

"And don't be strangers," Lotus adds.

"You know I won't be. I am after all your favorite student." Nova snickers in response.

"Nova you are absolutely my favorite student which is why I told your mom that I think you would be a great addition to the staff next year. You can be a guide and make sure that everyone is settled and happy," Lotus grins.

"You did not," Nova pouts.

"Did too," Lotus smirks.

"I hate to interrupt, but the cars will be arriving in about twenty minutes to take the out of towners to the airport. Everyone else who has personal rides coming, I expect they will be here shortly after." Zora joins us at the table.

"I guess that means me." I look around the table.

"I'll keep you company while you pack." Nova grabs both of our empty plates and puts them into the sink.

I walk back to my room to finish packing, and after a few minutes, Nova peaks her head in. She sits on the edge of the bed, staring at me with the same sad eyes from earlier. It is weird to think that saying goodbye will be so hard when I barely even know her, but I have a feeling that she is someone that I will stay in contact with long after this retreat ends. A few moments later, Alicia and Lizzy shuffle in wearing intense frowns. The two of them take turns blowing out air until Nova finally asks if they are okay.

"This weekend went by way too fast," Lizzy admits.

"It definitely went by faster than I expected it to, but if any of you are ever in Dallas, hit me up. We can go to lunch or something," I offer.

"Let's add each other on social media so that way we can keep in touch." Alicia hands me her cell phone while Lizzy passes hers to Nova.

"I have family in Dallas, and I should be there to visit in a few months." Nova hands me her cell phone.

"Okay, let's exchange numbers, so you can just text me if you really decide to come." I hand her my phone.

"Sorry to interrupt again ladies, but Willow's ride is here." Zora peeks her head into the room.

"Thank you, Zora," I say, sincerely.

"Did Zora get to have any fun this weekend?" Nova asks.

"She was too busy making sure the retreat ran smoothly, and according to Lotus, that will be your job next time," I say in a petty tone.

"I'm ignoring you and deciding to take the high road. Now, goodbye." She pulls me in for a hug.

"Bye ladies." I hug each of them before walking down the stairs.

"You weren't going to leave without saying goodbye to me, now were you?" Lotus gives me the same knowing smile that she gave when we met a few days ago. I should have known that she would be waiting for me by the door.

"No ma'am. I was going to come and find you before I left." I pull my suitcase down the last step.

"Well, I'm not one for long goodbyes. All I want to say is don't be a stranger, and I hope that one day our paths cross again. You are an amazing young lady and that is why I asked Zane to put me as your mentor. You thought it was by chance, but it was far from chance. I knew that you had some things to teach me, and I had some things to teach you in exchange. I just hope that you are leaving here with tools to succeed in whatever you decide to."

"I don't know what I could have possibly taught you, but I am so grateful that I got to spend the past few days with you as my mentor. I expected you to be different, but you were exactly the type of teacher that I needed. For now, all I can say is thank you and promise to apply everything that I learned going forward."

"You don't owe me any promises. Just be good to yourself." She pulls me in for a side hug.

"I will," I vow before turning to leave.

13

Three months later

I PULL UP to work and immediately begin to take three deep breaths, which has become my ritual lately. These three breaths have the ability to make or break my day, and I need all the armor that I can get working for a fool like Carter. He owns one of the biggest fashion companies around the world, and I was grateful when he first agreed to hire me but having no experience in the fashion industry meant that I had to start at the bottom of the totem pole. As head of marketing, Janae tries to help me out by assigning me to help on her projects, but Carter likes to keep me at his side to remind me of my place. I've considered leaving on many occasions, but he works with some of the biggest names in the industry, and I guess I'd rather be in the room with my face seen than to not be known at all.

I step off of the elevator and walk past Janae who is waiting for me with a worried expression. This is her usual greeting; she pretends to be holding her breath as I walk towards Carter's office. She calls it 'The walk of pain," which makes me laugh because even she knows that Carter can be a total ass the majority of the time. I walk into his office, mentally preparing myself not to react when he begins to complain about the temperature of his coffee or his lack of sleep.

"Good morning Carter, here's your coffee. Nice and hot just like you like it." I hope he doesn't notice the hint of sarcasm hidden behind my words.

"Good morning, Willow." He has a huge grin displaying the gap between his two front teeth. I scratch my head in confusion because Carter is never this nice.

"Um, Okay," I say taken aback. "Your wife requested to have lunch with you at 12. Should I pencil her in?"

"Yes, please call her back to confirm. Oh, and please add Noah Daniels to the schedule. He is stopping by for a meeting this morning." He flashes another toothy smile before leading me out of his office and closing it behind him. Apparently, he needs time to prepare for his meeting, and I would be a distraction.

Carter's words ring in my ears, and I feel sick to my stomach. It has been almost four months since my *almost encounter* with Noah which is what Janae and I decided to call it since we technically never met but exchanged glances. I speed walk to her office to share the news and to force her to help me plan an escape route out of this place before Noah arrives. Janae has gotten me out of sticky situations before by finding projects for me to help her with, so this should be a cake walk.

"Carter just told me that Noah Daniels is coming for a meeting this morning, and I need you to help me come up with an excuse to leave early, or I can play sick and hide in your office until he leaves," I whisper frantically as I pull her office door shut.

"Finally!" She lets out a sigh of relief. "I've known for the past two days, but I wanted you to be surprised because I knew you would try to run away, but you can't hide forever. Maybe he won't even remember you. Your little run-in with him was months ago." She shrugs her shoulders nonchalantly.

"We are no longer best friends. I can't believe you withheld something this important from me. I'm seriously starting to feel nauseous." I place my hand on my head to check for any signs of a fever.

"Best friends are allowed to withhold information if it is for the good of the other person. So, take some Pepto-Bismol and plaster on a smile because you know Carter will fire you if he has to walk to the front to get his own client. He expects you to bring them to his office with a smile in tow."

"He can fire me for all I care, and a real friend would have at least given me a warning." I cross my arms in defiance.

"Willow." She pulls my shoulders so that I am now facing her. "You are young, gorgeous, smart, funny, and one day you are going to launch your own business. You need to give yourself a chance to be happy. Maybe nothing will come of this but give yourself the chance to find out. You have to admit it's pretty crazy that you will be in the same room with him after almost meeting four months ago."

"You talk a good game, but you haven't allowed a man to get close to you since college. I'm proud of your success, but I know you want love too. I don't see you out here giving brothers a chance."

"Okay, let's make a deal. I'll put myself out there if you do," she says with confidence. But I know that she is nervous about truly putting herself out there again.

"Whatever you say, Janae," I respond angrily before running to look at myself in the mirror. I may not want Noah, but I refuse to look bad in front of a client.

◆ ◆ ◆

The elevator door opens, and two bodyguards that look like giants step out to greet me. Just as I am introducing myself, Noah steps off of the elevator, and I almost lose my breath. It is not a feeling of being star struck because in this line of work I've seen many celebrities, but I have never seen a man as beautiful as Noah in my entire life. His skin is the most perfect shade of brown as if the sun shines just for him. His curls are coiled loosely all over his head, and his beard is scruffy and somehow still well groomed. His height demands that I look up to him, and it is almost funny to see how skinny he is in comparison to his bodyguards, but, even so, he is much more handsome than I realized the night we crossed paths.

A few of the staff members walk by to greet Noah on his way in. He politely smiles at each of the staff members as they say their hellos, but he is sure to keep his distance. They don't seem to notice his discomfort, but I am fully aware of how he is using his bodyguards as a shield as if they are a mob of fans attacking him when there is only about twelve people welcoming him from afar. I roll my eyes, annoyed by his arrogance and instruct the group of men to follow me. Once we reach the door to Carter's office, I turn to walk back to my desk, but I am caught off guard when Noah tells Carter that he would like for me to be part of the meeting. Carter looks disappointed by his suggestion, and it is obvious that I am the last person he expected to be in his meeting. But, rather than expressing his dissatisfaction to a client, he clears his throat and lazily agrees for me to join them.

I find a seat towards the back of the room where Noah's bodyguards are, hoping that the distance will allow me to avoid Carter's scowl. I have no clue why Noah suggested that I be present for the meeting, but he just transformed Carter 's unusually good mood back to his typical angry self. As the two men talk, I take down a few notes, capturing Noah's ideas while also creating sketches, which is not part of my job description, but I do it anyways because I love making people's ideas come to life. In fact, I am damn good at it, but Carter doesn't seem to notice.

The meeting only lasts about thirty minutes because of Noah's tight schedule. His manager, Derrick, mentioned that they were pressed for time and would be leaving our office and going straight to the radio station to continue the press for Noah's new album. They agreed to come back next month to hear Carters pitch for Noah's upcoming red-carpet event. I made a mental note to call out sick that day. As I escort the men back to elevator, I feel Noah staring at me intensely, but I keep my head turned forward and pretend not to notice.

Janae walks over to where we are standing and confidently introduces herself to Noah and his staff. She grins wide as she passes her business card to Derrick and each of his bodyguards. I respect her for this because she is never afraid to be seen. Janae has a boss mentality, and she can talk her way into any room. Our mothers are best friends, and growing up, they taught us the importance of asking for what we want. We were both trained to be confident in our dreams, but my confidence usually wavers while Janae trusts that all will work out for the best.

The elevator finally arrives after what seems like eternity. I shake Derrick's hand first, offering my business card so that I can assist him in setting up the second meeting with Carter in a month. Then, I confidently reach out to shake Noah's hand. To the normal eye it would look as though I am cool calm and collected when really, I am nervous and sweaty. I watch as he moves to the back of the elevator, once again surrounded by bodyguards. I wave one more goodbye to the men before the door shuts, and our eyes connect for a brief moment. Though neither of us says a word, I am left still feeling his energy long after he walks away, just as I did months ago.

14

I AM ON my way to meet Janae for our weekly Sunday brunch. She is introducing me to a friend of hers, which is surprising because she typically keeps her dating life private until things become serious. She mentioned that he was a good guy and that she could introduce me to some of his friends, but lately, my days have been spent at work, home, or in the gym with little time for dating. I won't lie and say that I haven't been craving intimacy because I definitely have been, but after the retreat, I decided that it would be best to abstain from sex until I meet a man worthy of my body, and the few men that I have met weren't willing to respect that, so our time together was brief.

I walk into the restaurant and stride towards the booth that we have sat in every week for the past two years, but the table is empty, and Janae is nowhere in sight. We talked less than five minutes ago, and she told me that she was already here, so I dial her number hoping that she didn't lie to me and is actually going to be late. I wouldn't be surprised if she wasn't here yet because Janae is always late and always lies about it which is why I purposely showed up fifteen minutes after our scheduled meeting time.

"Hey, girl!" She answers on the first ring. The background noise is filled with loud laughter and conversation, but none of the voices sound familiar.

"Where are you?" I ask, confused.

"Sorry! I'm walking to the front to meet you now. We thought it would be a good idea to get a private table since there's a group of us. Please don't be a party pooper." Her request is both a warning and a plea for me to be on my best behavior.

"The only reason you would be warning me is if you did something that you know I wouldn't like. So, what is it?"

"I need you to smile first." She finally reaches me and ends the call.

"Just tell me what you did," I say, bluntly.

"Well David decided to invite his friends, and they decided to bring dates so there will be more people than expected, but it will be fun I promise!" She puts her arm around my shoulder.

"You've never cared about fancy private sections or introducing me to a guy this early, so this David guy must be someone special." I eye her suspiciously.

"Relax, we're just friends, and I'm pretty sure you've already met him before. Do you remember the bodyguards that came to the office with Noah Daniels? Well, he was one of them. The tall cute one." She flashes a smile and quickly walks to the table to prevent me from making a scene.

My nerves take over as we walk towards the table. If David is Noah's bodyguard then there is a small chance that Noah might indeed be here today, and if this is some kind of setup to get us together, I am never speaking to Janae again. I look around the table; paranoid that Noah is going to be sitting amongst the group of friends, but when I realize he isn't, I release the breath that I was holding.

Janae takes a seat next to David and introduces me to the group. I recognize Kaleb and Khalil from the Kansas City Chiefs football team. They are a brother duo that came on the scene a few years ago and have become an unstoppable pair. While the rest of the group have dates next to them, these two seem to be solo, and I wonder if they are part of whatever Janae has planned for me, but despite my suspicion, I behave nicely.

The conversation amongst the table flows smoothly, and I realize that I actually have a lot in common with each person sitting here. We are all young with dreams that we hope to one-day turn into careers, and we all seek love and purpose. While some of the group has already started living their dreams, they still don't have life all figured out and are on a similar quest to create happy lives. I realize that I shouldn't fault Janae for wanting to spend time with her new group of friends. Maybe they will become my friends as well. As long as Noah isn't a part of the group.

◆ ◆ ◆

I guzzle down my third mimosa, and my alter ego begins to rear her ugly head. In this moment, all I want is to release my pent-up sexual frustration, and drunken me only sees two options. I can call Ziggy and rehash an old argument, or I could ask David for Noah's number to see if he remembers me from our first encounter at the restaurant a few months ago. I look across the table, hoping to get Janae's attention, but she is gazing into David's eyes intensely and doesn't notice me looking at her, so I pull out my phone and send her a text, hoping that she will do my dirty work and ask David for Noah's number.

Willow: Can you ask David for Noah's number?

Janae: What's changed? You freaked out the last time I suggested you contact Noah.

Willow: Well, the mimosas revealed my true feelings, so be a good friend and get the number.

Janae: No. Ask me again when you're sober.

Willow: Okay, mom! I'm going to the restroom to freshen up my lipstick, and when I get back, I'll ask David myself.

Janae: You talk a good game, but when you get back from the restroom, you'll feel differently.

Willow: I wouldn't count on it.

I look up from my phone and shoot her a dirty look before standing up from the table. She is always telling me to put myself out there, but now when I decide to give it a try, she is standing in my way. I decide that the only way for me to get even is to send her another angry text on my way to the restroom, so I pull out my phone and begin to type when I bump into a body that almost sends me flying against the wall.

"Damn, just push me against the wall why don't you!" I say, without looking up. The collision is entirely my fault, but the mimosas mixed with sexual frustration are blocking my view of reality. The rude stranger with the apparent strength of a wrestler also disappeared around the corner so fast that I wouldn't have been able to apologize if I wanted to.

After freshening up my lipstick I head to the bar to order a round of drinks for the table. I decide to cut myself off after my run-in on my way to the bathroom, but I order an extra drink for Janae, hoping that she will do as I asked and hook me up with Noah's number. If this doesn't work then I will go home annoyed, unsatisfied, and reconsidering my friendship. The bartender tells me that they will deliver the drinks to the table since there are too many for me to carry, so I strut back over to my seat excited to be back amongst the group of like-minded people my age.

When I walk back to the table, my seat is occupied with one of David's friends, so I stand behind him hoping that he will catch the hint. Everyone else is so wrapped up in their own personal conversations that they don't seem to notice me. I have manners and believe in personal space, so I clear my throat hoping not to have to touch the stranger, but the sound goes unnoticed and I am forced to tap his shoulder. Janae finally notices me standing there just as I am about to reach out. She flashes a smile that screams "I told you so," and my stomach drops.

"Oh hey, I forgot to tell you that Willow was sitting there, but I can have the waiter pull up another chair for you." She smiles innocently at the man.

"Oh, my bad. My boy didn't tell me the seat was taken." Noah turns to face me and removes the ball cap from his head.

"Uh, it's okay. Stay here. I'll move to the other end of the table." I stumble over my words.

"My mother would not appreciate me sitting while a woman stands, so take your seat back, and I'll move to the other end of the table." He stands and towers over me.

"I have an extra seat for you, Mr. Daniels." Our nosey waiter rushes over with an extra seat, placing it right next to mines.

I try my best to avoid making eye contact with Noah by focusing directly on Janae, but she turns her head and pretends to be in deep conversation with David leaving me to entertain Noah on my own. I quickly turn to my right hoping that Kaleb and Khalil will have a good conversation going, but the two of them are engaged in their phones, so I begin to talk loudly to Marcus and Tara who are sitting three seats down from me. The two of them just so happen to be on the phone with their babysitter, so I am stuck sitting in awkward silence next to Noah.

"I remember you." He places his elbows on the table and leans over to speak in a hushed tone. His statement causes my armpits to sweat. I am not ready for the entire table to know that our first encounter consisted of him watching me cry and shake my keys in a valet driver's face like a madwoman.

"We met at Carter's office a few weeks ago but you're also the woman who bumped into me a little while ago without saying excuse me," he smiles teasingly.

"In my defense, I was going to apologize, but you ran off before I had the chance to," I joke back, feeling somewhat relieved. Maybe Janae is right. Maybe he doesn't remember our first encounter.

"It's okay. If it takes a cracked iPhone screen for me to get a beautiful woman's attention, it was all worth it." He smiles with his perfect white teeth.

"I cracked your screen?" I pretend not to notice that he called me beautiful.

"Yeah, but it's not a big deal. I'll get it replaced later today," he shrugs nonchalantly.

"Well, it's a big deal to me. Money does not grow on trees. I sincerely apologize for being rude, and I promise to buy you a new one." I feel guilty.

"No, I got it. No worries." He quickly rejects my offer, and we go back and forth like this for a while, me promising to replace his phone and him saying it's not necessary.

"I have an idea," Janae interjects, "Why don't you take him to lunch as a sort of peace offering?" My eyes stare at her like daggers, and I hope that she can hear the silent threats that I am sending her way telepathically.

"I like that idea. In fact, there's a new spot that I've been meaning to try. I hear they have the best chicken and waffles," Noah responds.

"Oh no." Janae abruptly spits her drink out of her mouth causing the entire table to focus on her.

"What'd I say?" He looks around, confused by the situation.

"You didn't say anything wrong. I'm a vegan so Janae found your suggestion to be funny but ignore her. I'll take you to one of my favorite spots if that's cool?"

"I was raised by a vegetarian, and I'm down to try new things, so teach me," he says with confidence.

"Say less. I got you," I assure him.

15

"I CAN'T BELIEVE you actually agreed to go on a date with Noah!" Janae squeals. "I guess I should add matchmaker to my list of skills now. I might even start a matchmaking service," she says with confidence.

"Let's not forget that you manipulated me into going on this date. So, you should add blackmail to your list of skills, not matchmaker," I tease.

"Hey, I did what was necessary, and I don't regret it." She hands me a dress to try on.

"I am not trying on anymore clothes." I bypass her.

We have been sitting in my closet for the past hour trying to find the perfect outfit for my date with Noah which technically hasn't even been planned due to his busy schedule. He is currently in Los Angeles putting the finishing touches on his album, so we haven't solidified a time or date to meet, but Janae insisted on helping me find the perfect outfit in advance, so here I am standing in my closet watching her gloat over the fact that she tricked me into going to lunch with Noah. What she doesn't know is that I have been considering canceling the date for over a week now. Noah seems like a nice guy, but he lives in the public eye, and I don't think that I could ever be comfortable with the world watching my every move. I also worry that if things get serious between us, I will end up feeling insecure and questioning his actions which I swore I wouldn't do in my next relationship.

"This is the last one I swear." She pleads with me. "As a best friend and professional matchmaker, it is my job to make sure that you look your best on this date, so please, let me help you."

"We haven't even set a date, so all of this is pointless," I whine. "And if I'm honest, I don't know if I can do this." I exit the closet and sit on my bed.

"You always do this," she says, knowingly.

"Do what?" I retort.

"You run away from any chance of romance. It's like your vow to practice self-care at that retreat has given you the idea that you have to be alone in order to be healthy."

"I've been on dates Janae," I scoff.

"Yeah and as soon as they started to like you, what did you do? All I am asking is that you give yourself the chance to go on a date and have fun this one time. You deserve to be wined and dined. And Noah sounds like a good guy from what David tells me."

"I'm not saying he's a bad guy. I wouldn't be going out with him if I thought he was, but don't you think it's weird that he still hasn't mentioned our first encounter?"

"Honestly, it is pretty strange, but that was so long ago. Maybe he doesn't remember you. You said yourself that you avoided eye contact, and when he finally saw you, it was only for a split second." She tries to justify his actions.

"And it was dark out," I add.

"Exactly, so maybe he doesn't know that you're the same woman, but if it bothers you that much, you should ask him about it."

"I wouldn't know where to begin. I can't just walk up to him and say, '*hey do remember seeing me shaking my keys in someone's face and crying hysterically?*'"

"Why can't you?" she asks strongly.

"Because it's embarrassing. Are you saying that if you met David the same exact way, you would ask him directly?"

"I would because I'm not scary like you," she teases.

"Well, I'll be scary then," I shrug.

"Hey, Willow?" she says, suddenly sounding playful.

"Yeah?" I notice that she is trying not to laugh.

"Now's your chance to find out if Noah remembers you." She carries my phone from the closet. It begins to vibrate in my hand, and we both stare at it as if it's a ticking time bomb.

"Oh, my goodness! We spoke him up! He's Face Timing me!" I nervously throw my phone on my bed.

"Answer it!" Janae picks the phone up and tosses it back to me.

"No, my hair is all over the place. I'm not letting him see me like this."

"So, you're going to ignore him when you were literally just talking about him?"

"Exactly," I say, firmly.

"Okay, well at least let me answer and tell him that you're busy, so he doesn't think you're ignoring him."

"That's a good idea," I say in agreement.

"Okay." She grabs the phone.

"Hey Noah! Willow just walked into the other room, but I'll go get her for you. Hold on for one sec." She pauses the phone and marches in place for dramatic effect. After a few seconds, she says, "Willow, Noah's on the phone!" She gives me a stern look, which means that if I don't talk to him, she is going to embarrass me, so I take the phone but avoid looking directly into the camera.

"You know you're supposed to schedule Face Time calls, right?" I say, candidly.

"Hi to you too, Willow." He ignores my comment.

"Sorry. Hi Noah. You know you're supposed to schedule FaceTime calls, right?"

"I wasn't aware of that rule, but maybe you can help me understand your logic?" He is still smiling.

"I'm not trying to be rude. I just think it's polite to inform someone of a call beforehand to give them a chance to make sure that they look appropriate," I explain.

"So, you're saying that you don't look appropriate enough to talk to me?" he replies, unaffected by my discomfort.

"Exactly, so can I call you back in a few minutes?" My question causes him to laugh uncontrollably.

"What's so funny, Noah?" I ask defensively.

"I don't mean to laugh, but women are so funny sometimes. My sister actually told me about the scheduled video call rule, but I thought it was just her being crazy."

"It's a woman thing, and you probably can't understand," I retort.

"I can understand that you don't want random men Face Timing you without permission, but I want you to understand that those rules don't apply to me." He smiles conceitedly.

"And why is that? Because you're not used to being told no?" I look into the camera, eager to hear his response.

"I won't lie and say that there aren't women and people in general who are willing to offer me things to get close to me, but I don't need 'yes men' in my life. I surround myself with genuine people because I'm a good man, and the people in my circle are very capable of telling me no."

"I didn't mean to insinuate that you weren't a good man." I suddenly feel the need to clarify.

"It may not have been your intention, but you definitely wanted to judge me. That's why you asked that question, but hey, I'm going to let you get back to what you were doing. Just know that you're gorgeous, and you don't need to be made up for a man to notice that." His confession causes a smile to spread across my lips.

"So, I offended you within the first five minutes of conversation, and now you're done talking to me?"

"You seemed disinterested in talking to me, and I'm not one to force someone to do something they obviously don't want to," he admits.

"Well, you have to at least give me a chance to prove that I'm not a judgmental jerk." I finally move into the full frame of the camera.

"Look into the camera and talk to me like a nonjudgmental jerk then." He laughs playfully, and that is exactly what I do. I look into the camera, and we talk for two hours, which turns into daily texts and calls for five straight weeks.

16

I MADE THE mistake of telling Janae that I was going to a restaurant to have dinner by myself because she showed up within fifteen minutes of my arrival with David in tow. She claims that she didn't want me to eat dinner alone, but she had no problem making me be their third wheel. After they kissed in front of me for the third time and then David's hand found his way onto her thigh, I decided to FaceTime Noah hoping that it would make things less awkward and that I wouldn't feel like a complete third wheel. He ordered room service from his hotel, and we turned our call into a virtual date which gave me the perfect excuse to ignore Janae and David.

"Are they seriously watching each other eat on FaceTime?" David whispers to Janae, but it's loud enough for everyone to hear.

"David, you've never been great at whispering." Noah laughs into the camera.

"Sorry bro, it's just funny seeing you so vulnerable. I haven't seen you this interested in a woman in a *very* long time," David confesses.

"Wow, are you purposely trying to embarrass me?" Noah chuckles. "I'm re-evaluating our entire friendship right now."

"It's funny you say that because I've been re-evaluating my friendship with Janae for weeks now. Ever since she met David, she's been trying to make me their third wheel." I jokingly join forces with Noah.

"Hey, I've been nothing but supportive of you and Noah's friendship. In fact, you two should pay for this meal to say thank you for my match-making skills. Oh, and Noah when you get back in town, you have to take my beautiful best friend on a proper date instead of these weird video dates. That's probably why she is so cranky all the time," Janae retaliates, causing us all to erupt with laughter.

"What you call cranky is actually fire. It's my Aries nature. I can't help her," I inform her.

"Yeah so don't ..." Noah starts to respond when his manager, Derrick, appears into the camera and hands him a piece of paper. His presence usually means that they have business to handle, so when Noah excuses himself from the conversation, I am not surprised.

"Hey, I have to go," he says, after looking over the document Derrick handed him. "I'll be back in town next week, so let's go to lunch or catch a movie," he offers.

"Okay, give me a call, and we can set something up." I am excited with the prospect of seeing him but disappointed that our conversation is coming to an end.

"Will do. Peace, Queen." He smiles into the camera.

"Peace, King." I blush in return.

When the call ends, Janae's words ring loud in my ear, and I second her desire to have Noah here with me on a real date. Our phone conversations have truly been amazing, but it will be nice to finally meet face to face after weeks of talking on the phone. So far, his energy feels authentic and familiar, which at times makes me feel uneasy because I have never dated a man who genuinely wanted to know the real me. We've discussed our childhoods, fears, heartbreaks, and life goals. I opened up to him fast, which is both scary and exciting thus, my reason for letting Noah know upfront that I am not looking to become intimate with anyone anytime soon, and he agreed that we should take our time and become friends before exploring a relationship.

It definitely takes effort to communicate as often as we do with me having a traditional work schedule and him being busy at random times, but he has proven that he is dedicated in getting to know me. What I most admire about him is his excitement for life. He has so much going for himself, and not once has he questioned my ability to accomplish my goals or tried to interrupt my workflow. For the past three weeks, I have worked my regular job and then come straight home to get the plans together for my clothing store. I have so many sketches, and I sold three new pieces thanks to the women at the retreat. This is the most motivated I've ever been and for the first time in my life I am learning to support myself and I believe that the universe is supporting me in return.

17

STICKING TO OUR original agreement, Noah and I decided to call this lunch a peace offering instead of a date, which means that I am planning and paying for today's outing as an official apology for breaking his phone all those months ago. I decided to meet him at Vegan Tingz, which is a local restaurant in the heart of Dallas. He isn't a vegan, and I don't judge people for their lifestyle, but I am impressed at how open he is to try new things. Due to heavy traffic, I arrive at the restaurant a few minutes later than expected. Once inside, I immediately notice Noah sitting at a booth in the corner of the restaurant with his head down reading a book. I walk over and gently re-adjust his hand so that his fingers no longer cover the title of the book. Though he is caught off guard, he instantly smiles when he realizes that it is me and not some random person invading his space.

"*The War of Art.*" I am impressed by his choice.

"To be honest, I started reading to waste time, but now I'm kind of digging it. Maybe you could read it for motivation while you're in the planning stages of your business?" He slides the book across the table and gives me the most genuine smile. I turn my head to the side, purposely hiding the reaction that he just produced inside of me. This man is absolutely beautiful and to refer to him as anything else would be an insult.

"Don't do that," he softly commands.

"Don't do what exactly?" I furrow my eyebrows in confusion.

"Don't hide yourself from me. Keep it real, and I promise to do the same."

"Hmm." I release an accusatory sigh.

"What just happened?" He studies me. "You just exhaled deeply, and you look like you have something to say, so let me know what's on your mind, lady?"

"I don't have anything on my mind," I lie and slide into the seat across from him.

"Willow," he says softly.

"Fine, I've been wanting to ask you something for a while now, and I don't mean to bombard you with questions, but it's important that we start our friendship in truth."

"I agree with everything you just said."

"Okay, so I was wondering if you remember the first time you saw me?"

He chuckles softly, "I was wondering when this was going to come up."

"So, you do remember me?" I peer over at him.

"Yeah. Of course, I remember you."

"Well, why didn't you say anything when we met again at my job?" I am puzzled by his discretion.

"I guess for the same reason you didn't. I just figured you would tell me about it when you were ready to."

"So, you would have kept pretending not to remember if I hadn't brought it up?" I feel embarrassed.

"No, I would have eventually asked you about it but not until I felt you were comfortable with me. Are you comfortable enough to share that part of your life with me?"

"I've shared almost everything with you, but I'm not ready to talk about that. Not yet."

"Okay then, so let's enjoy today and worry about the rest another day." He reaches across the table to offer me his pinky.

"What is this?" I laugh.

"We are going to pinky swear. I won't force you to talk about it, but you can't hide from me either. If we can't be real, what's the point in doing any of this?"

"Deal," I interlace my pinky with his.

◆ ◆ ◆

When the waiter came to our table, Noah insisted that I order for him. He proclaimed it as our first exercise in trust, so I kept it simple and ordered a veggie burger, which he swore had to have been meat. We sat in the booth for almost two hours allowing the conversation to flow effortlessly, just as it does when we are on the phone. After lunch, I invited him to check out the vinyl record store next door, and his face lit up with excitement. He shared that his mom collects records and listens to everything from gospel to reggae to country. She even added his favorite rapper, Nipsey Hussle to her collection after hearing his album *Victory Lap*.

"Moms is from the hood, but she's brilliant and highly spiritual. When I first decided I wanted to pursue music professionally, she told me that when I use my voice, I better make sure I have something to say. She actually sacrificed her career to raise my sister and me. That's why you hear me sing about women and love, but I also talk about consciousness and manifesting the things you want in life. My music will always allow people to dance and have fun, but it also has a message, and that's what matters most."

"Your mom sounds like a wise woman who raised a wise man," I admit.

"Yeah, she's a great woman. I couldn't have asked for a better introduction to love if I tried, and I feel the same way about my father. He was always softer in his approach to parenting, but his love and support echoes just as loud as my mom's."

"They sound similar to my parents. Their love languages are different, but I could never say that one is better than the other. I just always felt that I needed both if that makes sense.

"Makes perfect sense to me. You know the more we talk, the more I realize how much we have in common. I guess that's why you seem so familiar," he confesses.

"I always tell Janae that our conversations feel kindred. As if they were supposed to happen."

"So, you talk about me with your bestie? You must really like me," he says, playfully.

"Oh gosh. I'm second guessing my decision to invite you to the record store." I bump against him.

"Too late. We're here now." He opens the door for me. We both smile with recognition when we hear "Before I Let You Go" by Frankie Beverly and Maze playing from the speakers creating a nostalgic vibe.

"What you know about this young blood?" I joke. I begin to sway my hips to the music. I am only a year older than Noah, but I tease as if I am so much more mature.

"Nothing wrong with having an older woman. I happen to like cougars." He steps behind me and places his hands on my hips for me to move in sync with him.

"Don't get too handsy now." I warn him, but my body presses snug against him, and we rock back and forth as if we are at a family cookout jamming to the song that we both obviously grew up listening to.

I begin to move away from him when the music slows and "Ready for Love" by India Arie begins to play, but Noah holds me firm against him, moving his arms from around my waist and wrapping them around my entire body. With my back still to him, I move slowly and purposefully, allowing myself to get lost in the moment. Our bodies are connected, but our movements are not filled with lust. We create a sense of intimacy that liberates us, and for a few moments, we ignore the world going on around us. Then, the door starts to open slowly causing us to separate from one another.

"Oh my gosh!" A tall woman with long legs and a pretty face rushes towards us. "I heard you were always in Dallas without security, but I never expected to see you in a record store like a regular person. Can I get a picture with you?" She bats her long lashes at Noah.

"Sure thing, lady. I got you." He moves into the frame of the camera. He plasters on a smile, but his eyes reveal his true feelings. Without saying a word, he communicates his disappointment to me. Our moment ended as quickly as it started.

18

"So, he really didn't try to kiss you good night?" Janae asks, for the hundredth time today. She is supposed to be helping me grocery shop for the dinner that I am cooking for my parents and younger brother, Omari, but instead she keeps throwing back every item that I put into the basket and harassing me about my date with Noah.

"We have been over this a million times already. He walked me to my car; we hugged, and he said he would be in contact. That's it. There is nothing more to tell." I am annoyed with her constant prying.

"But that was over a week ago, and he hasn't contacted you since?" She looks confused.

"For the last time, no I have not spoken to Noah since our date."

"Well, I'm going to ask David if he's heard anything because this just doesn't make sense."

"Please, leave it alone. If Noah wants to speak to me, he will. I refuse to chase behind him or any other man. Celebrity or not," I say, honestly.

"Fine, I'll stay out of it then." She throws her hands up in surrender, but I don't believe her for a second. It is only a matter of time before she comes back to tell me what news she has of Noah.

"Please do, and maybe now that you're not in my business, you can actually help me figure out what to cook for dinner."

"Remind me again why Omari isn't cooking this meal?" she says sarcastically. She then turns to pick up more snacks that aren't on my list, and as soon as she does, I throw all of the junk that she's managed to pile in the cart back onto the shelf.

"Omari is staying as a guest in my home, so I'm not going to make him cook, and you eat my food all the time, so why are you being picky all of a sudden?" I respond defensively. Janae isn't a vegan, but you would never know by the way she is always looking up plant-based recipes and harassing me to cook for her.

"Yeah, but this is your parents first week back in the states. You don't want them to move to Jamaica permanently after eating your cooking, do you?" she teases.

"Whatever. Just make sure you don't show up asking for a plate," I say, jokingly. I am wasting my time threatening her because she will definitely be showing up at my house all week, taking in all of the parental love that she can get until she gets to fly home to visit her family.

19

I AM ON my way to the airport to pick up my parents when my cellphone begins to ring. Carter's name flashes across the screen for the third time today. He approved my vacation time three weeks ago, when he was in a good mood, but today he acts as if my time off is a total surprise and inconvenience to him. He originally agreed to give me the next three days off to spend time with my family, but he doesn't seem to comprehend what time off means. As tempted as I am to decline his call, it would only give him cause to pick a fight and threaten the security of my job.

"Is everything okay?" I am trying to mask my irritation.

"No, everything is not okay. I need you to come to the office to locate a file for me," he sneers.

"All of the files from last week's meeting are on top of your desk. Remember, I told you I would put them there for your convenience?"

"No, I do not remember having that conversation. Anyways, just make sure you are back in the office first thing Monday morning," he demands.

"I will be in bright and early like I am *every day*." I am no longer able to contain my sarcasm.

"Be here with a better attitude than the one you currently have or else don't bother showing up at all." He ends the call without saying goodbye.

I find an open space in the arrival section and decide that the only thing that would make me feel better is to change his name in my phone from "Employer" to 'Little man with an attitude." I hit save and immediately feel a sense of relief. Although my behavior is petty, it is also cathartic, and I refuse to let him ruin my good mood. My phone chimes, and I swipe to answer the incoming call from my mother. My mom blurts out in excitement, asking me where I am. Realizing that I am in the wrong part of the airport, I drive around to find her standing near the curb with her head rested on my father's chest. A look of youthfulness spreads across their faces as she leans in to kiss him. These public displays of affection are my mother's specialty. It's as if she can sense me coming and leaned in just in time for me to witness it and be grossed out.

"Must you do this in public?" I say causing their smiles to widen.

"Hey, Sup!" my dad says, calling me by my childhood name, which is short for superstar. I hop out of my jeep to give both her and my father a much-needed hug.

They've spent the past month traveling abroad, and now that they are finally stateside, they decided to spend a few days in Dallas before returning home to Atlanta. Omari has a project that will keep him in Dallas the next few weeks, so he will be flying in later tonight to spend some time with us.

"Are you guys hungry?" I hope they can't hear my stomach rumbling from hunger.

"We're starving, but don't worry about cooking right now, just take us to one of your hippie dippy food places," my father says, which causes me to laugh. My dad loves vegan food, but he also likes to give me a hard time.

"Okay, Pop. We can go out for lunch today, but after that I want to make you home cooked meals." I am proud to finally show them the cooking skills I picked up from Lotus.

"Oh, yeah?" My dad exchanges a look of concern with my mom.

"I'll have you know that I picked up a few cooking techniques recently," I say, proudly.

"Baby girl, we're not saying you can't cook. Your pasta is always amazing, but we don't want to eat the same meal the next three days."

"Yeah, just let your brother do the cooking this weekend. You know he likes to show off," my mom adds.

"Okay. If you think Omari is such a great chef, then let's have a cook off."

"So, you can accuse of us of playing favoritism? That sounds like a setup to me. What do you think, Sage?" My father turns to my mom.

"I say let them do it. Just don't get mad if the outcome isn't what you hope for sweetie." My mom reaches over to kiss my cheek.

My ability to cook has been the running joke in my family for years, and the only way to convince them of my skills is by action. What they don't know is that Lotus taught me a few recipes while I was in California, and I plan to whip up the soul food dish that she made our first night at the retreat and finally prove to my family that I can cook more than pasta.

"Wow, such supportive parents I have." I pretend to be offended. "Now put your bags in the car, so we can go eat."

◆ ◆ ◆

Perry, the owner of Vegan Tingz and his grandmother, Mrs. Davis, greet us as soon as we walk through the restaurant doors. Mrs. Davis is a true pillar of the community and has spent most of her weekends working here since retiring a few years ago, but she is by no means a normal hostess. Unlike most of the employees who work at Vegan Tingz, Mrs. Davis has the free-dom to spend the majority of her shift sitting and talking with customers. I have been a patron of this restaurant for over two years now, and many of those visits were spent sitting and enjoying lunch with Mrs. Davis. In the beginning, she didn't give me much of a choice, she spoke to me every time I walked through the door, and after a while, I began to rely on her being here. Now, I can't imagine how the restaurant would run without her, and I would be willing to bet that most of the patrons feel the same way.

"Mrs. Davis, come join us at our table. I need a full update on what this child of mine has been up to." My mother smiles deviously before taking her seat.

"I'll be right over, but I'm not sure how much help I'll be since she hasn't said anything about her love life in a while, but maybe we can double team her and pry together." Mrs. Davis grins playfully in my direction.

"You two better leave my baby girl alone." My dad comes to my defense.

"Thank you, daddy." I stick my tongue out at Mrs. Davis and my mother.

"I wouldn't have to pry if she would share with her mother more," my mom complains.

"Let me seat a few more people, and I'll be right over." Mrs. Davis holds up her index finger.

"No rush." I urge her to take her time.

"I would never rush you, but this is of the upmost importance," my mom says, adding dramatic flair to the conversation.

"Sage, are you talking to Mrs. Davis or the whole restaurant?" my dad teases.

"You know they both talk extremely loud every time they see each other. I honestly don't know why I keep bringing you here when you visit," I say, half serious.

"Quest, I love you dearly, but leave me alone, and Willow have you ever heard of rental cars, Ubers, Lyfts, or taxi's? I could utilize any of those resources and still find my way to this establishment with or without you." My mom rolls her eyes at the two of us.

"Let's just order please." I am hopeful that the waiter's arrival will put a stop to our current discussion.

"I will have the vegan BLT with fries, and if memory serves me correct, my handsome husband here would like the soul food plate with an extra serving of black-eyed peas." My mom waits for my dad to object, and when he doesn't, she beams with pride as if she just cracked a code when in reality, all she did was order the exact meal he gets every time we come here.

"I'll take the oyster mushroom po' boy with mac and cheese and greens on the side please." I hand the server my menu.

"Sorry ma'am, but we actually ran out of that item about twenty minutes ago. There are plenty of other amazing options to choose from, and I can make suggestions if you'd like." He places the menu back in front of me.

"I guess I will have the vegan nachos with extra guacamole." I reply dryly. All of the food here is amazing, but the po' boy is my absolute favorite dish.

"Yes, ma'am and sorry about that." He takes the menus and leaves.

"So, baby girl what's new in your world?" My dad restarts conversation.

"Not much. I keep saying that I am ready to revisit the business plan that I started working on a while ago, but most of my time is spent at work, the gym, and at the yoga studio. Oh, and I've sadly been a third wheel to Janae and her new friend more times than I can count."

"A third wheel?" Mrs. Davis interrupts the conversation.

"Mrs. Davis, out of everything I just said, that is the one thing you heard?"

"Sorry baby, I only heard the last few words you said. You can repeat it if you'd like," she says, sincerely.

"Well, I was saying that I haven't told many people but I…." My voice trails off as I watch David walk into the restaurant.

I breathe a sigh of relief when I don't see Janae or Noah following behind him. He has his phone to his ear and doesn't seem to notice me, so I turn and put my head down to hide in case he turns around for any reason. As Noah's close friend and confidant, he probably knows why Noah hasn't tried to contact me since our date. There is a small chance that Noah doesn't have an issue with me and that there was nothing to share with David, but I don't want to find out while sitting at the table with my parents and Mrs. Davis.

"David James Randall, I know you did not just walk past me like a stranger." Mrs. Davis says, using the table to pull herself up.

"Mrs. Davis you know I would never ignore you on purpose, and I definitely would have spoken if I saw Willow sitting over here," He is obviously surprised to see me.

"Are you two friends?" my mom asks curiously.

"Yes, ma'am we are. I'm David by the way." He smiles politely at my parents.

"I did not know you two were friends. What a small world!" Mrs. Davis eyes the two of us curiously.

"It's not like that." David addresses the suggestive tone to her voice. "My best friend had a meeting at Willow's company a few months ago, and she was kind enough to show us around. She's pretty great at what she does by the way, so you two should be proud." He addresses my parents.

"It turned out that we had a mutual friend in common, so we sort of became friends by default," he says, setting the record straight. I offer him a sincere smile because his answer just saved me from further prying about my dating life from the three nosey people at the table.

"Well, it's good to see you sweetie. Your being here so soon means that my grandson is doing something right with this restaurant of his. David and his friends were just here two days ago ordering the entire menu," Mrs. Davis says, filling us in.

"Oh, yeah? I didn't know you liked vegan food," I say, in an accusatory tone. I brought Noah here, and I wouldn't be surprised if he is one of the friends that Mrs. Davis is referring to.

"Boss man had me try one last week, and we've both been hooked on the po'boy ever since. I still can't believe it's not real meat." He chuckles in an attempt to lighten the mood.

"So, that's why I couldn't order the po'boy earlier. You got the last one."

"Hey, it's not my fault. Blame the chef," he chuckles. "Well, let me go grab this food. I have a meeting to get to. It was good to see you all." He excuses himself.

"I should probably be going too. I need to get back to the front to greet customers. Come say bye before you leave, now." Mrs. Davis follows David.

"Yes, ma'am." I say, putting my head down to look at my cell phone and avoid my mother's glare.

I can feel her eyes glued to the side of my head. She most likely assumes that David and I are more than friends or wants to ask me more about our mutual friend. David's choice of words mixed with my obvious annoyance at the mentioning of his best friend or "boss man" has her desperate to know what that whole conversation was about. Surprisingly, she doesn't bombard me with questions. Instead, we enjoy our lunch, and they share details of their vacations.

20

"HEY FAMILY!" JANAE yells as she opens the door to my condo. "I see you used your key." I eye the key that I gave her for emergencies only.

"Technically this is an emergency because I haven't seen your parents in nearly a year, and I missed them." She walks over to hug my parents.

"We missed you too, and your mama asked me to give you an extra hug for her." My mom pulls Janae into a tight embrace.

"Thank you for that," Janae says, with tears in her eyes.

"She told me to tell you that you are to shed no tears," my mom says, sternly.

"Well maybe if you had a present for me, I wouldn't feel sad about missing my mom so much," Janae jokes.

"I actually have a little surprise for you two." My mom smiles deviously.

"You didn't!" we say in unison.

"Oh, but I did." She walks away to grab her luggage. She returns with a big bag and begins to open it slowly for dramatic effects.

"Ma, come on already." I am eager to find out if she got the present I hoped for.

"You are so impatient." She tosses two separate bags towards us.

"What did you get?" I say, after seeing Janae frown.

"Tapestry with Bob Marley's face on it which I love because he is my favorite artist of all time, but this isn't what I was expecting," she pouts.

"I got a Bob Marley tee, but I'm jealous because I want the tapestry for my condo," I admit.

"I'll trade you, but I'm not going to lie and say I didn't half expect to find a joint in our bags." Her confession causes me to laugh because I had the same exact thought.

"Oh no, I'm too pretty to go to jail, but I did try some special tea when I was out there," she confesses.

"Yeah and she was reciting poetry and talking about how beautiful the sky was for three hours straight," my dad interjects.

"Wow, so you two were just living your best lives in Jamaica, huh?" I giggle at their middle-aged fun.

"Oh yes honey! We felt like teenagers all over again in Jamaica. We even made love under the stars."

"Dammit Sage, you always go too far. I told you about that!" my father says, frustrated with my mother's over-share.

"Yeah ma, some things are meant to stay private, and that was one of those things," I clarify in case she didn't understand how gross her comment was.

"Okay Miss judgmental. You obviously aren't interested in hearing about my trip, so how about you tell me who that guy was at the restaurant?" She directs her question at me but looks straight at Janae for a response.

"Wait, don't tell me you ran into him?" Janae is confused by my mother's question.

"Ran into who? Who is this mystery guy?" My mom stares at me intently.

"There is no mystery guy, and I need to go answer the door," I excuse myself from the conversation. Omari's arrival couldn't have come at a better time.

"Oh, thank God you're here!" I pull him into the house.

"Mom and Janae must be interrogating you," he says, knowingly.

"Mom has been interrogating me since we left the airport." I guide him into the living room where my mom and Janae are huddled together, whispering.

"Oh lord, I'm guessing I'm in trouble?" Janae realizes that she has been caught red handed.

"When your mom comes to visit, I promise I am telling her all of your business," I say matter-of-factly.

"You know how it is when mama Sage is around." Janae follows me into the kitchen where my mom is out of earshot. "She forces me to spill my guts, but I promise that I didn't tell her anything. I was trying to figure out who the guy in the restaurant was, but I pieced it together and realized that she was talking about David."

"I was just so shocked to see him getting food for Noah. I'm surprised he didn't call to tell you that we ran into each other. He did say he had a meeting though," I explain.

"Your mom said you seemed annoyed when he mentioned a mutual friend. I hope you didn't let on that you felt some kind of way about him ordering food from your spot," she shrugs. "But hey, you always say that divine timing is everything, so maybe this whole situation was meant to happen."

"I hate it when you use my words against me." I pretend not to realize that she might be right.

She has a point. Sometimes things align, and this could very well be one of those times when I was in the right place at the right time. I am not saying that I plan to reach out to Noah because I am definitely not doing that, but I can be more open minded like I was before I got hurt in past relationships. I did a good job in not assuming or making excuses for Noah's disappearing, but I haven't been upfront with the fact that I am disappointed that we haven't spoken in over a week.

21

"WILLOW, WAKE UP." Janae gently shakes me awake. My body instantly jolts into an upright position, and I am ready to fight if I have to, but I'm also ready to run away if the situation calls for it.

"Whoa. Relax it's just us." Janae moves out of reach.

"What is going on?" I am confused by her and Omari's smiling faces.

"Get up. We're going on the roof like old times," my brother says excitedly.

"What time is it?" I am still groggy from sleep.

"It's midnight." Janae reads the clock on my nightstand.

"So, we couldn't have scheduled this little conversation sometime earlier in the day?" I am annoyed by their timing.

"You fell asleep at nine-thirty like an old lady, so no there wasn't an opportunity to do this earlier in the night," Janae retorts.

"Just get dressed and meet us upstairs." Omari cuts straight through the long conversation that was sure to follow.

"Fine." I am annoyed with their timing but excited to rehash what I think is their attempt at participating in an old tradition of ours.

◆ ◆ ◆

"I've missed this place." Omari holds his head up to the sky with his arms stretched out wide. The three of us used to meet up on my roof every month to talk about our dreams, relationships, fears, and as cheesy as it sounds, we would look up at the stars and meditate.

"You're the one who moved away and ruined our tradition." I tease him.

"Yeah, you definitely ruined our tradition," Janae jokes. "But just last year, we were creating vision boards, and now you're actually living your dreams. I'm seriously proud of you." Her tone turns serious.

"Come on now. Don't get all emotional on me," he says sternly.

"How do you expect us not to get emotional when we see you out here accomplishing goals left and right? I haven't done half of the things that I set out to, and I'm your big sister," I admit.

"We are not allowed to feel sorry for ourselves up here, remember?" Omari reminds me. "And besides, tonight is a new moon which means that this night marks new beginnings for all three of us. Whatever we want is ours *if* we believe it wholeheartedly and work for it so no more feeling sorry for yourself. Get out there and grind, sis."

"You know your brother is right." Janae drapes her arm over my shoulder. "I dare you to put as much faith and support in yourself as you do everyone else," she challenges.

"I don't think she's up for the challenge," Omari taunts.

"I think you're right," Janae adds.

"Grow up. I know what you two are doing, and it's only working because I'm allowing it to." I glance towards the moon. "Give me a few months and things will look much different for me. I promise you that."

"You know I'm petty, so I will be watching you, and I hope I don't have to say I told you so because I'd rather congratulate you," Janae says, candidly.

The two of them have given me this same lecture many times, but tonight I hear them clearly, and my intuition says that now is the time to bet on myself and watch how things begin to unfold. So, with my boost in confidence I spend the next few hours with my best friend and brother dancing and howling at the moon like kids. For a short while, we are free from worry, doubt, and the realities of life, and we don't realize how long we've been out here until the sun comes up.

◆ ◆ ◆

"Grand rising, Queen." I greet my mom who is in the kitchen cooking bright and early. She taught my siblings and I that we are royalty by design early on, and after some time, this became one of my favorite ways to acknowledge her.

"Hey, mini me." She places a plate down on the table for me.

"Thanks, ma." I dig into the spinach and potato scramble.

"Anything for my baby girl." She smiles wide, revealing the small gap between her two front teeth.

"What are you up to, ma?" I ask suspiciously. If I had to guess, I'd say she is hoping to continue our conversation from last night.

"Can't a mother cook for her child without having an ulterior motive?" She places her hand over her heart to suggest that she is hurt by my distrust.

"Well, thanks again." I scoop more food onto my fork.

She waits until I take a bite to say, "Well, since you brought it up, I was sort of wondering how your dating life has been, and I've been traveling a lot, so I haven't been here for you as much as I usually am. I think it only makes sense for you to fill your mother in on your life."

"Okay, fine." I let out a breath. "Honestly, work has been crappy because my boss sucks, and I am working on a plan to open my own business, but I haven't told anyone yet. You're actually the first person I've said this to. Then, there's my love life, which isn't much of a love life at all. I've been on a few dates, but I didn't have chemistry with either of the guys, so I took the past few months to focus on myself. Then, a few months ago I met this guy Noah for the second time, which was really sort of the first time depending on how you look at the situation. But ma, he feels so familiar. I admit that at first, I was overthinking the situation because he's a singer and women throw themselves at him all the time, but the more we talked I started to realize that he is a regular guy, and I like the real him better than his R&B persona."

"I'm guessing he challenges you?" She laughs when a surprised look spreads across my face. "You're my child and your whole life you've been attracted to men who challenge you without trying to control you or dim your light."

"Most of our interactions have been over the phone, but I feel like he really sees me, ma. Not the fear I hide behind or the guard I keep up to avoid being hurt again. He genuinely tries to see the real me, but it doesn't really matter now. He hasn't called me since our date last week, and it feels like everyone expects me to freak out over it."

"Baby girl, why do you care what other people expect you to do? You know what you need better than anyone else." She looks me directly in the eyes, daring me to argue with her logic. I have no rebuttal, and I'm happy not to because my mom is right, and I need to acknowledge the great advice I've been receiving the past few months. Deep down I know that my focus has to be on creating the life I envision for myself. I've been going within and working to heal my past hurts, but I haven't fully surrendered to the process. I hop up and walk to my closet to grab the vision board I created at the retreat, and I prop it up on the wall for me to see every morning when I wake up. As far is Noah is concerned, I believe in giving people the space they need, so that's exactly what I plan to do.

22

I WALK INTO work in an unusually good mood. Not that I am a Debbie Downer or anything; it's just that Carter knows how to push every button and overstep every boundary that I have. He feels that as the alpha male he knows everything that there is to know about business, but he doesn't realize that half of his female clientele are unhappy and hate his communication style. Thankfully, I spent the past three days with my family and received some much-needed loving care, so my head is in a good space, and I refuse to let anyone steal my joy.

I turn the corner to walk towards Carter's office, but the hallway is crawling with employees standing a few feet away from his door pretending to be working when what they are actually doing is eavesdropping. I spot Sasha, one of the few people I trust at this company and walk over to her to find out what exactly is going on around here. She tries to fill me in on the situation, but with Carter screaming at the top of his lungs, it is quite obvious that he is on the phone having an argument with one of his clients. His office suddenly goes quiet, and the crowd scrambles back to where they came from, leaving me to do the job I've come to dread. I knock on the door lightly, but when Carter doesn't answer I knock again a little louder.

"Come in already, Willow! I know you heard the whole thing." He sounds defeated.

"I heard shouting, but I couldn't understand what exactly was going on." I am cautious, hoping to avoid an argument.

"Basically, the ungrateful models that I hired for an upcoming fashion show decided to drop out at the last minute and have been spreading rumors about my professionalism," he hisses.

"Well..."

"Well what?" Carter dares me to disagree with him.

"Well," I decide not to give away my power any longer. "I have to admit that your management style is different than most people's, so maybe they just aren't used to it."

"Excuse me?" He is surprised by my admission.

"Look at me for instance. You have clients that personally ask to work with me, yet you keep me on as assistant after promising to move me up to a junior designer. Why is that? Do you feel that I'm the wrong person for the job?"

"You can leave now," he says without emotion.

"Carter, please. I am asking for feedback on my work performance." I stand my ground.

"We can have this discussion during performance review times, but right now, I need you to do your job and bring the files for these models, so that I can do some damage control." His voice is stern but controlled.

"You seriously won't give me feedback?" I want to make sure I understand the situation fully.

"Okay, since you need feedback so bad, here is your feedback. You are a talented employee and designer, but you don't have enough drive to make it in this field. You've stayed on as an assistant for years because you don't believe in yourself, but you'd rather blame me. People always want me to be the bad guy, so I have no problem letting you blame me for your problems," he shrugs.

"Well excuse me for thinking that I could trust my supervisor and so-called mentor to keep his word and help me make my way up the totem pole. You can go get those files yourself because I quit."

"Whatever. I can have another assistant here in a matter of minutes."

"And in a matter of months, she will probably quit on you like all your other assistants, little man." I take a jab at his height.

"Clean out your desk and be gone within the hour!" he shouts.

"I'll be gone in twenty," I reply with a smile because he has gotten over on me for the last time.

◆ ◆ ◆

My phone begins to ring just as I am putting my key into the door of my condo. I am not surprised when I see Janae's name flashing across the screen. I received a lot of discreet thumbs up and pats on the back before I left the office earlier, so I wouldn't be surprised if someone called Janae to fill her in on what happened. She was out of the office today, but word travels fast around that place. I drop my grocery bags on the counter and press accept to answer her call.

"Hey, girl. What's up?" I pretend not to know her reason for calling.

"Girl, I heard you walked out on Carter." Janae screams through the speaker of my phone. "Everyone at work is saying how proud they are. We all knew it was only a matter of time before you got tired of his antics."

"Honestly, I should have left a year ago, but I was scared to lose the consistent paychecks," I admit.

"That's how the man keeps us down. The promise of consistent checks has us walking around like robots, clocking into jobs that don't even bring us joy. You aren't the only one. I lived like that for years."

"Yeah, I could easily be nominated as the spokesperson for people who hate their jobs but needed a check. Not anymore, though." I beam with pride. "I almost told you and Omari the other night, but now that I'm jobless I might as well let you know, so you two aren't worried about me or getting in my business on a daily basis. I've actually been thinking of selling my pieces online to bring in some extra money. I already have pieces to sell and two clients requesting custom designs."

"Online shopping is becoming really popular, so that's a great idea. In the meantime, keep building up your clientele, and let God do the rest. I mean, *The Most High* or whatever name you're using today with your hippie self." I laugh.

"Wow. I didn't realize how much I needed to laugh until just now," I confess.

"Well, how about we move our Sunday brunch to Saturday instead? We haven't had a Saturday brunch in a while, but I think there is definite cause for one."

"Sounds like a plan. But hey, I'm about to use my anger to get some work done. I don't want this momentum to go away and I get all comfortable again."

"Oh, miss thing, please hang-up. Use that energy to be productive because I don't need you to ask to borrow money," she jokes.

Despite our decision to cut the call short, we end up talking for another hour. She fills me in on how everyone at work called her with different versions of the same story. One person said I purposely spilled coffee all over Carter's desk before quitting and another person said I tossed several files of paperwork off of his desk. Though untrue, the stories are pretty entertaining, and I wish I could go back and make one of those things happen, but I am proud of myself for taking the high road. Brunch is two days away which means that for the next two days, I will be held up in my home, working on new designs and creating a social media page. The promise of girl-talk and mimosas is the motivation for staying in and working.

23

MY PHONE RINGS, which causes me to look over at my alarm clock. It's almost twelve in the afternoon, and I am supposed to meet Janae in thirty minutes for brunch. I jump out of bed and rub the sleep out of my eyes. The caller ID reveals that the person intruding my sleep is my older sister, Justice, who seems to have a knack for calling me during naptimes. We haven't spoken in a few days, but we never go more than a week without checking in with one another, so I answer the call to make sure that everything is okay with her.

"Hey, sis," I grumble into the phone.

"Whoa. Did someone finally have sex that was so mind-blowing it caused her to sleep in until 12 PM?" she says, excitedly.

"Relax." I say sleepily, "I was up working until 4 o'clock in the morning which is why I'm so tired."

"And grumpy." She cuts me off.

"Sorry sis but I had a long night. I quit my job on Thursday, and now, I'm late meeting Janae for brunch. Don't be mad that I didn't call to tell you, but I promise to fill you in later today."

"Well, I'll let you go since you're obviously busy, but I expect a call later with a full explanation. Now, go take a quick shower and throw on some clothes. I'm sure Janae will be just as late as you, so you should be fine."

"I promise to call you later. I love you sis. Talk soon."

"I love you too, and hey, try to have some fun today. You sound stressed."

"I promise to at least try." I use a similar line to the one I used at the retreat and on the roof top with Janae and Omari.

I end the call and walk straight to the bathroom to turn on the shower. The hot water runs over my body; after a few minutes I feel wide awake and ready to go out into the world without falling asleep mid conversation. I grab my hair pick, deciding to style my hair in an afro and throw on an oversized tee with Chuck Taylors. To the normal eye, it will look as though I am giving off comfy chic vibes, but really, this is all I have that's clean at the moment.

I unlock my phone to send a quick text to Janae and let her know that I am running late. I must have been sleeping hard throughout the morning because I have a missed call from her and what looks like at least a thousand notifications on my new social media pages. I only sent friend requests to a select group of people, including friends, family, and a few of the women that I met at the retreat, so I am confused by the high rate of notifications I received. I click on my *For the Love of Fashion* Instagram page that I created less than forty-eight hours ago. There are over three thousand likes on the design I posted and several comments from familiar faces saying congratulations. I scroll lower and my stomach does backflips when Noah's name appears on the screen. He not only followed my business page, but he also gave me a shout-out on his personal page.

"What the hell?" is all I manage to say. I haven't heard from Noah in over a week, but he decided to share my ventures with the world. I shrug it off deciding not to analyze his actions or make assumptions until I've had food in my system. I click on his post and add the praying hands image under the comments to symbolize that I am grateful for his support. Then, I leave the house to meet Janae for drinks.

◆ ◆ ◆

I tiptoe into the restaurant to make sure that Janae isn't setting me up like she did the last time we were here. When I spot her sitting in our usual booth alone, I let out a sigh of relief because I definitely need to have girl talk right about now. As I begin to walk over to the table, someone walks up from behind me and reaches for my hand. I turn to yell at whatever guy was bold enough to touch me, when I notice my sister, Justice standing behind me with a huge grin on her face.

"What are you doing here?" I say, in total shock.

"Damn, can a sister get a hello?" she says, jokingly.

"Sorry, I'm just surprised to see you, but I'm happy to see you," I confirm.

"Well, good because I've missed you." She pulls me in for a hug.

"Now that a hug has been shared between us, please tell me why you flew all the way to Texas without telling me." I circle back to my original question.

"I was worried about you, so I hopped on a plane to check on my baby sister. Is that a crime?" She places her arm around me and leads me to our table. "So, what's the deal with Noah?"

"See, I knew you were up to something. Janae and her big mouth!" I complain.

"You've been so busy lately that I had to go through her to find out the basics of your life. Now tell me who Noah is!" She gives me a stare down that only an older sister could give.

"We went on *one* date. He hasn't contacted me since then, and I haven't reached out to him. It's not a big deal. I was going to tell you everything when I called you later today but like always my best friend beat me to the punch."

"Don't be mad at Janae. She was looking out for you. She felt you needed me, and if she hadn't, I wouldn't be here. Now, back to this Noah guy. You haven't had any contact of any kind since the date?" She leans in close to study my eyes. She has always been able to tell when I am lying.

"Justice, you must have seen his Instagram post, or you wouldn't be leaning in all close to my face like you are inspector gadget." I take my seat across from Janae and fold my arms over my chest in protest.

"I saw it this morning, and that's why I'm curious as to how your date with him really ended." Janae clears her throat, making it obvious that she has something to add to the conversation.

"You obviously have something to say, so go ahead and inform us," I say, in a frustrated tone.

"Don't shoot the messenger, but David explained the situation to me, and I can see where Noah is coming from." She shrinks into her seat.

"When did you talk to David?" I reply quickly.

"He came over last night and explained the entire situation to me. It took some work to get the information out of him, but I threatened to join you in your vow of celibacy, and he gave up the information within seconds. I knew I had to tell you as soon as I found out." She sits up taller before continuing.

"Noah really likes you, and he enjoyed the date. David said that he even mentioned some lovey-dovey moment that happened in the record store, but apparently, your reaction to his fan interrupting you guys is what made him question if he should really be dating at this point in his life. He said that he wouldn't want to push you into a situation that you're uncomfortable with, so rather than hurt you, he decided to give you space and support you from afar."

"If that's true then why did he make a post on social media telling thousands of people to support my new business venture? And what does he mean he saw my reaction? Yeah, the fan bombarding him for a picture freaked me out a little, but I didn't say anything to him about it."

"Now, you know your face says how you feel without you ever needing to say a single word." Justice confesses.

"Yeah, and it's not like he said he didn't like you. He was trying to protect you from his world. The thought was sweet but misguided," Janae adds.

"The question is what are you going to do now?" They say in unison.

"I'm going to call him and set him straight. He has no right to assume that he knows what is best for me without even discussing it with me first." I grab my phone confidentially and dial Noah's number, but when he answers on the first ring, I chicken out and hang up.

"What just happened?" Justice says, confused by my reaction.

"I got nervous!"

"So, you hung up in the man's face? He is going to call back, you know?" Justice pinches me like she did when we were kids, and just as predicted, a second later, my phone begins to vibrate in my hand, and his name appears across the screen.

"Girl, pick up already!" They shout in unison.

"What if he was right? What if I'm not ready to date?" I ask, nervously.

"You know what? You're right, Willow. Just keep doing the same thing over and over and expect different results." Justice is obviously frustrated with me. Her tone of voice sounds just like my mother, which causes me to remember that I am a grownup who needs to answer the call.

"Hey, Noah," I say casually as if I didn't just hang up in his face.

"Hey, Willow. What's up?" His voice sounds calm, as if nothing has transpired over the past week and a half, which annoys me even more, but I refrain from letting it show in my voice.

"I just wanted to call and say thank you for helping promote my business. You didn't have to do that, so I appreciate it." I hear him smile in reaction to my words.

"Well, your work speaks for itself. I just wanted to give people the opportunity to see for themselves," he says, without hesitation.

"Well, thank you for that." I say again except more awkwardly this time.

"Hey Noah, we have that conference call in three minutes." I hear his mangers voice in the background, and it is obvious that Noah is busy but doesn't want me to know. He covers up the phone with his hand and sighs heavily.

Returning to the phone he says, "Hey, not sure if you heard that but ..."

"Hey, you're a busy man. I understand," I say, jokingly.

"I'm a tired, man who needs rest," he says, sleepily. "But, hey, thanks for calling. It was good to hear your voice."

"No problem, and thanks again for your support." The call ends; I pick my head up to find Justice and Janae staring at me eagerly.

"That was a quick conversation, and you were definitely smiling the entire time!" Justice teases.

"I was eavesdropping, and I feel like that manager of his was definitely blocking." Janae takes a sip of her mimosa. She misses her mouth, and Justice and I look at each other and laugh uncontrollably.

"Well, he just released a new album, so he's bound to be busy. I just hope he's taking care of himself." I come to his defense. Justice begins to play an invisible violin while Janae makes the heart symbol with her hands.

"Hey, mock all you want, but I reached out to him, so I don't want to hear anymore judgment from either of you. It's obvious that we are meant to be friends and nothing more, and I am fine with that," I say, firmly.

"You are so right. Friendly vibes were written all over that conversation." Justice mocks me once again, and Janae takes over playing the invisible violin. We laugh at one another's childishness and agree to spend the rest of our brunch catching up on their love lives instead of mine.

24

I AM EXTREMELY happy to finally have my own business, but I did not expect things to take off this fast. I have received nine requests for custom-made pieces this week alone, and my online store has only been open for two weeks. According to several of my former co-workers, the news of my starting a business is being shared around the office, and Carter is not happy about my newfound entrepreneurial spirit. Word on the street is that he has badmouthed me to a few of his clients, but with Noah's endorsement and my strong work ethic while at the company, I believe that people will give me a fair chance to dispel Carter's lies. One of the nine requests came from my friend Nova who wants me to design a dress for an event that she's attending in a few weeks, but business is business even if it comes from a friend. She kept her word and reached out to me shortly after the retreat ended to schedule a lunch when she visits her family near Dallas. We were originally supposed to meet a month from now, but due to a change in her schedule, she is coming to Dallas sooner, and I couldn't be more excited.

25

"WILLOW!" NOVA SMILES as she walks over to the table where I am seated. Her curls are now straight and flow past her shoulders. Her dark brown skin looks flawless, and she looks even happier than she did when I last saw her.

"Being in person is much better than texting every few weeks. I'm glad you came to visit early." I stand to hug her.

"It's definitely better to talk in person because you're such a bad communicator via text!" She laughs and takes a seat across from me. "It's really good to see you, though. You're actually one of the reasons for me flying in sooner." My eyebrow rises in confusion.

"Right, you mentioned needing a dress for an event. Do you need it sooner than expected?"

Her genuine smile turns into an uncomfortable grin. "I do need a dress for an event, but that's not what brought me to Dallas sooner. Don't freak out, but I asked you to lunch because I wanted to ask how you know my brother, Teddy." Her question causes me to choke on my lemonade.

"Teddy? I don't know a Teddy." I think back to the men I've went on dates with over the past few months. There were only three and none were named Teddy.

"Willow, you definitely know my brother." She turns her phone so that I can see the screen. A knot forms in my stomach when she points to image of me on Noah's social media page.

"I swear I had no clue you two were related. You said that your brother's name was Teddy!" My stomach starts to feel queasy.

"Teddy is a nickname because he was chunky when we were kids. I started calling him that when I was six, and the name sort of stuck."

"But why wouldn't you tell me that Noah Daniels was your brother?" I am confused by this entire situation.

"Teddy is a very private person, and I'm protective of him, so I don't go around telling people who he is. He is sort of a big deal now, and I just can't risk people using me to get to him, so I don't mention him unless it comes up."

"Damn." I feel dumbfounded.

"Yep," she says, awkwardly.

"Well, I promise that I didn't know he was your brother or else I definitely would have told you. Noah and I crossed paths about nine months ago, but we didn't actually meet until four months ago. There is nothing going on between us. We're just friends or more like acquaintances actually. We talked on the phone and video chatted for a few months, then we finally went on a date or something like a date, but he never called me after that. His social media post was a big shock to me."

"He is such an idiot" She reaches across the table to touch my arm. "I didn't mean to insinuate that you were lying or using me to get to know him. I'm just shocked is all. I haven't even mentioned this to him yet. I wanted to talk to you before I jumped to conclusions."

"Well, that's pretty much the story of Noah and Willow. There isn't much to tell," I shrug.

"I am going to tell him off as soon as I speak to him. I don't want our friendship to be messed up because of my brother. We've grown close the past few months, and I don't have many friends that I trust."

"This won't come between our friendship, and I'm not mad at Noah. Things didn't work out romantically but I'm grateful for his support. I'm working hard to grow my business, and I'm actually enjoying spending time with myself. I'm actually a pretty great woman," I laugh.

"You've definitely changed since the retreat. You seem different, more confident. I have to be honest with you, though. My brother's decision to broadcast you on his page means that he cares about you. As I said before,

Noah is a very private person. Fame is not something he ever expected or wanted, but now that he has it, he doesn't want to do anything to tarnish his brand."

"I can understand that, and it makes me appreciate his support even more."

"Do you think the friendship could blossom into something more?" A sly smile spreads across her face.

"Nova, please don't pry. I don't want him to think that I'm trying to force him to date me. I honestly don't know if I even see him *that way* anymore," I lie.

"Fine, I won't pry, but I have to tell him that I know you. You've been a great friend to me these past few months, and I refuse to let our friendship be ruined because of my idiot brother."

"It won't. Now, please promise to stay out of it."

"I promise." She offers me her pinky, which I assume, is a family tradition. Noah made the same gesture when I saw him last.

◆ ◆ ◆

An hour goes by before we realize that we've been doing nothing but laughing and gossiping the entire time we've been here. Nova shared stories about her and Noah's childhood, filled me in on her recent engagement, and showed me pictures of her four-year-old daughter, Lexi. She even tossed in a few details about Noah's past relationships. Apparently, he was in a serious relationship that ended three years ago. Nova didn't go into many details, but her stories had a way of making me feel guilty. I felt as though I was prying into sacred spaces that Noah never intended me to see, so to make things fair, I told her about my breakup with Ziggy. I didn't go into details, but I gave her just enough to make things even between Noah and me. I know that she is going to go back and tell him what we discussed, but at least now we are on even playing field.

After lunch, we shopped for fabric and handled the business side of things. Nova insisted that I come to her grandmother's house when she is back in town in a few weeks. She claims that it would be the perfect time for her to try on the dress in case we need to make any adjustments and then she briefly mentioned that she is also hosting a game night and thinks that it would be a great idea for me to stop by to meet some of her friends and drum up more business. She says that her intentions are pure, and she simply wants to help promote my brand, but I'm wary of the situation. Nova and I are friends, but I do not want to interfere in Noah's life. I told her that I would think about it and let her know. If I do go, I will most definitely be brining Janae or Omari for support.

26

I AM SPENDING the day with Omari to give myself a mental break from all that has occurred over the past few weeks. He is hosting a day party for a group of millennial aged entrepreneurs, which could turn out to be a great networking opportunity for the both of us. He hired a DJ, and there will be tons of vendors selling food, clothes, jewelry, and art. As the host, Omari will have a booth to promote his artwork, and he agreed to sell a few of my pieces as well. I haven't painted anything new in a while, but since I no longer have a steady income, I figured I might as well put some of my old artwork up for sale and a few of the new outfits I designed. The venue is forty-five minutes away, so I have just enough time to take a quick shower, make lunch, and get dressed.

I hop out of bed and connect my phone to my Bluetooth speaker. Summer Walker's "Girls Need Love" begins to play and my mind automatically goes to Noah. I haven't been physical with a man in so long, and right now, I can't help but wonder what it would feel like to have him in here with me. First, washing my back then running his fingers through my hair. I close my eyes and allow myself to imagine what it would feel like for us to surrender ourselves to one another. My hand travels down to the sensitive bud between my thighs, and I move my fingers in slow precise circles, feeling closer to climax with each movement. Just as I begin to pick up the pace, my phone rings, startling me out of my fantasy. Moving the shower curtain back, I take a peek at my phone.

"Shit! Why is he calling me?" I feel slightly panicked, as if Noah could somehow see what I was doing. I grab my towel and quickly throw it on my body before answering the call.

"Hey." I try to catch my breath.

"Hey, did I catch you at a bad time? You over there exercising or something?" I attempt to keep my laughter contained but a soft giggle manages to escape.

"Yeah, I was doing a little yoga. You know I'm all about self-care." My cheeks redden from my lie.

"I heard yoga is really good for the body. Maybe we can check out a class together one day." His suggestion catches me off guard because less than a month ago, Noah felt that he shouldn't date me, and he's been awkward about it ever since.

"Oh yeah? What's changed since the last time I saw you?" He sighs heavily into the phone a few times before responding.

"Willow, I know Janae told you what I said. David told me he spoke to her, and I'm sure she told you what I said about you, but it was not personal. It's just that my lifestyle can be difficult at times. Strangers expect to have a piece of me whenever they demand it, and I saw your face when that lady asked for a picture. I decided then that I can't pull you into what I have going on."

"So rather than explain how you felt, you decided to ignore me? I bet if I never called you to say thanks a few weeks ago, we wouldn't even be on the phone right now." I finally share my frustration.

"You're probably right, but one thing you have to know is that I will always support you even if we never speak again after today."

"But why, Noah? You barely even know me."

"Willow," he says, firmly, "Why don't you trust me by now? I haven't known you long, but I think I've proven that I care about you."

"That's just it. You keep saying you care, but your silence speaks volumes. You ignore me then you support me then you're quiet again for weeks. I can't keep up with your moods. I bet Nova put you up to this phone call."

"Nova can't make me do anything. She told me you two knew each other, but I planned on calling you long before she told me anything."

"Okay, so if your sister didn't ask you to call, please help me understand what's been happening with you? I feel like there are things you haven't said."

"This isn't a conversation I wanted to have over the phone."

"Too late." I cross my arms in protest.

"Okay, but please listen, and once I explain everything, you can ask questions." I hear the pleading in his voice, and I relax a little.

"I promise to stay silent until you finish." I cross my fingers in case I have to break the agreement.

"Okay so, I guess I should start by explaining why I care about what happens to you?"

"That would be helpful." I sound tough, but I'm full of nerves.

"When I first decided that I wanted to meet with Carter to discuss a possible joint venture, my manager, Derrick, decided to ask around to see what other people thought about his work. I was at my parent's house having dinner with my mom and her friend Lotus when Derrick stopped by to tell me what he learned of Carter. According to his sources, Carter isn't the easiest person to work with, so we started discussing possible alternatives. That's when Lotus joined in and gave her opinion. She said that if we worked with Carter, we needed to make sure that his assistant was part of the team. I was surprised to learn that she found his assistant to be equally as talented as him, but I trust her, so I followed her instructions without question." He pauses for a second before continuing.

"That morning, we arrived at the office, and I walked off of the elevator and saw you standing there. I *never* expected Carters assistant to be the same woman from the restaurant months before. You probably couldn't tell, but when I saw you, I was nervous, and more than anything, I was afraid that my presence would make you uncomfortable and take you back to whatever you were going through that night, so I kept my distance and hid behind my guards. Despite my reservation, I did as Lotus instructed and had Carter bring you in for the meeting."

"I wondered why you were acting so weird when everyone tried to approach you. I thought you were a pretentious jerk," I laugh.

"Nope. I was just nervous," he chuckles. "After the meeting, David told me that he saw you sketching my ideas as I explained them to Carter. I immediately knew that I needed to see your work, so I suggested it to

Carter, and he said some disrespectful things. Without a second thought, I decided to part ways with him and his company. I figured I would never see you again, but then you bumped into me at lunch a week later, and I was grateful for the chance to finally talk to you. I decided to keep things on a personal level and leave business dealings out of it. It felt like a selfish decision once I realized how bad you wanted to be a business owner. That's why I posted you on my social media accounts."

I sit on the other end of the phone trying to soak in everything that was just said. Lotus obviously wanted our paths to cross. She kept our meeting at the retreat confidential but found a loophole to getting what she wanted which seems to be having Noah and I in the same room. I'll have to reach out to her soon to figure out why she wanted us to meet so badly, but I am grateful for her prying ways. I can't decide if I am angry with Carter or thankful for his spitefulness. His actions led to me taking a leap of faith that I otherwise might not have taken. What impresses me the most about Noah's confession is that in all our months of knowing each other, he never boasted about his attempts to help me. In fact, I was blindly aware of everything until this very second. A request for a video call appears on the screen, and I wrap my towel tighter, hoping that he doesn't realize that I lied about what I was doing at the beginning of our phone call.

"I don't like unscheduled FaceTime calls, remember?" I say, jokingly.

He chuckles, "Those rules don't apply to me remember? But I won't keep you long. You got quiet for a while, so I wanted to give you the chance to ask me whatever questions you have face to face." He rubs his hand over his tired eyes. I'm guessing his schedule hasn't slowed down since we last spoke.

"Well, first I want to say thank you for everything that you've done for me. I guess I just need to know what you hope for going forward."

"I'm not demanding anything of you, but I hope for a fair chance to spend time with you now that everything is out in the open," he says without hesitation.

"Okay, let's do it. I'm in."

"Whoa. That's it? No long speech or sarcastic response?"

"There will be no fussing from me today. All I ask is that you be respectful of me, and I'll give the same in return."

"Deal." He grins into the camera. "Now hurry up and hop back in the shower funky lady." The call ends before I get the chance to respond.

27

I RUSH INTO THE restaurant where the event is being held. I planned on arriving early to help setup, but when Noah called, I lost track of time. I can't help but be suspicious of the giddy feelings that Noah's call produced inside of me. I want to enjoy the moment and not stress over the past or future, but I also do not want to have my heart broken. Shaking those thoughts from my head, I walk inside the venue, prepared to hear complaints from Omari.

"What took you so long to get here? Everything is already set up now." He is pretending to be annoyed, but the place is swarming with staff, so I am sure he had plenty of help.

"Sorry baby bro. I ran into traffic." I decide to keep my conversation with Noah a secret.

"Willow, you suck at lying, but I'll let it go for now. Just make sure you tell whoever he is that he better treat you right or else," he says, matter-of-factly.

"I could ask the same of your friend." I eye the chick standing in between his legs.

"Where are your manners?" she rolls her eyes at him. "Hi, I'm Carmen. I've heard a lot about you." She reaches out to shake my hand.

"Is that right?" I accept her hand. My brother is tense with nerves.

"Yeah, your brother always talk's about how amazing his sisters are," she says, proudly.

"That's good to know. He never says anything nice to our faces," I tease. "Has mommy met your girlfriend, Omari?" My words sound sincere to the untrained ear, but Omari knows when I am teasing him. He is a total mama's boy, and although she is the most loving woman in the world, she can be protective of her youngest child and only son.

"Does mommy know about your boyfriend?" He grins back at me. "Yeah, Justice filled me in on your love life. I know all about Noah," he retaliates.

"Forget I asked." Damn Justice and her big mouth. "Take me to my booth please." He thinks that he has won, but we are going to continue this conversation later. In the meantime, I send Justice a text to let her know that I am never sharing details of my life with her again.

28

*A*FTER TWO WEEKS of negotiation, Nova finally convinced me to attend game night. She marketed it as the perfect opportunity to network with other entrepreneurs in Dallas, but my decision to attend was mostly to get to know her better. We have grown fairly close over the past few months. She reminds me a lot of myself, and with my sister living in Atlanta and Janae being in a new relationship, I figured it wouldn't hurt to keep building the bond that we developed at the retreat. Noah is out of town, so I invited Janae to come with me. It turns out that David beat me to the punch, so once again, here I am stuck being their third wheel. To make matters worse, they have me driving while they sit in the back seat as if I am their chauffeur.

"Okay love birds, we're here." I pull up to the house.

"Is this really their idea of a small get together? There are at least twenty cars out here." Janae looks out the window.

"This is pretty small compared to last year's event," David explains.

"So, this is an annual thing?" I ask.

"Yeah, it became tradition almost four years ago when Nova's boyfriend, well her now husband-to-be, started his own tech company in California. Game night is her way of bringing everyone together when she's in town, and we've done it every year since they moved."

"So, is any of Noah's family in there?" Janae takes the words from my mouth.

"Yeah, it's mostly his family and some of my family as well," David mumbles before hopping out of the car.

"Excuse me? Why am I just now learning that I am about to meet your family?" Janae does not like being caught off guard.

"I didn't think it was a big deal." His inability to look her in the eye suggests otherwise.

"Not a big deal? So, you wouldn't mind if I brought you to a party to meet my family without warning?"

"Guys, please don't argue especially with the old man on the grill starring at us. You have David with you. Meanwhile, I'm here without Noah, and he didn't give me any kind of warning that this was a family tradition." I am hoping to diffuse the situation.

"It probably slipped his mind. His schedule has been hectic with the upcoming album release." As always, David comes to Noah's defense.

"Don't try to take up for your best friend. He's in trouble for keeping pertinent information from me, and you better hope tonight goes smooth or Janae will never forgive you." I glare at him.

"Yeah, what she said," Janae utters before walking ahead of us with her arms crossed over her chest.

"Everything good over there?" the old man on the grill says, squinting his eyes in our direction.

"Yeah, Uncle Buzzard. Everything is good. I just did something stupid is all." David reaches for Janae's hand, but she softly pulls away.

"Sounds about right," the old man chuckles. "Please forgive the knucklehead for whatever foolish thing he's done. I've tried to teach him and my nephew how to be smooth their whole life, but some things just aren't teachable."

"You know what, Mr. Buzzard? I might consider forgiving him if you hook me up with a plate of barbecue," Janae negotiates.

"Sure thing, darling. As long as you call me Uncle Buzzard, everyone else does."

"Let me do formal introductions," David says. "Uncle Buzzard, this is Janae and Willow. Ladies this is Noah's uncle, Buzzard."

"Oh, so *you're* Noah's special friend that I've so much heard about?" Uncle Buzzard looks me over before continuing. "He told me you might be joining us tonight. I've got to warn you, our family can get a little crazy, but I got your back. Noah tasked me with looking out for you tonight, so if you need anything, I'll be out here on the grill until it's time to go in and whoop some ass in spades."

"Your nephew didn't tell me I'd be meeting his family tonight, so I wasn't prepared, but I come from a lively family of my own, so I think I'll be fine." If Uncle Buzzard is the standard, then I think I'll enjoy Noah's family just fine.

"Alright, now. I see you're a tough one, but I'm here if you need a break from all the noise. Now, go in and make yourselves a plate. Oh, and Willow, there's some fake plant burgers on the stove for you. Noah said you'd like those." He offers a sincere smile.

"Thank you. I'll save you one, so you can see what the hype is about," I tease.

"You see me throwing down on these ribs, and you offer me plants? No thanks but go on in now and enjoy yourselves." He winks before shooing us away.

We walk inside the house, past the foyer where a group of kids are dancing in the living room. David instructs us to sneak past them, but they notice him and run straight towards us, calling out his name in excitement. I laugh as the kids swarm him before quickly returning to their post to continue dancing. The youngest of the bunch is slower to walk over, and when she finally reaches us, David leans down and takes her into his arms. She holds onto his neck tight, eyeing Janae and me suspiciously.

"Hi, I'm Willow." I reach out to shake her hand. "And this is my best friend Janae." She studies me, ignoring my hand, and reaches over to whisper in David's ear. He whispers something back, and whatever was just shared between the two is enough to make her suddenly feel comfortable taking my hand into hers.

"Hi, my name is California, but everybody calls me Cali." She smiles and my heart melts.

"Like the state," I smile. "My parents named me after a tree. My mom loves Willow trees." That causes her to giggle.

"I've never seen a Willow tree, but mommy and daddy might take me to see one when I'm bigger," she shrugs. "I love trees and flowers so much, but last time we went on a hike, my little legs tired out, and daddy had to carry me all the way back to the car. I wasn't sad for long though because Uncle Noah painted my room with giant trees, all sorts of cute birds, and a big yellow sun." She peeks over her shoulder to where the other kids are dancing, and I can see her interest in this conversation slowly fading away.

"Are you a good dancer, Cali?" I give her an exit strategy.

"I'm the best dancer of the family. Want to judge our dance contest? My uncle Noah put me in charge, so it's my job to make sure that everyone is nice to you, but if you'd rather spend time with the grownups, I understand." She pouts and my ovaries do a back flip. She is definitely using her adorableness to charm me.

"I'd love to judge the dance contest." I talked a good game to Uncle Buzzard, but truth be told, I am nervous to meet the rest of Noah's family. So, this dance contest is a much-needed diversion.

"Do not force her to play with you all night. Okay, peanut?" David kneels in front of her.

"I won't, Uncle David. I promise." She places two crossed fingers behind her back, and he walks away, oblivious to having been tricked by a four-year-old.

"So, how do you know my uncle?" She turns her attention to me.

"Well, our best friends became friends then we became friends. Sounds complicated, huh?"

"A little." She giggles, but her face turns serious. "Uncle Noah is always so busy. He needs friends to help him remember to take care of himself. I try to do it, but I'm only a kid, and mommy makes me go to bed by 8 o'clock every night."

"Your mommy is a good friend of mine, so if you win this contest, I'll see if I can convince her to let you stay up until 8:10. Then, you can take care of Uncle Noah for ten extra minutes. How does that sound?"

"I always win, so get ready to talk to mommy." She runs off to dance, and I find a seat on the sofa to judge the competition. I notice a vinyl record player and giant collection of records in the corner of the room. On our first date, Noah mentioned his mom's love of music, which leaves me wondering if these records belong to her. I can't imagine that he would want me to meet her this soon into our friendship especially without him being here to witness it, but I realize that I shouldn't put anything past him. Afterall, here I am meeting his family without him.

"Girl, why are you hiding out with the kids?" Nova takes the seat next to me.

"Cali asked me to be a judge, and I couldn't say no. You see how cute she is. She's your daughter," I joke. "And I sort of promised that I could convince you to move her bedtime back ten minutes. Sorry." I squirm in my seat.

"Willow! You haven't even become her official aunt yet, and you're already making changes to her schedule. She played you, you know that, right?" She shakes her head.

"Hey, don't blame me. I was duped by her cuteness."

"Yeah, she is pretty cute!" she says, admiring Cali from afar. "But hey, come to the kitchen and grab some food with me." She stands.

"I would, but I promised to be a judge."

"Girl, these contests are rigged. She uses the routines that she learns in her dance classes and wins every time. So, join me, and I'll consider changing her bedtime."

"Deal." I follow her to the kitchen.

◆ ◆ ◆

After spending a few minutes in the kitchen, I realize that Nova purposely picked the spot in the house with the highest amount of traffic. The kitchen seems to be the central place to where everything is happening. For starters, anyone who wants to eat has to come in the kitchen, and most of the family are only a few feet away playing cards. The kitchen is also the central spot for gossip. So far, the kitchen gossipers have shared that David isn't just Noah's bodyguard. He actually owns a very lucrative security company but does occasional bodyguarding as a personal favor to Noah when he is on the road or goes to certain events. They have been best friends since they were ten years old, and according to Aunt Leola, his bringing Janae to this party means that he wanted her to meet the people that are most important to him. Aunt Leola also mentioned that Noah's mom took her mother to get a prescription filled but would be back shortly. Nova assured me that her mom and grandmother are the nicest of the bunch, but I feel nauseous knowing I'll meet them soon. Needing some air, I go outside to sit with Uncle Buzzard and offer him one of my burgers. I plan to use our alone time as opportunity to gather as many embarrassing stories about Noah as I can. He will regret introducing me to his family.

"Who's your friend, Buzz?" says the woman pulling into the driveway. I can tell from the resemblance that she is related to Noah. She has beautiful brown skin with dreadlocks that go past her shoulders. She hops out of the car and walks over to the passenger side to help an older woman out.

"Hey baby sister, this here is actually Noah's friend." Uncle Buzzard looks back and forth between the two of us knowingly.

"So, you're the pretty lady that I've heard so much about?" she says with a genuine smile.

"Yes ma'am." I respond, seemingly lost for any other words. I did not expect for Noah to talk about me with his mother. We've technically only been on one date, and we agreed to keep things casual while we get to know one another.

Walking over to me, she reaches out for a hug, "I'm Noah's mom, Yvette, and this is his grandmother, Ruth."

"Nice to meet you both." My nervous stutter comes out right on cue.

"No need to be shy around us," his grandmother giggles. "I'll let you have a teaspoon of my cannabis oil if you need something to help you relax. Buzzard usually has medicinal marijuana somewhere around here, so if you prefer to smoke, just let him know," she winks.

"No need to be nervous. When we welcome friends into our home, we treat them like family," his mom seconds.

"That's right," Uncle Buzzard says proudly.

"Don't keep her out here too long, Buzzard. You know its tradition for me to beat you in a few rounds of Spades and then beat you all over again in UNO. Maybe this year I'll add Willow's name to the list." She talks smack just like my family, and I decide that I'd rather be the real me then some nervous version.

"You don't want none of this Ms. Yvette; I'm the UNO champion in my family. I'm new to spades, but I'm sure I can beat you in that too." I brag, playfully, and she laughs. When she reaches the door, she turns around and winks at me.

"Be careful playing cards with the old folks, Uncle Buzzard warns. "They look innocent, but they are sharks."

"Thanks for the warning, but I think I can handle them." I follow Yvette and Ruth inside the house to play a round of Spades.

29

MS. YVETTE KEPT her word and beat me in UNO six times, reinstating herself as the official UNO Champion of the world. I was so desperate to redeem my title as champion that I forced Janae to partner up with me in Spades. We won two games, but Ms. Yvette overshadowed our wins by bragging to her family about her wins in UNO. Despite all the teasing and trash talking, the energy at the party is very positive and genuine. They plan to have another game night in a few months when Nova and her husband return from Los Angeles, and the entire family gave Janae and I a personal invite.

Another round of spades starts, but I decide to take a break and spend some time in the back yard after hearing Ms. Yvette talk about how beautiful her garden is. She was right; the area is peaceful, and since it's further from the city, there is distance between the houses, which allows for more privacy and space between each yard. I slide off my sandals and place my feet in the grass, allowing the sun to kiss my skin. Before Ziggy and I started dating I hated being outside in the Texas heat with bugs crawling all over the place, but I eventually learned to be comfortable in nature. The two of us would go on long walks, and Ziggy would put his feet in the grass and meditate. I would be embarrassed and afraid of what people might think of us, but I soon learned that these types of acts instilled a sense of peace and freedom within me.

I spent less time in nature when we broke up because I was afraid that admitting Ziggy taught me things somehow meant that he still owned a piece of me, but being out here right now with my feet in the grass reminds me that I don't have to lock away our memories just because he is no longer in my life. He isn't my enemy. That would give him power over me, and I fought too hard to get my power back. I don't plan to give it away ever again. I hear the sliding door open, which causes me to open my eyes. Nova lifts up a bottle of wine and drinking glasses for me to see before placing everything on a table and walking over to stand next to me.

"Needed some quiet time?" She bumps her hip against mines playfully.

"Honestly, this view is amazing, and I couldn't miss the chance to spend a few minutes out here."

"Yeah, I'm grateful for it." She stretches her arms out wide, lifting her head to the sky.

"You live in California, so I'm sure you see beautiful views all the time."

"There's nothing like being home though. The air here is just different. I don't know how to explain it." She has appreciation in her tone.

"Yeah, this view makes you pay attention. It's almost like it's demanding that you stop and give thanks for it," I admit.

"Respect." I hear a deep voice say from behind me. I smile when I realize that I know the voice all too well, but it's been a long time since I've heard it up close and personal. I look back to find Noah standing near the doorway with his hands stretched out wide towards the sun.

"I guess that's my cue to leave." Nova points towards the wine sitting on the table.

"Thanks, Nova." Noah hugs her and moves towards me. I bend down to grab my socks and shoes, but he stops me.

"You look at peace. Keep doing your thing." The confidence in his voice spreads warmth all over my body. He takes a seat at the table, pouring a glass of wine in each of the cups, but he doesn't take a sip from either. He just stares, watching me intently.

"Noah Daniels. Are you really going to keep looking at me like that?" I smile, giddily, and he releases a low chuckle that turns into a yawn. He tries to hold it back, but another yawn escapes his lips which causes me to yawn.

"Sorry. I hopped on a late flight to make sure that I could be here, and I'm jet lagged."

"I have no excuse. I'm just tired." I walk over to him, placing my arms on his shoulders. Even sitting down he is much taller than me.

"You smell good." He leans his head against the side of my neck.

"Thank you." I am surprised by how natural it feels to have him close to me. We stand like this for minutes; him breathing deeply against me as I stand between his legs with my arms wrapped around his neck.

"Sorry to interrupt, but the family found out that you snuck in without speaking, and they're looking for you," Janae warns us. I move from between his legs, and the interruption automatically leads me to think back to our first date that was almost our last date.

"Tell them to give us a few minutes without them spying on us, and we'll be right in." He's calm but frustrated. She disappears into the house, and I step back between his legs and place my hand on his chin, guiding his eyes to meet mine.

"Before you go making decisions for the both of us again, please don't push me away because of a little interruption." He stares at me with a blank expression.

"Fine. Push me away again, but I promise I won't chase you." I walk towards the house, but he quickly stands, blocking my path to the doorway. He takes my hand and guides me so that my back rests against a tree, and we are out of everyone's view. He reaches down, placing his hands on my waist and places a soft kiss on my lips. His tongue finds mine, and we explore one another almost forgetting where we are. After a few seconds, he breaks our kiss, allowing his lips to rest against my neck. He inhales a few times, taking in my scent.

"I won't disappear on you again. My word is bond," he promises.

30

W E WALK BACK into the house to find Janae, Nova, and Ms. Yvette in the living room, scrambling to their seats to pretend that they weren't just spying on us. Janae is in the middle of the room acting out a scene from Coming to America, and David is sitting in the corner, shaking his head in disbelief as he watches her bark like a dog and hop on one foot. They are pretending to play charades, but it is obvious that they are trying to refrain from laughing. When Noah and I walk deeper into the room, they all break out into laughter, no longer able to contain it.

"Well if it isn't my son, prince charming." His mom crosses her arms over her chest. She frowns and pretends to wipe away tears.

"Yvette, leave the boy alone," his aunt Leona interjects.

"It's okay, mom. He has a new woman in his life, but I'll always be here for you." Nova smirks in Noah's direction.

Ignoring his sister, he walks over to his mother and places a kiss on her forehead. He casually sticks his middle finger at Nova, which seems to go unnoticed by everyone except for me. Nova opens her mouth to respond, but when she sees the way their mother is looking at Noah, she stays quiet allowing them to have their moment. Their sibling rivalry reminds me of Omari and me. She made sure that he was here today, and I know that he is grateful for it.

The rest of the group starts another game of UNO, deciding it best to give Ms. Yvette and Noah some alone time after months of being apart. After he finishes talking to his mom, he spends a few minutes with the rest of his family but quickly excuses himself with the promise to visit in the morning. He offers to give me a ride home, but as the designated driver of our best friends, I decline. Earlier tonight, I planned to ditch them, but now I'm glad to have them as an excuse. If our kiss was any indication of what's to come, I think it's best that I'm not left alone with Noah tonight. It takes serious effort to remind myself that we agreed to take things slow.

31

*T*HERE IS LOUD banging at my door, which forces me to wake up. I roll over to check the time on my phone and notice that I have two missed calls from Janae and a good morning text from Noah, which was sent three hours ago. I rarely sleep in past nine, but my body obviously needed to rest. I throw on my robe and walk to the door, grabbing my bat along the way. Looking out of the peephole, I see Janae with her hand balled up about to knock again.

"Why are you knocking like the police?" I ask, sarcastically.

"I figured you weren't going to make it to brunch, so I brought you a drink, but I can leave. Just know that the smoothie is coming with me." She holds up a mango smoothie, which is my favorite, so I decide to go easy on her.

"Sorry, Nae. You just had me worried that's all," I respond in a soft voice, hoping that she doesn't throw the drink away. She hands it over and watches me take a few sips before she explains the reason for her visit.

"Well, since I'm already here maybe you should get dressed, so we can go on a double date," she smiles innocently.

"Wait, who put you up to this?" I ask, suspiciously.

"Noah knows that we have weekly brunches on Sunday, but he wanted to spend time with you, so he included me which is a bonus if you really think about it." She smiles wide.

"Okay," I quickly respond, and Janae's eyebrows rise in confusion.

"When did you become so agreeable?" She watches me as I search for an outfit to wear.

"I like him. Plus, I've been saying yes to life lately, and I think that a date is one of those things that I'd like to say yes to," I answer without hesitancy.

"So, you're basically saying that you're grateful that your best friend invited him to brunch all those months ago because if she hadn't, you wouldn't be all optimistic and in love?" She pats herself on the back both literally and figuratively.

"Yes. All the credit is due to you." I roll my eyes and guide her out of my room so that I can shower and get dressed in peace.

◆ ◆ ◆

"Where are we going?" I ask, anxiously. Noah is standing behind me with his hands covering my eyes. He made me promise not to peek because he wants our first *official* date to be a surprise. I hear Janae squealing in front of me, and from the sound of it, David accidentally guided her into something causing her to stub her toe.

"David, I love you, but you can never guide me blindly again!" She suddenly halts in front of me, and I jump backwards, accidentally bumping my head into Noah's body. The contact feels as though it had to have hurt him, but he doesn't complain. Instead, he moves in front me and grabs my hand.

"Trust me." Noah tries to guide me.

"Did you just admit that you love me?" David asks Janae.

"No, I said *like* not love. It's way too early for love," she says, frustrated with herself for her choice of words.

"Go ahead without us," David tells Noah. It is obvious that they need to talk now that Janae confessed her love after only six months of dating. In all of our years of friendship, I have never seen her fall this quick for anyone. Her last relationship was almost four years ago. She fell in love with a guy who she believed to be the one, but after two years of dating, he got another woman pregnant. After that, she refused to take anyone serious, and she mostly dated immature guys who she was too ashamed to bring home to her parents. It's nice to see her with a good guy like David, and I can tell that she's happy, but she's also afraid to be vulnerable again.

"Okay, don't take too long though. I have both of the things with me," Noah says to David, trying to be discreet and keep the surprise concealed.

"Noah, can I please take this blindfold off?" I am annoyed with being led blindly.

"We're almost there," Noah says, excitedly.

"Is that water I hear?" I instantly reach for my blindfold.

"Willow. Trust me." He reaches for my other hand. He guides me backwards so that I am leaning against what feels like a tree.

"Okay, now sit down. I'll help guide you." He supports me as I find my way to the ground. He then takes off my shoes and removes my socks. Luckily, I moisturized my feet with shea butter before leaving the house.

"This is starting to feel weird," I say, nervously. "I don't let anybody touch my feet without me knowing," he laughs and instructs me to open eyes. To my amazement, I am sitting on a yellow piece of tapestry, which he is using as a picnic cloth, surrounded by a sketchpad, an old school boom box, and three picnic baskets that are filled to the top. We appear to be at some kind of Nature Park with giant oak trees and beautiful sunflowers blooming all around us.

"We can explore first, or we can eat." He picks up one of the giant picnic baskets. His smile is so energetic and downright contagious.

"Let's eat first," I say, curious to see why he brought three picnic baskets.

"This one is actually for David and Janae." He moves one of the baskets to the side.

"Wow, I must be special to get *two* baskets." I mock him. He removes the lids, and I quickly regret my sarcasm, realizing that he put a lot of thought into planning this date. One basket is filled with my favorite brand of spring water and mango juice. I open the second basket and my mouth begins to water from the alluring smell of food. There are two plates filled with roasted kale, black-eyed peas, fried oyster mushrooms, sweet potatoes, and mac and cheese.

"And it's all vegan too." He hands me a fork.

"Mm," I moan after taking a bite. "Where did you get this from because I am definitely adding it to my list of restaurants." He chuckles as he watches me scarf down my food. I would usually feel self-conscious about being observed so closely, but he seems to be enjoying watching me just as much as I am enjoying the food.

"I wouldn't suggest this in any other case, but I think you should kiss the chef," he grins, playfully.

"Wait, you made this?" I am surprised. He's a celebrity and a mama's boy, so I assumed that he would have someone cooking meals for him on a regular basis. Obviously, I was wrong.

"Don't act so surprised," he says, defensively. "I rep California all day, but I spent every summer in Dallas in my grandmother's kitchen, so please believe she taught your boy how to cook. Now kiss the chef." He leans in.

"I'll thank your grandmother for passing down her cooking skills." I bypass his lips and scoop more food onto the fork. I have a feeling that he's used to getting his way, so I feed him some of my black-eyed peas instead of giving him a kiss. He doesn't complain; instead, he grabs the sketchpad and sketches me as I eat.

"Aren't you going to eat?" I am puzzled by his actions.

"I ate before we came, but I'll eat again in a little while. Now, stop moving so much. An artist is at work."

"Let me see it," I reach for the pad.

"Chill out," he laughs, avoiding my reach.

"Have you ever seen *Jason's Lyric*?" I ask, noticing the pond up ahead in the distance. My question seems simple, but it's really more of a quiz than a question. *Jason's Lyric* is one of my favorite movies, and I've always wanted to be with someone who was goofy enough to re-enact the scene where Jason washes Lyric's feet in the bayou.

"It's one of my favorite movies, so I already know what you're thinking, and the answer is no. I'm not washing your feet with this dirty water." He scrunches his nose up at the thought.

"That's okay. I guess you aren't as romantic as Jason," I shrug.

"I am ten times more romantic than Jason. All they had was the bayou, and I respect the fictional character for washing her feet, but I'm not limited to this pond, and you are worthy of having your feet washed in clean water. If you act right, maybe I'll wash your feet on our hundredth date," he chuckles.

"Okay, fine," I say, reaching for the sketch pad. This time, he lets me take it.

"You drew me as a stick figure!" I punch his arm lightly.

"Chill," he says, snickering at my reaction. "Come here."

"Okay, but only because I want to," I warn him.

"Breathe with me," he says, softly in my ear. I look back to see if he is serious, but his eyes are already closed, and I feel his chest expand against my back, so I close my eyes to do the same, and our breaths quickly become in sync. We sit quietly, like this, for a while, taking in the sounds that surround us. It is so quiet out here and yet so loud. I'm reminded of my childhood when my friends and me stayed outdoors until the streetlights came on. We played so long that my dad would have to whistle to signal that it was time to come in. As an adult, I lost that sense of freedom. Working eight hours a day towards someone else's dream convinced me that I wasn't worthy of days like this because I hadn't earned it yet. I hadn't gotten to retirement or put in enough years, but now, I know the truth. The days when I was solely working towards someone else's dream, I should have also been creating a vision for myself, but I am now, and that is all that matters.

Yelling voices in the distance snaps me out of my thoughts. Noah stands up to look up the trail and see what the commotion is about. Janae is walking in front of David with her arms crossed. She looks back to yell at him every few steps, but he doesn't respond. He looks tired and defeated, so I quickly run to Janae to see what is going on, and Noah does the same with David.

"Let's go over here, so we can talk." I lead her away from the guys.

"He told me that he is falling in love with me." She drops her arms to her sides dramatically.

"Yeah, and you told him first. I was there, remember?" I am confused by her emotions.

"Yeah, but I took it back shortly after I said it." She crosses her arms again.

"But, did you mean it when you said it? That's what matters."

"I ..." She opens her mouth to speak, but no words come out. She is never quiet, so this is my chance to get her to listen.

"You always tell me that I'm worthy of love, but what makes you think you aren't? Are you really going to hold David accountable for a jerk who wasn't worthy of your presence let alone your love?"

"Ugh," she says, rolling her eyes and walking back towards David.

"Can I talk to him alone for a sec?"

"Of course," Noah says, stepping out of the way. Her tone is much softer when she approaches David this time, leaving Noah and I to feel safe to go and sit back under the tree just as we were, him with his back against the tree and me with my back against his chest. Except this time, his arms are wrapped around me.

"Is she always like that?" He moves his chin to rest on my shoulder.

"Honestly, she usually doesn't allow anyone to get this close to her. I can tell she really cares for David, which means that she is probably terrified of those feelings. They just need to talk, and I think she'll be okay." I lean into him.

"What about us? Do we need to talk?" His voice is laced with concern. We've had several conversations over the past few months, but I still haven't let on to how much Ziggy meant to me. I don't want to be seen as damaged, and I feel that discussing my past with him somehow means that he still has claim to my heart which he doesn't. I plan to share the details of my past relationship with Noah, but right now I just want to focus on what we're building together.

"Sing to me," I am hoping to lighten the mood.

"I just asked you to talk to me, and you tell me to sing?" His concern is replaced with confusion.

"You're being too serious. Today is supposed to be a day of fun."

"I understand that, but I just want to make sure we talk so that we don't end up pushing each other away like our best friends almost did just now." He unwraps his arms from around me and stands. I expect him to walk away, but he just stands in place, staring at me, so I stare back intensely.

"My ex broke my heart. He embarrassed me, and you saw the results of that the night you saw me at the restaurant. What more do you want me to say?"

"I just want to make sure that I'm not competing with someone from your past. I saw you that night, and I never want you to feel that broken again, but I don't even know what happened. How do you expect me to see you crying and yelling *in public* and never ask you about it?"

"I never said you couldn't ask me about it, but the night you saw me, my world had been turned upside down. The man that I loved for five long years asked me to dinner, and like a fool, I went because I was desperate to salvage what was left of our relationship. So, there I was, sitting in a fancy restaurant looking over the menu when he sits down at the table with the woman he had been cheating on me with for over six months. I have never been so humiliated in my life. I wanted to fight. Hell, I almost fought, but I remembered where I was and *who I was,* and I walked away. I walked out of there, desperate to get in my car and leave, but the valet driver ignored me. Let's just say, he picked the wrong night to be an asshole. I bet he won't treat anyone else that way, and as for my ex, I've moved on. He didn't break me. I remembered I was seed, and I'm standing in front of you, blooming."

"That you are," he smiles seductively. "You still want me to sing to you?"

"That's the least you could do for ruining our date," I joke.

"I'd say we made progress. We didn't ruin a thing." He walks back to me and starts singing "Let Me Love You" by Mario. After the third note, I forget what we were even discussing.

32

A month later

I HAVE OFFICIALLY been a business owner for three months now, and I am happy to announce that things are flourishing. I've made new business connections and added a nice amount of money to my savings. I am currently on my way to meet a potential client who is considering hiring me to design her wedding dress and then later today, I am meeting Noah for dinner. We have spent almost every day together the past few weeks, but it has not been easy to pull off. We agreed to keep our relationship private from the media, which means that we have to do a lot of sneaking around. At first, my request to keep things private bothered Noah, but after a few long conversations between the two of us, he understood my feelings and decided to honor my wishes. He has also continued to respect my three-month celibacy rule which is something that I am not even sure I want to stick to. Technically, we have been dating for more than three months if you count our first unofficial date but neither of us has forced the subject. I am buying myself more time to make sure that sex doesn't complicate our entire relationship, and he is working hard to prove that he cares about me even without the physical act.

I walk inside the coffee shop and wave to the employees, who I happen to know well, since I use their shop for most of my business meetings. I pull out my phone and text my client to let her know that I arrived a little early and would be sitting in my private booth near the back. She quickly responds, letting me know that she is running late but would be joining me soon. With extra time on my hands, I decide to walk to the office to talk to Doc, the 70-year old owner of this establishment. Doc's coffee shop is a staple in Dallas. I used to host open mic night here when I was in college, and this was the first place I performed one of my poems. I haven't been on a stage in years, but still, Doc makes me feel like a celebrity every time I walk through these doors.

"Hey there, Willow tree," he smiles.

"Hey, old man," I say, playfully.

"Old man? So, I guess you don't want the tea I was about to go out and make just for you? You know I don't get behind the counter much except for people near and dear to my heart." He pretends to be offended.

"You know I didn't mean it, Doc. At seventy, you can keep up with the best of us," which is actually true.

"Alright, then. Now follow me little lady." He leads me out to the front. "Here you go, Stella. This is for whatever Doc is making me. He likes to surprise me," I pull out my wallet to give the cashier a ten-dollar bill.

"As always, your money is no good here," Doc says, interrupting the transaction.

"Thanks, Doc," I toss the money into the tip jar before he notices.

"Anything for you. Now, go have a seat. I'll send your client over when she arrives." He points me towards my private booth.

"You always have my back, don't you?" I walk over to listen to music and return emails before my client joins me.

"You know it. Now, go work," he winks playfully.

◆ ◆ ◆

A few minutes late turns into thirty minutes late, and I begin to predict that my client will be a no show. I start to pack up my belongings, and just as I do, my phone chimes with a text message from my client, Alexis, informing me that she just drove up and would be right in. I am tempted to tell her to reschedule, but I need all of the business I can get right now, so I decide not to make a big deal of the situation. I respond to let her know that I am still here, and a few seconds later there is a knock on the glass partition that separates my table from the rest. My heart begins to race when a familiar face appears, grinning widely at me. A familiar face that was sitting across from me over a year ago, confessing that she stole my fiancé from me.

33

"So, you're the client that's been emailing me the past two weeks?" I ask, in a calm tone. A laugh escapes my lips, and surprisingly, I am not bothered by her intrusion. In fact, I find her to be quite desperate. The woman even created a fake name.

"Yes, and my husband-to-be is outside finishing his cigarette. He'll be in shortly," she brags.

"Oh, he smokes now. I guess he picked up some bad habits after we broke up. Stress can do that to a man, you know?" I laugh at my own joke, and she doesn't like it one bit.

"I …" She opens her mouth to respond but is interrupted by the chime of the door.

"Willow, what are you doing here?" Ziggy says, obviously caught off guard.

"Babe, this is the designer I was telling you about. I want her to design my dress for the wedding." She gives him a stern look, and he suddenly catches on.

"Oh yeah, the wedding planner, right." He plays along. He makes the mistake of reaching out to shake my hand, and I leave it hanging in the air. If I had any respect left for him after our last encounter, I can honestly say that I have no more after today.

"Let me make sure I understand this. You tricked me into meeting you here just so you could brag about your upcoming nuptials?" I turn to her and laugh. She got the best of me when we last met, but it won't happen again.

"Willow Tree, I'm sorry about this," Ziggy says. I am not sure if he is apologizing for today, for the last time we met, or for the past few years we spent together, but his approach is all wrong.

"Do not call me that. My nicknames are reserved for my family and friends," I snap at him.

"Yeah, babe. You aren't a family or friend anymore. I guess that ended when you chose me," she gloats.

"Listen sweetie, I haven't spoken to or seen Ziggy in a very long time, so I am not sure why you feel the need to throw your relationship in my face *again*, but what I do know is that this isn't some rich restaurant we're in. This is my stomping ground, and after these next few words, I promise there will be no more talking. Try me and watch me make a believer out of you." She opens her mouth to speak but thinks it over and quickly closes it.

"Mia, give us a few minutes to talk, please'" Ziggy's eyes plead with her. She scoffs but does as asked.

"It's not what you think." He finally looks me in my eyes. "I did not know that you were the person we would be meeting today. I wouldn't do that to you."

"Again, you mean. You wouldn't do that to me *again*."

"Right. I wouldn't do that to you *again*, and I'm sorry for doing it the first time. I tried to call you and apologize, but I guess you blocked me."

"I had nothing else to say to you, so yeah I blocked you the night I walked out of that restaurant."

"I deserve that, but I hope you know that I really did love you. I didn't know how to communicate to you that I needed more than what you had to give at the time. We were draining each other. I needed to be a man and stand on my own, but you wouldn't walk away, so I forced your hand by getting with Mia."

Tears stream down my cheeks, and I release a breath that I have been holding in for far too long. Ziggy moves closer to me, placing his hand on the small of my back. His words are confirmation to my own thoughts. After the retreat, I spent a lot of time alone to figure out when I became so unhappy. The first assignment was to figure out why I stayed with him as long as I did. Then I realized that I forgot how to love myself. I knew how to as a child, but as I grew in age, I lost my way. Ziggy literally gave me the kind of love that I was giving myself. I set the standard, and he simply followed.

"I still love you, don't cry." He comforts me.

"I am not crying because I want you to love me, Ziggy. I'm crying because I realize that I'm over you. I realize that I've grown, and here you are being the same old Ziggy. I wish you and your wife-to-be nothing but the best." I swat his hand from my body.

"Alright, Willow. You win," he grunts before walking over to Mia. He angrily grabs her hand, and they exit the coffee shop together like the two miserable fools they obviously are.

34

"HEY, IS EVERYTHING okay?" Noah says through the phone. I try to hold back tears, but they keep welling back up.

"I won't lie and say that I haven't been crying, but they aren't sad tears. I promise to tell you everything when I see you later tonight."

"Okay, so what do you need right now?" he asks, concerned.

"Let me finish talking to Doc and then I'm going to one of Janae's yoga classes for about an hour. I promise to call you after." I say, hoping to reassure him.

He huffs out a low grumble. "Alright, but I'm holding you to that promise."

"Okay, I will talk to you soon." I end the call.

I look up to find Doc, leaned over his desk, staring at me with concerned eyes. The two of us have been sitting here for the past twenty minutes, as I filled him in on everything that happened between me, Ziggy, and his minion Mia. I tried to sneak out of the front door shortly after Ziggy made his dramatic exit, but Doc saw tears in my eyes and stopped me right in my tracks. Although he is a seventy-year old man, he still has a no-nonsense attitude, so without a second thought, he grabbed his bat to meet Ziggy in the parking lot. Luckily, the two of them were gone before he even made it outside.

"Is that the new fella you were just talking to?" Doc says, with a worried expression. I reply with a nod of my head.

"If there's one thing I've learned over the years, it's that communication is the key to a balanced relationship. A man can't fix what he isn't aware of, and he can't protect you if you pretend to be strong in moments where you actually need support."

"Doc, you just heard me promise to call him later and explain the entire situation. That's *if* you ever let me out of your sight." My words come out harsher than I hoped, but Doc doesn't understand that I need time to think right now, not explain the story to yet another person.

"Go on to your yoga class now and release some of that frustration before you meet up with that fella and push him away," he says, in an authoritative voice.

"Yes, sir." I follow his command.

"And Doc?" I turn back before closing the door. "Thank you."

◆ ◆ ◆

Janae is in the middle of teaching a class when I finally make it to the studio. I tiptoe inside, hoping to find a good seat without causing a commotion. The rusty door, which I have told Janae to oil on more than one occasion, squeaks and everyone looks up from their pose to watch me as I walk to the open space near the back of the room. It isn't like me to be late, so I am sure Janae is curious as to why I'm strolling in with only thirty minutes left of class, but lucky for me, she is teaching and can't harass me until after class. I kick off my shoes, lay down my mat, and jump into the warrior one position like the rest of the group.

"Let's go into warrior two." She studies me, but I adjust my face so that I look neutral and unbothered.

"Nice job, ladies. Now, let's make our way into the downward dog pose. Hold it for about ten seconds and then make your way down to your belly."

"Great job, everyone. Now, we've spent the first half of class practicing balance and stretching our bodies, so I would like to use the rest of our time getting still. I don't know about you ladies, but sometimes, I just need a little quiet time with myself. So, find a comfortable position with your legs crossed and close your eyes for meditation." I have a feeling that her sudden change of direction is for my benefit, but I do as she instructed and close my eyes.

"Wait for me after class." I hear a voice whisper from behind me. It's Janae.

"You are being really unprofessional right now," I whisper, sharply.

"I don't care. I can tell something is up with you, so wait for me once class ends."

"Fine," I whisper-yell in response.

"Shush." Ms. Cathy, an older lady who is always quieting people, looks back at me.

"Sorry Ms. Cathy, we have a talker back here," Janae points down at me. "She is now fully aware that this is sacred time, and she assures me that she will respect the rest of the class and stay quiet." I roll my eyes at her and Mrs. Cathy and then I use the rest of the yoga class to get in a peaceful state of mind.

When the class ends, I stay on my mat, doing some extra stretches while I wait for Janae who is speaking with one of her students at the front of the class. Mrs. Cathy shuffles past me and rolls her eyes. I am tempted to give her the finger, but I immediately think of how rude I was to Doc and decide to give her a pass just as he did for me. Plus, she is my elder, and I would regret disrespecting her, but boy am I tempted. Janae witnesses the exchange and covers her mouth, concealing a grin.

"Ms. Cathy is crazy. Don't let her get to you." She joins me on the floor.

"I'm glad you're enjoying this so much." I toss a foam yoga block at her.

"Hey, you're the one that came to class looking like you were ready for war. I'm just glad that Ms. Cathy is fifty-seven, and you have rules about respecting your elders because if she was a little bit younger, I probably would have had to kick you out of class for fighting."

"Girl, I was not going to fight Ms. Cathy, and it was your fault anyways!" I giggle.

"Well, your body language suggested that something was wrong, so I had to find a way to check on you discreetly, but you started whispering all loud and what not."

"I am not falling for that. You were being unprofessional, and due your behavior, Ms. Cathy almost got slapped."

"Don't take your attitude out on an old woman," she laughs. "Besides, I see you don't need me anymore anyways."

"What are you talking about? I came here to talk to you. I will always need my best friend," I assure her.

"I know, but now you have him too." She points towards the door. I re-adjust my body to look in the direction that she is pointing. Noah is standing in the doorway with a nervous grin, holding a plant.

"Did you know he was coming here?" I whisper to Janae.

"I'm not really sure what is going on for once, and I have no clue why he is here, but I'm going to let you two talk if that's what you want," she replies.

"This is your studio. You stay, and me and Noah will talk outside." I stand up.

"Hey," I say to Noah.

"You seemed really upset over the phone, so I brought you a plant because I know you hate flowers, and I know you said you would call me, but I was worried and didn't think you would mind me checking on you, so I asked David for the address to Janae's studio, so I could meet you here after class and take you to dinner. The idea seemed great in theory, but now that I'm here, I'm not sure if it was a good idea," he laughs, nervously.

"I know I had you worried, and I'm sorry for that. Let me finish helping Janae clean up really quick and then we can grab dinner and talk."

"No need to help me. This was my last class of the night, so feel free to stay and talk. You have the extra set of keys, so lock up and call me later? Oh, and Noah, I will be the first to call the police if this is some type of stalker move." She turns and leaves without saying another word.

35

BY THE TIME Noah and I finish talking, it is dark outside, and the entire building is empty. He is lying with his head in my lap and has a stunned expression written all over his face. When Janae left earlier, we agreed that tonight would be the night that he and I shared the most important parts of our past with one another, and tonight, that is exactly what I did. I let go of everything that I had been holding in. All of the drama with Ziggy, my journey since our breakup, and all the lessons I have learned since the retreat. I didn't even realize how much I had to say until I finished talking. For years, I tried to attract a mate that would love me the way that I couldn't seem to love myself. Now, I know that love is choosing to come into a relationship having done the work and self-reflection. Love is being supportive of your significant other but never expecting them to be the solution to your happiness. Love is starting to become synonymous with Noah.

"All he did tonight was prove how great you are without him," Noah says, reassuringly.

"Yeah, he thought he was dealing with the Willow that he once dated. Instead he got the Willow that doesn't tolerate bullshit. From *anyone*." I eye him jokingly. He readjusts his body, so that he is facing me.

"I am not him, and my actions will continue to prove that."

"I believe you, but we still have to talk about you. Is there anyone you need to tell me about from your past?" I say, realizing that I've done most of the talking.

He nods, "I guess it is my turn to speak, huh?"

"Yeah, I spilled all my tea. Now, it's your turn."

"Well, I haven't had as much drama as you," he teases. "But there was one girl who I *used* to say got away. We dated all throughout high school and college. Our families thought we would get married, but we broke up when we were twenty-three and twenty-four. I won't lie; the breakup was entirely my fault. I started getting recognized for my music, which led to more club appearances, studio time, and whatever else it took to get my name out there. The more popular I became the more women seemed to want to come around."

"That sounds like a lot of drama if you ask me." I try to hide a worried expression.

"Just to be clear, I was young and new to this life, and I didn't really know how to handle it. I never physically cheated, but I was tempted to on numerous occasions. At the time, I hadn't officially moved to Dallas, so I was always going back and forth between Dallas with my grandma and California with my mom. Nina, my ex, was in college and couldn't travel as easily as I could, so we started spending less and less time together, and after a while, she ended things."

"Did you ever try to fix it?"

"Yeah, but she changed her number and moved out of state, so I had no way of getting in contact with her until we ran into each other years later at the grocery store and she could no longer avoid me. We follow each other on social media now, and she checks in on me every once in a while. She's married with a little daughter and one more on the way."

"You're happy for her, aren't you?" I notice how his face softened at the mention of her becoming a mother for the second time.

"Absolutely. We were meant to be each other's introductions to love, but that's it. Now, she is with the person she's supposed to be with, and I'm sitting in a yoga studio on a funky mat with a woman that I really like," he smiles.

"It is kind of funky, huh?" I laugh, "Janae usually disinfects the mats, but she left me to do the dirty work tonight."

"I say you get revenge by kissing me all over her studio," he says matter-of-factly.

"I'm a lady. I can't do that," I tease.

"You weren't worried about being a lady all the other times you had your tongue down my throat." He leans over to kiss me.

"Alright, one kiss but then you have to help me disinfect these mats." I meet him halfway.

"That's it?" He is surprised by the quick peck.

"Yeah. I told you I'm a lady." I reach past him and grab the bottle of disinfectant spray to wipe off our mats. He stands, following my lead and neatly folds up each mat before tossing them in the bin.

"When we finish with this, I expect a real kiss," he says, matter-of-factly.

"You really like kissing me, don't you?" I ask, playfully, but his phone begins to ring just as he is about to answer me. He is standing a few feet away, but I can hear his manager, Derrick's voice through the phone. Letting out a frustrated sigh, Noah mutes the call so that he can talk to me without Derrick hearing him.

"I need to take this. We have a meeting with the label tomorrow, and he wants to go over a few notes really fast. I'll be back in a few minutes." He slips into the hallway.

Their calls usually take a while, so I decide to play music while I wait for him to return. When Nipsey Hussle's voice begins to play over the speakers Noah peeks his head in the window, and he watches me inquisitively from the doorway. On our first date, he told me that Nipsey Hussle was one of his favorite rappers, and I've heard him play his music almost every time I've been in his car. He is supposed to be focused on his phone call with Derrick, but he is too busy studying me through the window.

"What are you doing?" He walks back into the room after a few minutes. I ignore his question and rap the lyrics to "Last Time That I Checked." I even throw in a few dance moves, C-walking like a L.A. native.

"Oh, so you want to battle, huh? You know I lived in Cali most of my life, right?" I answer his question by dancing even harder causing us both to erupt with laughter. His world is constantly full of seriousness, so I take the opportunity to provide a little fun, even if only for a few minutes.

"I love this side of you. The goofy confident Willow." He pulls me towards him.

"I love this side of you. Relaxed and fun."

"I'm starting to realize that you bring this side out of me. I am grateful." He leans down to kiss me.

"As am I." I get lost in his embrace but then my phone chimes, interrupting the moment.

"It's Janae's ringer, so I need to check it in case it's something serious." I reach for my phone.

Janae: Don't forget to lock up.

Janae: Oh, and please make sure the dance contest stays PG-13. I don't need my cameras picking up on any inappropriate behavior ☺

I shake my head in disbelief before handing my phone to Noah so that he can read the messages. He laughs as I stick my middle finger up at the camera. I try to convince him to do the same, but he takes a more mature approach and switches the music to a slower paced song. When "Sexual Healing" by Marvin Gaye begins to play, we grin into the camera and slow dance on purpose just to annoy her. Getting an even better idea, I toss my jacket over the camera to leave her in suspense.

36

"*J*UST TELL ME the truth, did you have sex with Noah in my studio?" Janae stands across from me with her arms folded against her chest.

"You were the one watching us on camera, so you tell me," I shrug, knowing that the suspense is killing her.

"If I knew the answer to my own question, I wouldn't have asked. I just hope you weren't on my desk!" She reaches for the bottle of disinfectant spray.

"What are you doing?" I say, suppressing my smile. Noah and I did not have sex last night, but I am enjoying making her think otherwise.

"You won't tell me what happened, so I'm cleaning my desk in case you two decided to be gross all over it." She moves around me and sprays a copious amount of disinfectant onto the desk.

"Be sure to get that spot. We *really* enjoyed ourselves over there." I point to the edge of the desk.

"I knew it!" She grabs my hand to guide me to one of the mats on the floor. "I'm your best friend, so you have to tell me everything that happened."

"Do you really think our first time was in a sweaty yoga studio with you texting me every few minutes?"

"No, I don't, but in my defense, it's been a while since you've been with anyone, and you covered the cameras, so I wasn't sure if I needed to hire a professional cleaning crew to disinfect the entire studio," she smirks.

"For your information, all we did was kiss and dance, and it was one of the most fun and intimate experiences I have ever had."

"Damn." She is impressed by my confession.

"Yep." I think back to how Noah and I turned Janae's yoga studio into our personal nightclub. We played around for hours, singing, dancing, and taking turns laying with our heads in each other's laps as we talked. Things got really intimate when Noah dared me to watch us in the mirror. At first, I was shy, but each time I tried to put my head down in embarrassment, he would lift my chin back towards the mirror so that we could watch our reflections.

"I have a confession," I admit

"What?" Janae says, excited.

"The way we kissed last night was different than all the other times. It was gentler and hungrier, and I sort of had a momentary lapse in judgment and threw myself at him." I cover my face in embarrassment.

Janae's eyes go wide. "How?"

"Well, let's just say that I felt something hard pressed against my leg when we were dancing, and I tried to unbutton his jeans, but he stopped me."

"Oh, my goodness. Noah had my best friend throwing the cookies his way. You are in trouble, girl. I'm worried for you," she says in a serious tone.

"I never move this fast, and he straight up denied me."

"Did he really, or are you being dramatic?"

"Janae his exact words were, *I can bend you over this desk if that's what you want, but once it's over, you would analyze the situation and regret it, so let's not do this tonight.* Then he walked me to my car and gave me a church hug. You know the kind where the person pats you on the back? Well, he gave me one of those."

"It sounds like he was trying to be a gentleman and follow your three-month rule. You're the one who made the rule, so don't start looking for excuses to run away."

"How am I supposed to act normal around him after embarrassing myself like that?"

"Easy. You act the same way you have been except this time don't stick your hand down his pants, and now is your chance to practice because he's coming this way." She nods her head towards the entrance. In walks David and Noah.

"Hey, what are you doing here?" I am surprised to see them. Noah squats and places a kiss on my lips, and David follows suit and kisses Janae.

"We just came from the gym. David said he was coming over to take Janae to lunch, so I figured we could all go together. Give me a chance to make up for all the times you were stuck being their third wheel?" Noah says with a playful grin.

"I wish I could, but I'm really busy at the moment. I have some sketches to work on, deadlines and all. You understand, right?" He looks confused but quickly recovers with a smile.

"Yeah, I understand. I guess I'll just grab something and go home. Call me later?" He reaches down to kiss me goodbye.

"Of course." I return his kiss. *What the heck am I doing?*

37

I AVOIDED NOAH FOR two days, using work as an excuse not to see him, but Justice and her husband Zion come into town today, and the four of us made plans over a month ago to have dinner, so I am forced to finally come out of hiding. To make matters worse, Omari overheard our plans and demanded that he be included in the festivities, so later tonight, I am hosting a dinner at my place for the five of us. I already gave my siblings a list of pre-approved conversation topics, and they promised to steer clear of doing or saying anything even remotely embarrassing. Justice is aware of the recent incident between me and Noah, and though she accused me of being overdramatic, she agreed to be my ally tonight and help me steer clear of creating additional awkward moments with Noah. Omari, on the other hand, has always tried to intimidate the guys that I dated in the past, so I can't guarantee that he will be on his best behavior.

My phone chimes three times in a row. I glance down to see a message from Justice letting me know that their flight just landed, and they will be at my house as soon as they grab lunch. The other two messages are from Noah informing me that he is still coming for dinner tonight unless I no longer want him to. He then sends another text to let me know that if he does join us for dinner, he expects an explanation for my recent change in behavior. I reply to his message, letting him know that I still want him to come and offer an apology. Three dots appear on the screen, suggesting that he is typing a response, but after about thirty seconds they disappear. They reappear a minute later, and I assume that he is debating on whether he should respond to my apology now or wait to talk to me in person.

When the dots disappear again, I toss my phone back into my bag, grateful for a reprieve and continue shopping for tonight's dinner as if nothing is wrong.

I am fully aware that I am being immature about the entire situation, and I plan to give him a sincere apology later on tonight, but that doesn't mean that I am any less embarrassed by the situation. To be fair, I was the one who set rules, all of which he has followed without complaint. When he first attempted to get to know me, I questioned his motives, and when he wanted to go public with our relationship, I said that I needed more time. Despite his confusion, he continued to be patient with me each and every time I tried to push him away. I guess I just never expected him to be strong in following the one rule that pertained to sex. He literally has women throwing themselves at him all of the time, and when he became my voice of reason that night in the yoga studio, I began to revert back to my old way of thinking. The last thing I want is to become another woman that he can easily obtain, and though that wasn't my intention, I fear that he now sees me that way.

38

O MARI AND I are in the kitchen cooking when we hear a light knock at the door. Despite my refusal, Justice runs to open it, announcing Noah's arrival. I wanted to be the one to greet him in hopes that I could smooth things over before bringing him into the fold of my family, but she beat me to the door, and now things will linger throughout dinner until we finally have the chance to talk at the end of the night. I hear the two of them exchange pleasantries, and Justice says something that I can't quite make out, but it apparently was funny enough to produce a hearty laugh from Noah. As they approach the kitchen, I immediately busy myself, grabbing a spoon to stir the food in the pot that doesn't actually need to be stirred. Noah is all smiles as he introduces himself to my brother, but when his eyes reach me, the smile subtly fades. To the normal eye, it probably isn't noticeable, but his smile is one of my favorite things about him, so I noticed, and I have a feeling he wanted me to. He looks exhausted and in no mood to be around people, yet he still showed up.

"I didn't mean to interrupt. I came early to see if Willow needed some help in the kitchen, but I see she has it covered," he addresses Omari and Janae.

"That was nice of you man, but the food is basically done; it just needs to simmer for a little while longer. Why don't you join me and my brother-in-law on the couch to watch the game?" Omari offers, and Noah quickly accepts. His lack of energy only seems to be directed at me.

I wait until they are out of earshot before turning to Justice. She seems to have picked up on Noah's energy towards me because she instructs me to follow her to the room, so we can talk. She hasn't bossed me around since we were kids, so I know I am messing up right now. Like the younger sister I am, I follow my big sister into the room to get the lecture that I deserve. I can feel Noah eyes follow me as I walk past him. I glance back to smile at him before closing my room door. He returns my smile, but in his eyes reveal his confusion.

"Girl, what is going on with you two?" Justice asks as soon as I shut the door behind me.

"So, you picked up on his energy too? He's all smiles when talking to everyone else but cold as ice as soon as I look his way."

"Do you blame him? I love you sis, but you are doing the very thing you promised you wouldn't do. You shut down on this man again, and he has no clue why. This whole thing is overdramatic. You attempted to make a move, and he openly communicated that he didn't want to your first time together to be that night in a *yoga studio,* but he is here now meeting your family. Doesn't that tell you something?"

"I know, and I plan to apologize after dinner, but I can't do that if he doesn't allow me to."

"Nope. I am not defending your actions this time. Take responsibility and move on or just end it now." Justice walks towards the door.

"Ugh." I am annoyed with myself. "Can you tell Noah to come in here, please?"

"Of course, but since I'm doing your dirty work, you better give me all the details later." She winks at me.

Justice leaves, and a few seconds later Noah walks into my room. I am seated on the edge of my bed waiting for him to join me, but he stays standing and leans against the doorframe. He left the door cracked open rather than closing it completely, and I know that my family is probably eavesdropping on our conversation, but Noah doesn't seem to care.

"I owe you an apology for my immature behavior and for ignoring you. I was embarrassed and felt insecure, so I shutdown which I know I promised not to do anymore."

"Okay." He is unmoved by my apology. Noah is usually a very understanding person but tonight is a different story.

"That's it? That's all you have to say?"

"Let's just go enjoy your family and have a good meal. We can talk about the rest when we're alone. I don't want to argue." His tired eyes plead with mine.

"Okay, but if we're calling a truce does that mean I can have a hug?" I give a childish grin.

"Nope." He exits the room.

39

*J*USTICE AND OMARI grin at me from across the dinner table. I am not sure whose idea it was for them to sit next to each other, but I should have realized that I would need to separate the two of them at the start of dinner when I watched them eagerly take their seats. For the past hour, they have been asking Noah question after question, all of which he answered with ease. I guess I should consider it payback for all the times I teased them over the years, but I can honestly say that I have never embarrassed them as much as they have embarrassed me tonight. My brother in law, Zion, even chimed in with a question or two which is surprising because he is usually quite reserved.

"Willow told me that you were born and raised in Cali. You should check out my art exhibition next time you're in town," Omari offers Noah.

"Your sister brags on your work all the time. I'll definitely hit you up next time I'm in town," Noah agrees.

"Alright. Wait, is that cool with you, sis?" Omari grins at me.

"Noah is a grown man, Omari. He doesn't need my permission." I make a mental note to pinch my brother as soon as I get the chance to. As annoying as his offer is, it is a good sign that he invited Noah to spend more time with him. In the past, Omari was usually reserved about forming bonds with guys that Justice and I have liked until he saw that the relationship was becoming serious. I am not sure if he is taking a different approach this time around, but he seems to really like Noah.

"Omari, leave Willow alone." Justice comes to my defense.

"Yeah, leave me alone *Omari*," I sneer.

"Whatever, I have head out anyways. I have an art event to get to." Omari excuses himself.

"Yeah, and we should be getting back to our hotel to get some much-needed rest." Justice takes her and Zion's empty plates to the sink. I know that this is her way of giving me the alone time that is needed to fix whatever is happening between Noah and me.

"It was good meeting you all." Noah stands from the table.

"Alright man, it was good to meet you. You seem to be a good guy, so I won't threaten you. All I ask is that you treat my sister with respect. Oh, and please forgive her for whatever crazy thing she did. She's still learning how to be normal in relationships." Omari offers unsolicited opinions on his way out the door.

"Yeah man, it was good to meet you," Zion adds. "I don't usually say much especially when it's not my business, but my sister-in-law has been through a lot, so if she's letting you into her world, that's a good sign. Plus, I hear her and my beautiful wife gossiping about you all the time, so I know she cares about you. Just treat her right, man." Zion's confession causes me to spit some of my wine out.

"Yeah, I agree with everything both of them said." Justice chuckles on her way out the door.

"Have a good night and be safe." I slam the door in their faces.

I can feel Noah's eyes follow me as I walk into the kitchen. I prepared a speech in my head during dinner, but now that we are alone, I don't know where to begin. He leans against the kitchen counter and folds his arms across his chest. I can tell that he isn't as frustrated as he was earlier tonight, but he is definitely still perplexed by my actions. He stares at me intently as I wash the dishes which causes a nervous smile to spread across my lips. He shakes his head in disappointment and turns away forcing me to finally make a decision. Not wanting him to leave, I turn towards him, offering a more sincere version of my previous apology.

"Noah, hold up. I meant it earlier when I said I was sorry."

"You said sorry three times now, but I'm curious to know what exactly I did to make you feel like you had to ignore me?" he says, guardedly.

"I feel so silly for trying to have sex with you at Janae's studio. I honestly don't know why I did that because I am the one who made the decision to have the three-month rule, and I am usually calm and collected in those type of situations. Maybe it's because I haven't had sex in over a year or maybe it's because you cause my body to react without thought. Either way, my actions were dumb, and being denied made me feel like an idiot," I shrug.

"So, me saying no in that situation made you question my attraction to you?"

"I am very aware of how attracted you are to me, and I am not saying any of this makes sense, but you gave me a weird hug after we left the studio, and I felt like I turned you off. In my defense, you have women throwing themselves at you all the time, and I'm sure you've had your fair share of hookups. Just to clarify, I am not a random hookup."

"We've been dating for months, and I have never made you feel like you were a random hookup. I was not about to let our first time be with you bent over a desk or on a yoga mat. I thought you would appreciate that," he says, in a frustrated tone.

"I do appreciate it, but I was also embarrassed. Why does that not make sense to you? I have only been intimate with two men in almost thirty years of life, both of which I was in long relationships with. You, on the other hand, have women throwing themselves at you on a daily basis, and I have not tried to or felt as if I had to compete with them, but your reaction scared me, and I started making assumptions. However, I am fully aware that my insecurities led to this conversation, and I sincerely apologize for trying to place them onto you."

"You should be." He stares at me blankly. "But I understand why you felt the way you did. Your ex was a fool who wanted to occupy your body, space, and time without earning it."

"Yeah, you're right about that, but that's no excuse for my behavior. It's obvious that I still have a lot of work to do." I feel frustrated. "I thought I was further along in my journey of healing, but apparently, I still have a long way to go."

"We all have work to do. Don't be so hard on yourself. Use that energy to move forward." He rubs his hand over the stubble on his jaw.

"Where did you just go?" I notice the shift in his stance and the concerted look on his face.

"I'm still here with you. Don't worry." He drops to his knees in front of me.

"What are you doing, Noah?" My voice is shaky. My hands are still wet from the sudsy dishwater, but he doesn't seem to care. He lifts my dress above my waist and places a kiss on my stomach. When I let out a soft moan, he grins in approval.

"Slide your panties down and feed me," he says, in a raspy tone.

I do as he instructs, spreading my legs for him to gain full access to me. He lifts one leg over his shoulder, covering me with his tongue. He licks and sucks, sending me to a blissful state, and when I attempt to close my eyes, he pleads with me to watch him. It's been so long since I've had any contact like this that after only a few minutes, I climax. I put my shaky leg back on the ground and lean against the counter for support. For a second, I feel as though my legs are going to give out, but Noah lifts me and carries me to the couch. He spreads my legs once again and places his face back in between them.

"It's too sensitive," I whisper, but I give up my protest when he starts back up. It goes on like this until I can no longer handle it. He literally makes me tap out as if we are in a wrestling match. Though I am exhausted, I slide down to the edge of the couch, ready to return the favor.

"Nope. Tonight, is all about you. Now, let's hop in the shower, so we can clean up and go to sleep," he whispers, and I do as he instructs.

40

THE NEXT MORNING, I wake up in Noah's arms. He is snoring softly, and his curls are sprawled all over his head. I ease out of bed and head towards the kitchen to make breakfast for the two of us. Justice and Janae would laugh if they could see me. They would probably say, "*Dang, she woke up early just to make him a meal, and they technically haven't even had sex?*" and I would respond, "*Yes, haters that is exactly what is happening, and it's the least I can do.*" Last night, the man washed my hair, washed my body, and kissed me all night without attempting to have sex. I could feel his hardness pressed against my thigh when we cuddled, and from his tossing and turning throughout the night, I could tell that his restraint took effort. He wanted to prove to me that he wasn't after my body, and I commend him for being so dedicated to the cause.

There have been several times when I have tried to run away from our friendship which has naturally blossomed into a relationship, but last night was the last straw. I have grown sick of my own childishness, and this breakfast is a peace treaty to not only Noah but also myself. I am making a final promise to myself. I will live in the present and enjoy each moment, and if something doesn't feel right, I will walk away, but I am also honoring my agreement with Lotus to keep my heart open to love even if this thing with Noah is short-lived.

"Hey, sleepy head," I say to Noah when he walks into the kitchen. His shorts are resting low on his hips, and it takes real effort for me to lift my eyes to his face and not his body. The man is beautiful.

"Grand rising, beautiful. What are you cooking?" He raises an eyebrow.

"Just a little freshly squeezed orange juice, roasted potatoes with peppers and onions, vegan sausage, and I'm going to hook you up with one of my famous acai bowls. I'm about to show you how I get down in the kitchen." I beam with confidence, but my answer seems to cause a nervous smile to spread across his lips.

"What was that look you just gave?" I ask suspiciously.

"Don't be mad, but I was sort of warned not to eat your cooking." The warning had to have come from my siblings.

"Was it Justice or Omari? Or, maybe it was Janae?"

"I was sworn to secrecy, so I can't tell you, but I can honestly say that everything looks and smells edible, so maybe the person was wrong," he grins.

"Okay, let's make a deal. If you try my food and love it, you have to tell this anonymous food critic, slash, hater that my food was delicious. If you do me this favor, I will owe you and have to do whatever you ask me to, but don't get any weird ideas," I warn.

"What if I don't like the food? Do I still get the favor?" he asks, curiously.

"Yes, as long as you eat at least three bites of food."

"Okay, cool." He reaches for a fork, cautiously taking a few bites of the potatoes and sausage.

"So?" I await the verdict.

"It's really good, and I will let your haters know that I enjoyed the food," he pauses. "But between you and me, the sausage is store bought, so I'll have to judge you off of your acai bowl to get a true understanding of your skills. When do I get to try that?"

"Are you serious?" I whine.

"Wait. Are you seriously upset?" He looks up from his plate.

"No, I'm not mad, but I think it's rude that you would say something like that to me when I am working hard to become a better cook."

"Wait. So, you're telling me that you've been working *really* hard to prove yourself, and people continuously doubt you without giving you a fair chance?" he smirks, and I quickly connect the dots.

"Okay, point taken. I knew you hadn't fully forgiven me for last night. This breakfast is actually supposed to be a final apology or my version of peace treaty, but you don't seem to want peace." I shrug and walk towards the stove to fix myself a plate.

"I would like nothing more than peace with you. That's all I've been trying to do, but you fight me at every turn. There's only so much I can do to convince you that I'm a good man." There isn't a trace of anger or frustration in his voice. He sounds clear and determined for me to understand his side of things.

"Do you believe in fresh starts?" I ask sincerely.

"I do, which is why we should start over by enjoying this amazing breakfast you made. Then, if you don't have plans, maybe you can come with me to mom's house for lunch? Lotus is in town and wants to see us." He diverts his eyes at the mentioning of Lotus and walks over to the stove to get more food. My eyes stare into the back of him like daggers because I smell a setup coming my way. Lotus and I built a bond at the retreat, and it grew even stronger when I learned that she was the one who suggested Noah come to the agency to work with me. We don't talk every day, and most of our communication is via text, but it seems unusual for her not to send a personal invite. I, however, just made a deal with Noah, so I plan to go with the flow. I just hope I'm not walking into an ambush.

◆ ◆ ◆

We pull up to Ms. Yvette's house, and I turn to Noah as soon as he puts the car in park. I've been around Lotus and his mom enough times to know that they have big personalities which is usually fun but could also be intimidating, and I can only imagine how bad it is when they are together. The three of them have lunch together every time Lotus comes to visit which is why I feel the need to go over a few ground rules before we exit the car. Technically, there is only one rule, but I plan to emphasize the one so much that it feels like there are at least three.

"Do not gang up on me with your mom or Lotus," I warn him.

"I would never do you like that," he chuckles softly.

"Promise me, Noah," I say, reaching over to offer him my pinky to make a pact.

"Baby, I promise you. Everything is going to be fine." He links his pinky with mine. "But you know Lotus can read people, so relax." He removes the key from the ignition.

"Okay, fine. But let the record show that on this day Willow agreed to follow Noah's lead."

"Noted. Now can we go in?" He takes my head in his.

"Following your lead, sir." I exit the car.

◆ ◆ ◆

"Hey ma, we're here." Noah announces himself from the foyer.

When our calls go unanswered, we walk deeper into the house. The smell of food fills the air, but Lotus and Yvette are nowhere in sight. Muffled voices and laughter catch our attention, so we follow the sounds coming from the backyard. Uncle Buzzard is laying in a reclined chair with his arms propped behind his head for support. He is smiling adoringly at Lotus and Yvette who are kneeled down in the garden a few feet away, laughing and examining their kale crop. Uncle Buzzard is the first to spot us, and without warning, he rushes towards us with his arms extended in excitement causing Lotus and Yvette to look up.

"Hey nephew. Hey Willow." He pulls us in for a hug. Noah's face scrunches in confusion, and if I am reading his body language correctly, he was not expecting his uncle to be here.

"Hey, Unc. I'm happy to see you, but I'm surprised to see you." Noah returns his uncle's hug.

"Well, your mama said you wanted this pretty lady of yours to spend some quality time with her and Lotus, so I suggested that me and your father join you in case you needed some male energy around. Lotus and your mom might get paid to go around speaking and giving advice, but us men know a thing or two. Plus, I missed you, nephew." Uncle Buzzard beams with pride, unaware that he just revealed a vital piece of information.

This lunch was Noah's idea, not his moms or Lotus'. Avoiding eye contact with me, Noah stalks over to talk to his mom and Lotus.

"Did I say something wrong?" Buzzard turns to me.

"In my opinion, you didn't but I can't say the same for Noah," I chuckle.

"Aw Hell. Yvette or Lotus should have warned me," he lets out a long sigh.

"I'm glad they didn't warn you. If I don't get a warning neither should he," I say, turning my head in the direction of the garden where Noah is now standing with his arms crossed over his chest.

"He better not be fussing at them either, or I'll put him over my knee like I did when he was a kid." He tries to sound harsh, but his words are gentle, a threat with no power behind it.

"So, when is Noah's dad coming?" I ask apprehensively. Noah's dad is the only member of the family that I haven't met.

"He wanted to be here, but he's in L.A. for another day or two, spending time with Nova's little girl. I swear that baby has Isaac and Noah wrapped around her little finger," he chuckles.

"Well, I'm glad you're here, and I'm sure Noah is too." I try to defuse the situation.

"Thank you for that, but it's obvious that he isn't happy about me being here. I just want you to know that my nephew does not bring women around his family. In fact, I think the only girl he has ever brought around the family was his high school sweetheart, so your being here is a good sign, especially if he wants you to spend time with his mother and honorary godmother."

"And with that knowledge, I can breathe easier," I say, jokingly but Uncle Buzzard's words genuinely provided much needed comfort. Here I was assuming that Noah wanted to use this lunch as some sort of test or intervention. I figured that this may have been his way of getting me and Lotus in the same room so that she could get me to open up again like she did at the retreat, but Buzzard just discounted those theories in a matter of seconds. Noah may not be aware of the significance of his Uncle being here today, but I am. Uncle Buzzard just helped me understand one very important thing. Noah really wanted me to be here today.

After a few moments, Noah returns with Lotus and his mom at his side. They both pull me in for hug and then Noah steps up to apologize to his Uncle for the way he greeted him earlier. They repeat the hug they shared a few moments earlier, and Yvette invites us all to join her inside. After washing our hands, we each take our seats at the table, ready to eat the lunch that was prepared for us. Uncle Buzzard claims the seat next to Lotus, which is directly across from Noah and me, while Miss Yvette sits at the head of the table.

Lotus glares at Uncle Buzzard when he drapes his arm around the back of her chair. I seem to be the only one to notice, but there is definitely something awkward going on between the two of them. Buzzard seemed comfortable with the action, but Lotus seemed like she wanted to bolt from the table. I giggle silently to myself as I watch him quickly remove his arm and place it carefully in his lap. I turn to look at Noah to see if he picked up on their body language, but he is too busy devouring the bowl of gumbo to notice.

"Noah, since you started eating first would you like to say grace?" Ms. Yvette looks at him disapprovingly.

"God is great. God is good. Thank you, God, for this food," Noah smiles proudly.

"Strong prayer, nephew. Very good," Buzzard beams with pride.

"Really?" I giggle at their silliness.

"Ignore them, Willow. Their manners go out the window when food is placed in front of them." Yvette is trying to sound authoritative, but I can tell that she is happy to see them enjoying the food.

"Are you sure this is all vegan?" Uncle Buzzard turns towards Lotus and then towards his sister.

"Yes, it is, and it tastes just like mama's gumbo doesn't it?" Yvette beams with pride.

"It does indeed. I might have to give this vegan lifestyle a try." He glances at Lotus, and the corner of her mouth curls into a slight smile.

"Noah seems to be enjoying your gumbo just as much as he enjoyed the breakfast I made this morning," I add to the conversation.

"Yep," Noah smiles, nervously.

"Okay, so I might be exaggerating a little." I nudge him with my elbow.

"We could always continue our cooking lessons over the phone," Lotus offers.

"I can also teach you a few recipes if you're interested," Yvette adds.

"My sister may not be a well-known chef like Ms. Lotus over here, but she can throw down in the kitchen. Maybe, she can teach you a few of her best dishes since she's always trying to force somebody to eat that quinoa and kale stuff. Then Lotus can teach you on the video chat technology. You know when you use your phone to see each other's faces? That way you get to learn from the best of the best," Uncle Buzzard suggests.

"Great suggestion, Uncle Buzzard. I would really like that. As long as Noah is comfortable with us spending so much time together." I realize that none of us asked if he was okay with his family spending so much time with me.

"My son is not our boss." Yvette looks over at Noah almost daring him to object.

Raising his hand, Noah says, "For the record, her son has no issue with you spending time with his family."

41

Ms. Yvette and I are sprawled out on the living room floor listening to Al Green as we wait for our food to finish cooking. This has become a routine for us over the past three weeks, her teaching me a new recipe and then the two of us going into the living room to lay on the floor and groove out to old records until the timer goes off. This is also the part where she would normally show me pictures of Noah as a baby, but she has literally gone through every photo album that she owns, and as of last week, there are no more pictures for her to share with me.

It just so happens that Ms. Yvette is just as bad as I am when it comes to having small talk, so we were forced to bypass any awkward conversations that otherwise may have ensued and go straight to having deep conversations about our life experiences. Prior to meeting Yvette, Noah shared basic details of his mom's life, but from speaking to her, I gained deeper insight into her life and learned how she became the woman that she is today.

Her childhood dream was to be a famous singer, and she was on track to accomplish those goals, but when she was twenty-one, she became pregnant with Noah and decided that it was more important to be at home with her son instead of carrying him around from city to city with strangers around at every turn. So, she put her singing career on hold and pursued what she, at the time, believed to be a more suitable career. She enrolled in community college and obtained a degree in nutrition and holistic healing. She compiled the knowledge that she learned at school with the history she absorbed from her mother and grandmother early on.

She shared that Noah's grandmother, Ruth, is actually the person who was always interested in healing, but she never had a fancy title to go with it. Ruth was an herbalist who had a natural understanding of plants which she used to help people in the neighborhood whenever they got a cold or had small ailments that affected them. Ruth also taught the youngsters in the neighborhood the importance of knowing self. According to Yvette, it all started with her great grandmother, Rebecca, who passed down her knowledge to Ruth before passing away. That knowledge was then passed on to Yvette who studied the information further and became the neighborhood healer and historian, teaching black history in her living room to people in the neighborhood on the weekends and working her regular job during the week. I have been around strong women my entire life, but with my mom living in another state, it is revitalizing to be around a woman with similar strength to hers.

Last week was the first time that I truly opened up and gave her a look into my life, and I am so happy that I did. I shared funny stories from my childhood, and I even showed her a self-portrait that I painted when I came from the retreat. She is much like Lotus when it comes to listening and sharing wisdom. She told me that my art spoke loudly, and after seeing it, she suggested that I never put my dreams aside or hold onto things that aren't meant for me because it will only hurt more in the long run. These are lessons that I learned the hard way, but I won't make the mistake of repeating those mistakes again.

"Looks like it's time for us to check the food." Yvette moves the needle from the record.

"I'm praying that this turns out right because my friends will definitely be providing feedback if it's nasty."

"I watched you make it and nothing that is made in my kitchen could ever taste bad. Now, come on," she says, confidently.

I follow her into the kitchen and pull out a ladle to stir the gumbo that has been simmering on the stove for the last three hours. In exactly thirty minutes, this house will be filled with a few of our closest friends and family members, giving them a chance to judge my new cooking skills. Though, we used most of the cooking lessons as a way to get to know each other, we had at least three actual lessons, so I feel pretty confident in my ability to pull this off. Plus, if it turns out bad, I can just blame my instructor.

"Alright now let's taste it." Yvette hands me a spoon.

"On the count of three?" I dip the spoon into the pot. "One, two..."

"Oh, that is good!" Yvette tastes it on the two rather than three.

"It really is," I say, amazed at myself for making the dish. I quickly realize that I have nothing to worry about. I think my batch is even better than the one Yvette made a few weeks ago, but that is an opinion that I will be keeping to myself.

◆ ◆ ◆

Omari and his date Carmen are the first to arrive. He is staying in Dallas for another month while he finishes up an art campaign, so I invited him to join us for dinner along with David, Janae, Noah, and Noah's Dad Elgin. Yvette and Elgin divorced a few years ago, but they are great friends, and she insisted that he be here tonight to finally meet the woman she describes as *Noah's perfect match who was handpicked by Lotus, but she would have set it up first if she met me first.* I laugh every time she refers to me this way.

"Hey Squirt." I lean over to hug Omari.

"I told you not to call me that anymore." He groans but returns my hug. "You remember Carmen from the art show?" She steps closer and gives me an awkward side hug.

"Of course, I remember her. It's nice to see you again Carmen."

"You too!" she says enthusiastically.

"Where is everybody? Don't tell me they passed out from trying your food?" Omari releases a deep laugh.

"Ha-ha, very funny," I roll my eyes. "They should be pulling up any moment."

"It looks like two cars just pulled into the driveway," Carmen adds.

"Young man, did I hear you say the food was going to be nasty? It's my recipe, so I know I didn't hear what I thought I heard," Yvette catches Omari off guard.

"No ma'am. I wasn't saying that at all. I was just giving my sister a hard time is all," Omari stutters causing us all to erupt in laughter.

"Oh baby, I was only joking with you. Welcome to my home. I'm Noah's mother, Yvette." She introduces herself.

"Nice to meet you. I'm Willow's brother Omari, and this is my girl-friend Carmen."

"Ms. Yvette, he was not joking. He would have been disrespecting your recipe and our cooking lessons if you hadn't walked in." I try to keep a straight face.

"Willow, stop being so dramatic. If this wonderful mother said that she has taken the time to mentor you, then I am sure the food will be amaz-ing," he retorts.

"Ma, are you picking on people?" Noah catches the end of Omari's statement.

"Actually, it was Willow who was picking on me. You know how she is. You're the one who's dating her," Omari teases.

"I have no clue what you mean by that." Noah avoids the trap.

"I see I taught you well." David walks in with Janae. A man who looks exactly like Noah except for his gray beard is trailing behind them.

"*You* taught him?" The man questions David.

"Well, you and Uncle Buzzard taught us and then I taught Noah because you know I was a better listener than him," David clarifies.

"Oh ok. That's what I thought I heard you say," Elgin teases. "So, you're the young lady that I've heard so much about?" He turns his atten-tion to me.

"Pop, this is my girlfriend Willow. Willow this is my dad, Elgin." Noah introduces us.

"It's nice to meet you," I smile nervously. His father is even more charming than him if that is even possible.

"Now that introductions are out of the way, let's wash our hands and share a meal together. I think we are all in need of some good food and conversation," Yvette suggests.

"Sounds like a plan to me," I second her notion.

Omari rolls his eyes when Noah announces that the men should serve the women since Yvette and I cooked the meal. My brother is usually a gentleman and would have agreed to Noah's suggestion without hesitation, but he isn't used to me having a man around who shows affection without concern of looking weak. He will be sure to make fun of Noah when he gets the chance to, but I know that deep down he respects him for taking such good care of me.

I claim the seat next to Janae, leaving room for David to sit on the other side of her and for Noah to sit next to me. The two of us haven't spent much time together over the past few weeks due to our heavy workloads, so now is my chance to spend some much-needed quality time with my best friend. I watch as Yvette smiles adoringly at Elgin as he goes around the table pouring each of us a glass of red wine and giving us a hefty portion of gumbo and cornbread. They have been divorced for over five years, but I can tell that there is still a lot of love between them.

After the men take their seats, Yvette enlists Omari to say grace. We each bow our heads as he rattles off the same prayer that Noah said less than a month ago, making me realize that Uncle Buzzard isn't here to defend the effectiveness of the prayer like he had for Noah. According to Ms. Yvette, Buzzard went to California to visit Nova, but I have a feeling that he also went to visit Lotus. I still haven't shared my theory with Noah, but I suspect that there is definitely something going on between the two of them. After grace is said, the seven of us dig into our food. I can't help but smile as each person goes back to the stove to grab seconds and then thirds. Janae is usually full after eating one or two plates, so her nonstop munching is all the proof that I need to know that the food is good. After about an hour, Yvette brings out the peach cobbler that she made for dessert. I laugh as everyone groans in approval; they seem to be confused by their desire for dessert when they are still full of dinner.

"I can't lie. This was really good, sis." Omari admits what I already knew.

"Yeah babe this is just as good as mamas." Noah grabs a napkin and wipes a crumb from my mouth, ignoring Yvette's playful glare.

"Hey son, watch what you say" his dad teases. "We ought to give thanks for the teacher *and* the chef." He winks at Yvette.

"Mr. Elgin is right. Give Ms. Yvette credit for teaching me, and after that, I need everybody in this room to put some respect on my name because I am no longer a bad cook." The message is for everyone, but I focus in on Omari and Janae who are my biggest critics.

"Hey, I always eat your cooking," Janae feigns offense.

"And I just gave you credit," Omari adds.

"I will definitely be putting respect on your name from this moment on." Noah kisses my neck, and Omari immediately covers his eyes.

"Hey, no PDA, man. I do not want to see you all up on my sister."

"Yeah, no nuzzling each other's necks in front of your parents either," his mother warns.

"Sorry," Noah grins.

"Anyways." Omari changes the subject. "I know you two agreed to keep your relationship private a while longer, but I have an art show coming up on the eighteenth of this month if either of you are interested in coming." The night was going so well, so of course my idiot brother had to bring up a sensitive subject and change the mood.

"Man, I wish I could, but I'm scheduled to attend a charity event, and my manager would never forgive me if I missed it. Are you going?" Noah turns to me.

"I was thinking that I should …," I begin to speak when Carmen interrupts me midsentence.

"I know it's none of my business, but you should totally go to Noah's event with him. The women at those types of events can be so aggressive, and it's our job to keep our men focused. That's why I will be front and center at Omari's art show." She beams with pride.

"Anybody want desert?" Ms. Yvette saves me from having to respond in front of everyone.

"I wish we could stay, but I have an event that I'm hosting, and I can't be late. Thank you for the hospitality Ms. Yvette, and I'll see you back home later, sis. I won't be in too late." Omari stands and says his goodbyes.

Carmen may have been trying to help, but I think she created a situation for herself. Omari did not appreciate her comment.

"Yeah, we're going to be on our way too." David pulls Janae's chair out for her to stand. The two of them have been surprisingly quiet throughout tonight's dinner, which is far from their normal behavior. Something is definitely up with them, but I'll worry about that tomorrow.

"We still on for brunch tomorrow?" Janae asks.

"Wouldn't miss it for the world." I pull her in for a hug.

"Do you need any help cleaning up," Elgin offers Yvette.

"No, I think I have it covered. Go on and enjoy your night, old man," Yvette replies, softly.

"Okay then. It was a pleasure to meet you, Willow. I'm sure I will be seeing more of you if my son has anything to do with it." Elgin offers me a sincere smile.

"I guess I will walk everybody to their cars." Noah closes the door behind him.

"You two go on and enjoy your night. I can clean the kitchen in the morning," Yvette offers.

"No, ma'am. I can load the dishwasher before we leave. You've done enough, and I truly appreciate it." I walk to the kitchen. I watch as Yvette disappears into her room.

My back is to the doorway, but I can feel Noah's presence when he re-enters the kitchen. Things have been great between the two of us since we agreed to keep our relationship private, but after Omari's comment earlier at the dinner table, I worry that an argument is brewing, and the last time we argued in the kitchen, things ended with me in a comprising position. We can't do that tonight, at least not with Yvette only a few feet away in her room.

"You cooked; let me clean." Noah takes the plate from my hand.

"Is this what I have to look forward to when we get married?" My mouth forms the words before my brain has time to catch up.

"I hope so." He places the plate into the washer. "Things feel natural with you, and I trust you in my space."

"The feeling is mutual," I admit.

"Good to know." He loads another plate into the dishwasher. "So, are you going to Omari's showcase?"

"I've been to almost every show he's ever had, so he will understand if I'm not at this one, but my family is flying in to support him, so I figured I might as well be there."

"Oh ok." He plays it cool, but I know my response isn't what he wanted to hear.

"We promised to have open communication with one another, so I feel it's only right that I consider your feelings before making a final decision. You haven't formally invited me to this event with you, but I have a feeling you would like to ask me."

"I don't want to control you; you know that's not my style. But if I'm being honest, I would love to have you by my side at some point. I would rather be at Omari's event with you, but I'm performing at the benefit, and I can't miss it. I'm still new to all of this," Noah says, apprehensively.

"I would love for the world to see us together, but I don't think I'm ready for the pressure and negativity that can come from being in the spotlight."

"I understand." He looks me directly in the eye. There isn't any apparent judgment or resentment in his eyes, but I worry that I am making the wrong decision.

42

ANAE RUSHES INTO the restaurant wearing leggings and an oversized tee. She looks as though she hasn't slept in days, but I know that isn't true because we were together last night, and she seemed happy and well rested. She slides into the booth, saying hello with a wave of her hand, using the menu as a barrier to avoid making eye contact with me. I stay quiet, deciding it best to study her before jumping into conversation, but when the waiter comes to take our drink order, I can no longer contain myself. She asks for orange juice instead of her traditional mimosa, and I know for a fact that something is going on with her because out of all of our years of friendship, she has never come to brunch solely for the breakfast. Our tradition has always been to sip champagne mixed with orange juice, gossip about our love lives or lack thereof, and discuss how we plan to make the upcoming week better than the last.

"Okay, what is going on?" I get straight to the point.

"What?" She smiles nervously. "I had wine last night, so I'm not in the mood to drink today. It's not a big deal." She shrugs casually, and I consider her words for a moment before quickly realizing that she did not drink any of the wine that was poured for her last night.

"Janae, what is going on? I'm not saying you drink a lot, but you never turn down mimosas, especially when it's my turn to treat."

"Fine." She leans in closer. "My period is five weeks late, and I'm pretty sure I'm pregnant." She bites her lip nervously.

Reaching for her hand, I ask, "Have you taken a test?"

"Yes." She exhales deeply. "I took three tests last night before dinner, and they all had a plus sign"

"That explains you and David's awkward silence last night. You two are never quiet," I tease.

"I wanted to tell you as soon as I took the test, but I needed time to sort through my emotions."

"What did David say when you told him?"

"He's excited. Me on the other hand, I am freaking out. This is not what I expected at all. We *always* use protection except for this one time. Ugh. I can't believe I did this to myself."

"Have you decided what you're going to do?" I ask.

"Oh, I'm definitely going to be a mother to this baby. I'm just shocked is all, but I'm also really happy."

"I can't believe I'm going to be an aunt!" I squeal. "Wait, this also means that Noah is going to be your baby's uncle." Her face lights up at the realization.

"Yes, it does, so you two are stuck in each other's lives no matter what." She teases, "Now you have to get pregnant, so our babies can be born around the same time."

"Not going to happen," I laugh. "I can't even commit to being Noah's date let alone having his baby."

"I'm glad you brought that up. I've been trying to stay out of your business lately, but last night I almost lost it. Carmen definitely overstepped by giving her opinion, and she's lucky I was too distracted with my own problems to yell at her. If anyone had the right to give their opinion, it would be your friends and family, not Omari's flavor of the week. I'm sure everyone at the table wanted to tell you not to be an idiot, but we also know that this is your decision, so how dare she tell you what to do?"

"Wow." I say feeling slighted. "So, you think I'm being an idiot?"

"I think your concern for going public and having the media being all up in your business is valid, but are you sure that's your only concern?"

"What if we go to this event, tell the world that we're together and then break up shortly after, or what if he does something to hurt me publicly? I don't think I can go through that again."

"First of all, Noah is not Ziggy. Secondly, Noah *is not* Ziggy."

"So, what you're saying is that I should stop being an idiot and go to the event with Noah?"

"I can't make the decision for you. All I am saying is that you need to make sure that you aren't bringing old baggage into this new situation. I don't want to have to start calling you bag lady. Do you need me to run up and down these Dallas streets to find Erykah Badu to sing to you?"

"Not funny." I roll my eyes. "How could I ever be a bag lady when I have you, *pregnant lady*, keeping me in check?" My words come out as a joke, but the realization that life is changing for the both of us suddenly kicks in.

43

*A*FTER DAYS OF careful deliberation, I finally agree to accompany Noah to the charity event, thus my reason for being in a dress shop with Nova and Janae who have quickly become two peas in a pod. So far, I have tried on seven dresses all of which they scrunched their noses up to in disapproval. They claimed that the dresses were either too old fashioned, didn't compliment my body type, or just weren't red carpet worthy. I can't say that I disagree with them, but this dress shop is the closest I could find within my price range, and I refuse to live above my means for a one-night event. Noah offered to pay for my dress, but it didn't feel right to accept money from him, which led to a lecture from my mom, his mom, Justice, Janae, and Nova for my declining his offer. While I appreciated their advice, I wanted to be independent and foot my own bill, but I have almost fainted three times since we entered the store because the price tags on most of these dresses are outrageous. My business is doing well but not $800 dollars for a dress that I would only wear once kind of well.

"Wait, why are we dress shopping when you could easily design your own dress?" Janae poses a good question, but I am almost positive that everyone at this event will be wearing well-known brands.

"That's actually a brilliant idea." Nova eyes the dress that I am wearing in disapproval. "Everyone loved the outfit you designed for me. They kept asking who I was wearing, and I proudly let them know that it was a Willow Westbrook original, darling." She stands and pretends to walk down a runway.

"I do have this one dress that I made recently, but it's kind of out there. I'm not sure it's appropriate for this kind of event."

"Hmm," Janae says examining me. "I know you pretty well, and when you describe something that you've made as *out there*, it usually means you're about to shake shit up, so I'm going to take a wild guess and say that it has a big African symbol somewhere on it?" Janae teases.

"For your information it does not."

"Does it have a fist somewhere on it?" Nova takes a guess.

"For your information it does not." I laugh. "I guess you two will have to watch the broadcast to find out."

44

THE DOORBELL RINGS, and I look out of the peephole to find Noah standing in all of his six-foot glory, wearing a fitted black suit with a dark emerald green tie and loafers to match. His beard is long but well-groomed and his hair is tapered on the side with the top twisted into a bun. I, on the other hand, am only halfway dressed, and though I wanted him to see the final result, I'll have to settle for him seeing me in my robe wearing only half a face of make-up and gold earrings.

"You're early," I place a kiss on his lips. He looks at me in unreserved amazement, and I swear I just fell harder for this man if that's even possible. I reach up to hug him and the smell of soap and natural oils fill my nose, sandalwood mixed with peppermint.

"I know," he grins. "I had to make sure you weren't going to change your mind about coming."

"I was just about to text to tell you that I needed to cancel." I disappear into the bathroom to finish getting ready before he has a chance to respond. I realize that now probably isn't the best time to tease him, but I can't help myself.

After applying a few final touches to my makeup, I put on my dress and walk out to meet Noah who is sitting on the couch where I left him. He pulls his gaze from the television and focuses in on me, his eyes trailing up my body and landing on my face. We haven't broached the subject in weeks, but there is definite sexual tension in the air, and though we are well over the official three months of dating, neither of us has said anything. We have however been pushing the limits by kissing and exploring each other more intimately, learning what intimacy is outside of sex. We meditate together, pray together, read books together, work in comfortable silence together, and I've even read a few of my poems for him.

"You look beautiful," he admits.

"Do you think the dress is too much?" I ask, nervously.

"Not at all. I wish we could skip the event and stay here, but the world deserves to see you in this dress."

"See that's why Omari always rolls his eyes at you," I joke. "You say the sweetest things."

"I speak the truth," he says. "Now, let's go so Omari can see us on the red carpet and hate some more."

I smile as the driver comes to open the car door for me and find myself laughing in disbelief when Noah insists on being the one to help me in. His smile grows even wider than it did a few moments earlier when he appeared at my door, and if I had any doubts about my appearance, he is sure to wipe them away from my memory. Once we are seated in the back of the car, he reaches over to grab my hand. I watch as he glances out of the window, his energy suddenly shifting from confident to nervous.

"Everything okay?" I squeeze his hand gently.

"Yeah, I'm okay. I just get nervous every time I do one of these things. I'm glad you'll be with me this time." He leans in to kiss me on the forehead.

"Will they ask me any questions?" I prepare myself for what is to come.

"They will most likely ask who you're wearing and want to know who you are to me," he says the last part faster than the first.

"I don't know if I can do this," I admit.

"You can. Just hold my hand and show them your amazing smile."

Just as the words leave his mouth, he reaches for my hand, and we exit the car. The place is swarming with reporters holding cameras and people moving in every direction. Noah introduces me to a few well-known celebrities who I recognize but never expected to meet. They all seem nice, but it's not them that I am worried about. Paparazzi and Noah's fans are the ones that will be most likely to judge me and our relationship. After he promoted my business on his page a few months back, I received an endless number of messages from fans demanding to know who I was. Then, there were people who pretended to be interested in supporting my business but really only wanted to get to know me for their own personal agendas. I was able to ignore all of them over the internet, but once we step onto this carpet, I am opening myself up to the public and going unnoticed won't be as easy as it once was. Then again, maybe I am exaggerating. Maybe nothing will change.

"Just breathe, Willow. You look amazing." Noah leads us to the first group of cameras.

He wraps his arm around my waist, and we smile as camera flashes go off. We pose confidently together, him in his fitted suit with green accents that match my emerald green dress, which has a split that goes up to my right thigh. I decided to wear my natural hair, which is styled in a curly Afro. I don't wear makeup often, but tonight I decided to go with a very subtle shade, and I added gold earrings and black open toed stiletto heels to accentuate the dress.

"Noah, who's your date?" one reporter asks.

"Is she the same woman from your social media pages?" another asks.

"Who are you wearing?" a third yells.

He smiles and looks down at me before answering, "Well, this beautiful woman standing next to me is Willow Westbrook. She is a talented designer, and to answer your question, she designed my outfit for tonight. As for her dress, well, why don't you ask her?" he gloats.

The reporter places the microphone towards me, and I answer without hesitation, "This is an original design from my new line called *For the Love of Fashion*."

"What a beautiful gown," the woman responds as more flashes go off. The reporters attempt to ask more questions, but Noah's manager pulls us away and leads us to our seats.

45

*N*OAH WAS THE first performer of the night, and I cheered like a fan sitting in the stands at a football game. I received a few disapproving glances from people in the audience, but I brushed them off as quickly as they came. Overall, this has been an amazing experience though I admit I could hardly concentrate throughout most of the show with Soleil Chante sitting next to me. She is one of the greatest Neo Soul artists of all time, and tonight I learned that she is also one of the most down to earth souls that I have ever met. She was featured on Noah's album, and I knew that they were good friends, but I never expected to spend hours singing and laughing with her. I won't lie; I freaked out when I first took my seat, but after she kicked her heels off to dance, I realized that she is a regular human being, and I needed to stop treating her any differently, so I joined her in dancing, and by the end of the show, we were exchanging information to discuss me styling her for an upcoming project.

Noah received at least five invites to five different parties on our way out the door, and I am not sure how we are going to choose which one to attend. It feels strange to miss Omari's show after being at nearly every event he has ever had since childhood, but tonight I was exactly where I needed to be. I came to support Noah, who used every opportunity to support me by informing people that I designed my dress and styled him for the tonight's event. I am not sure how well I will fit in at these parties, but I'll use them as another opportunity to support Noah while having some fun of my own and networking with some of the biggest names in the industry.

Maurice, our driver for the night, pulls up and comes around to open my door, but Noah, once again, insists on being the one to help me in. Maurice laughs at the gesture but nods his head in understanding. After claiming the seat next to me, Noah gives the driver the address for the venue where Omari is hosting his art show and asks him to take us there. I love my brother but going to his show was not a part of tonight's plan.

"Don't look so disappointed." Noah studies the confused look on my face.

"It's that obvious, huh?" I laugh. "I love my brother, but I think he'd understand if I missed this one show. He's the one who basically forced me to be here with you tonight."

"And for that I will always appreciate him," he grins slyly. "But your mom really wants to meet me, and I promised Omari that if we had enough time, I would stop by to support him, but if you aren't ready for me to meet your parents, I can text and tell them that things ran long, and we can't make it."

I glance down at my phone to check the time and realize that Omari's show ends in less than thirty minutes, and we have at least a fifteen-minute drive ahead of us. There won't be much time to mingle, but I can tell that being there is important to Noah, so I choose to appreciate his effort instead of complaining about it. I lay my head on his shoulder and stare out of the window, thinking how grateful I am to be here in this moment with Noah.

"I can't believe my mom guilted you into coming, but they won't be back in town for a while, so let's do it."

◆ ◆ ◆

The venue is nearly empty by the time we arrive, but my parents, Carmen, Omari, and a few stragglers are still inside checking out the art and socializing. My mom is the first to see us, and she rushes over in excitement, pulling us both in for a hug. One would never know that this was their first-time meeting by the way her and Noah interact so comfortably with one another. My dad, on the other hand, takes longer to warm up to people, so he is quietly standing back, studying their interaction before introducing himself. When my mom releases Noah from her grip, my dad steps up and shakes Noah's hand. This is the part where I would usually interrupt their interaction and warn my dad to be nice and go easy on him but tonight, I think I'll see how Noah handles himself without me stepping in.

"So, you're the guy that my daughter's been talking about?" My dad watches Noah intently.

"Yes sir, that would be me. It's nice to finally meet you," Noah responds with confidence.

"We only have a few minutes before we have to be out of this place, and we have an early flight to catch, so I won't beat around the bush. I've heard a lot of good things about you, and according to my daughter, you're a good man. Now, I don't know you well enough to say if those things are true, but as long as you continue to treat her with respect, you will continue to have my respect." His words are strong, but he offers a soft smile and another handshake.

"Yes sir, I understand." Noah's eyes never leave my dad's. I know my dad well enough to know that he was somewhat impressed by the certainty Noah carries.

"Shouldn't you be out partying with the rich and famous?" Omari says, making his way over to us. Carmen's arm is in linked with his, and I imagine this is what she meant when she said she would be here to keep the vultures from stealing my brother away.

"They chose to spend time with you instead of going to party. Isn't that sweet?" My mom cheerily answers.

"You mean *Noah* chose to support me over the Hollywood crowd? I know Willow would be partying right now if she could." Omari releases Carmen and puts his arm around my shoulder, squeezing me tight like the annoying little brother he is.

Chuckling, Noah answers, "Hey, my word is bond. I told you I would be here if I could, and it turns out that I could. I just hate that we missed the whole event."

"Yeah, you missed one hell of a show." Omari looks around the now empty venue proudly.

"Well, let me look around for a few minutes to see if there's a piece that would look good in my house. Then, we can take a picture to post on social media to let people know that I was here." Noah winces at his choice of words, and though no one else seems to notice, I instantly recognize the discomfort. He is still getting use to people caring what he does and where he goes.

"That would be amazing." Carmen answers on my brother's behalf.

"It would be, wouldn't it?" My mom is obviously irritated by Carmen. "Omari, why don't you show Noah around? *Alone.*"

"Yes, ma'am." He moves his arm from my shoulder and leads Noah further into the studio. Carmen frowns but is sure to hide her irritation from my mother.

"I should get going. It was a pleasure to meet you all. Omari, I'll see you back at my place later." Carmen waves and makes a quick exit.

"Did you really just do that?" I turn to my mom who is grinning.

"Yes, she did, and if your friend *Noah* gets out of line, he will get the same treatment." My dad answers for my mom.

"Daddy, I love you, but please understand that I can handle myself. I will not be repeating any of the mistakes that I made in my past. I promise."

"Okay. I respect that." He ends the conversation just as Noah returns with a giant painting under his arm and a smile plastered on his face.

46

I WAKE UP TO an empty bed, but the smell of food and Noah's singing fills the air. I decide to shower and freshen up before joining him, taking a few minutes to replay last night's events in my head. I still cannot believe that I actually walked the red carpet, announced my relationship to the world, and introduced Noah to my parents all in one night. I purposely logged out of my social media accounts before the awards show started, deciding that I would rather focus on the present moment instead of being distracted by my phone all night. At some point today, I will need to check my social media accounts and respond to a few business emails, but until then, I plan to spend the next few hours alone with Noah.

I walk into the kitchen, and there are two breakfast burritos from Vegan Tingz and a pitcher of freshly squeezed watermelon juice waiting for me on the counter. Noah is standing on the balcony, shirtless, leaning against the railing. His back is turned to me, but I can tell that he is working from the way that his head is moving in sync with whatever beat is playing in his headphones. He reaches down to grab his guitar and notepad, seemingly lost in the moment. I have seen him do this several times since we started dating, and I've come to learn that this is what he does when he has a new song in his head that needs to be released. I hate being disturbed when I am working, so I eat one of the burritos, drink a glass of watermelon juice, and make my way to my healing room to create some art of my own.

◆ ◆ ◆

"Hey." Noah leans against the door of my healing room.

"Hey, thanks for the breakfast. I would have said it earlier, but I knew you were working, and I didn't want to mess with your vibe."

"I saw you watching me," he laughs. "You weren't as subtle as you thought you were."

"At least I tried to be considerate. You, on the other hand, have no problem interrupting me." *I was finished with my work over an hour ago, but he doesn't have to know that.*

"You were in here for a while, so I figured now would be a good time to come and talk."

"Okay, let's talk." I pat the seat next to me.

"Last night, was a new experience for you, and I wanted to see how you were feeling about everything."

"Honestly, I feel okay. I can almost guarantee that some people will be annoyed that I was there with you instead of them, but that's not my problem. I have no regrets about the event or about you meeting my parents."

"I'm relieved to hear you say that because people are not happy about seeing us together, but I want you to know that none of their opinions matter," he says, sincerely.

"Are you serious?" I pose the question without giving him time to answer. "It's probably just a bunch of groupies that wish they were in my place, and I refuse to let them kill my mood, so let's not even continue this conversation."

"Yeah, forget them." He mimics my serious tone with a playful grin.

"Is this a joke to you?" I am obviously annoyed by his delivery.

"Are you mad?" He straightens up. "Okay, before this joke turns serious, let me assure you that people loved your dress, and I have about five messages from people asking if you're available to style them for their upcoming events. But honestly, I wouldn't care if they didn't like it. You're talented, and anyone who can't see that is a fool. You've come too far to start doubting yourself now."

"So, they loved it?" The worry lines around my eyes begin to slowly disappear.

"Yes, baby. They loved you. I love you. We would be crazy not to," he says the words so casually.

"Excuse me. You what?" I pretend to clean out my ears.

"You heard me," he says in a frustrated tone.

"I don't think I heard you clearly. Say it again."

"I said, I love you." He tries to contain his smile, but a grin escapes his lips.

"You love me?" I stand in front him.

"Yes, Willow Renee Westbrook, I love you even though you have tried to do everything in your power to convince me not to."

He watches as I reach up to place an innocent peck on his lips. Wanting to remain close to him, I repeat the action, this time letting my intentions be known. Noah's hands find my waist, guiding me until my back is against the wall, and with each passing second, our kiss deepens, and our tongues collide. He picks me up and carries me to my bedroom. He lays me on the bed and hovers over me, grazing his mouth hungrily against my neck. A soft moan escapes my lips in reaction to his movements, and I feel his body stiffen in response. As if my noise somehow rouses him from the moment, Noah breaks our kiss and moves backwards until he is off of the bed and staring at me intensely.

"Are you sure you want this? We can wait as long as you need to." His words are sincere, but his eyes are blazing with need.

"I love you, and I want this." I reach out to him, but he doesn't budge. He stands in place, rubbing his chin as if he is in deep thought. I am about to walk away when he strides over to me and once again parts my lips with his tongue.

"Take your clothes off, Willow," he softly commands, and I do as I'm told.

His eyes trail the length of my body as I undress, making me feel empowered at a time when I would usually feel self-conscious. Once all of my clothes are removed, he reaches for his shirt and slowly removes it from his chest, revealing the most chiseled body which I saw less than three hours ago but now appreciate on a whole new level. Our eyes connect just as he begins to tug on the string of his joggers, and his manhood springs free. It's been well over a year since I've had sex, and I am not sure how he is going to fit inside of me.

He lays me on the bed, guiding my hips closer to the edge and spreading my legs so that he now has full access to my body. He returns to my mouth, and we kiss hungrily for a while before he moves lower. He teases me, placing soft kisses on each of my thighs and hovering over my most sensitive area. Desperate to feel his mouth, I plead for him to touch me, and with one swift flick of his tongue, he parts my lips and devours me. My back arches off of the bed; I thread my fingers in his hair and move in rhythm with his tongue. I close my eyes, feeling closer to climax, but he instructs me to keep them open. He watches as I come undone, and when my body tenses his cocky grin returns.

He walks over to his pants and grabs a foil wrapper from his wallet. After sheathing himself with the condom, he returns to me, connecting our mouths once again. I position him at my entrance, giving him full access to my body. He pushes in slowly testing how much I can take before pulling back out again. He does this a few times until our bodies form a rhythm that neither of us seem to be able to control. He slides his full length into me, and I feel myself falling apart. I have never achieved an orgasm this way, and though my body craves it, I am not sure what to do.

"I'm right here with you. Come for me," His voice is raspy as he groans against my neck. I push away my thoughts and find my way back to the present moment. His pace quickens, and I move hungrily, matching his thrusts. Pleasure spirals through my body, and I experience something with him that I have never experienced with anyone else.

"Damn Willow." His body beings to tremble.

We lay together for a moment, both breathless and satisfied. This weekend was filled with a lot of firsts for Noah and me, and though I did not expect sex to be on the agenda, I am more than okay with the way things turned out. Noah stands to dispose of the condom, and I go to the bathroom to clean up. We make our way back to the bed and position ourselves so that my back is against his chest. I stare out the window as he snores softly behind me. I laugh silently to myself as I realize that I just put this man to sleep.

47

"**H**AVE YOU CHECKED your social media pages? It's blowing up with comments and most of them are positive!" Janae says excitedly.

The two of us are in her dining room, sitting across from David and Noah who are smiling at us like two lovesick teenagers. After Noah woke up from his nap, we made love two more times then decided to get out of the house and spend time with our best friends. I can't help but laugh at the satisfied smile he has been sporting ever since we left my house.

"See, I told you people had good things to say." Noah beams with pride.

"There were a few haters here and there, but you know to ignore those comments. Most of those people are just jealous, especially once they saw Indigo Soul's comment. He wants to meet up and discuss you styling him for his next video," Janae squeals.

"Indigo who?" I laugh at her excitement.

"Indigo Soul. The rapper?" She sighs after seeing my confused face.

"The one who was sitting behind us at the award show," Noah clarifies.

"Oh, I heard Soleil Chante speaking to him towards the end of the show, but I didn't want her to think I was being nosey, so I didn't look back."

"Yeah, you were in the restroom when I spoke to him, or else, I would have introduced you," Noah replies.

"Just be careful with dude. He has a reputation for starting drama," David interjects.

"My baby is a professional," Noah reminds him. "She already has Soleil Chante and a few other people interested in working with her and more will be lined up once they see her work. Plus, Indigo knows not to cross me."

"He slept with his best friend's girlfriend. You two aren't friends, so what makes you think he won't try to something with your woman?" David asks.

"Excuse me. Willow is sitting right here, and Willow can handle herself." I look at Noah and David, so they both comprehend.

"I apologize for talking about you instead of to you, but if Indigo tries something, you can call me, and I promise to kick his ass," David says, unapologetically.

"That won't be necessary," Noah pats David on the back. "If anybody messes with Willow, she can call me, and I'll be there with the quickness."

"And me." Janae rubs her pregnant belly. We all laugh because we know that she would fight if she had to, pregnant and all.

◆ ◆ ◆

After dinner the guys clear the table, and Janae and I make our way to the couch. I smile in awe as I watch David bring Janae a pillow to prop her feet up. She smirks the entire time, and I can only imagine how bratty she is going to act when she is further along in her pregnancy. When the guys finally disappear onto the patio, Janae tosses the pillow to the side and leaps onto my couch.

"You have a glow, and Noah is smiling from ear to ear, so you might as well tell me what happened between you two."

"Not much. We did the usual kissing and spending time with each other. You know how it goes." I play coy.

"Bullshit." She rubs her belly and pouts.

"Fine, we had mind-blowing sex. The best I have ever had, but it is not a big deal, so don't be dramatic about it."

"Not a big deal? Girl, I know you. You wouldn't have gone there with him if you weren't in love. It's written all over your face, and it's obvious that he loves you."

"I do love him, and what we have feels different than anything I've felt before. I feel all giddy and lovestruck which you know I hate, but I am totally and utterly myself when I'm around him. I feel like I'm dating my best friend. No offense. You know you will always be my number one."

"Trust me when I say I know the feeling. I never expected to be in a serious relationship this soon. In fact, I avoided commitment for so long, and now, here I am pregnant and grateful to have met David."

"And none of it would be possible if Carter hadn't set up that business meeting with Noah," I admit.

"Let's toast to Carter. The world's biggest jerk who accidentally brought love into our lives." She lifts her cup, and I clink mine against hers as we giggle.

"Seriously though, Willow. I'm really grateful because I've seen you smile more the past year than I have in a really long time. Some of that is due to Noah, but most of it is because of your hard work, and I'm not referring to your clothing line. You've put true effort into loving yourself, and I couldn't be prouder."

"Stop it. I don't want to start crying," I say, firmly.

"It's too late for me. The waterworks have begun." She swipes a tear from her cheek.

"Is it wrong for me to admit that I'm scared of success? So much is happening so fast, and I want to make sure that I can handle it." Relief washes over me as I finally say my fears out loud.

"You don't need to judge yourself for being afraid. But you have to keep going, to keep working and prove that fear doesn't control you."

"You're right. It's just intimidating knowing that Noah's name *will* and already has opened doors for me. It's important that I make a name for myself, but I never want to lose sight of who I am and why I started this in the first place."

"So, don't." Janae's words are like daggers, straightforward and to the point.

"I won't," I say, meeting her eyes to affirm my promise to her. The sliding door opens, and she quickly wipes away the evidence of her crying.

"What did we miss?" David joins the two of us, making the couch dip lower from his six-foot three-inch frame. Noah takes the seat on the couch across from me and looks between Janae and I worriedly.

"Don't worry, we're fine. We were sitting here, giving thanks for the beautiful men in our lives, and I got emotional. I blame the pregnancy hormones," Janae covers for me.

"You sure you're okay?" Noah looks to me.

"Yeah, we're fine babe. Don't worry."

"Okay." He nods his head in understanding.

"Well, can we play spades now?" David eyes the deck of the cards sitting on the table.

"We can play a few rounds, but then I need to take Willow home to show her how much I appreciate her." Noah wiggles his eyebrows playfully.

"Just don't end up like us," Janae teases.

"Yeah, wrap it up kids," David adds.

"Get your mind out of the gutter. I was referring to the bubble bath that I plan to run her and the foot massage I plan to give her." He leans down to kiss me, and I know there will be much more than bubble baths and massages on tonight's agenda.

48

I WAKE UP to an empty bed and a note from Noah. I check the time, and it is only seven in the morning. According to his note, he had an early meeting and needed to go back to his place for clothes, but he promises to call me later. In the past, something like this would have bothered me, but I trust Noah, and I also realize that I can care for him without needing to be possessive of him. So, I roll over to get a few more hours of sleep before my meeting with Soleil Chantae later today, but my phone chimes five times in a row disrupting my plan. I stretch my arms and reach over to grab my phone from my nightstand. I rub my eyes, hoping that I am still dreaming, and misread the name that appears across my screen.

Ziggy: So, he's the reason for your newfound outlook on life?

Ziggy: You all over social media with this dude! You got my friends asking if you were cheating on me all along.

Ziggy: We should meet up for coffee, so we can talk about us. I hate the way things ended.

Ziggy: I was going through some things when we were together, and I lost sight of what was important.

Ziggy: You were important. You still are.

I laugh after reading each message because he cannot be serious. At first, I consider ignoring his messages, but I want to get this conversation over with once and for all.

Me: First of all, we are not friends, so do not text me multiple times in a row. Second, I don't have anything else to discuss with you, but I truly wish you nothing but happiness. Please don't text me anymore, beloved.

Ziggy: So that's it? You're just going to walk away from a five-year relationship?

Ziggy: Just do me a favor and look out for yourself. He has women around him all the time. I bet you already had an argument about it. If I had a hard time being faithful, he will too.

And that's when I block him. I don't change his name to *Liar, Cheater, or Deceiver* like I did every other time he did something to hurt me. Instead, I remove his number from my phone, and I delete every message that either of us has ever sent to one another. He doesn't know me. He knows the old me. I haven't felt insecure since Noah and I made our relationship official, and I don't plan to start now. He trusts me, and I will continue to trust him until I have a reason not to, and I hope that day never comes.

49

I PULL UP to Soleil Chantae's house, and I am instantly impressed. She lives in a two-story home on three acres of land surrounded by rows and rows of trees. Soleil waves from the porch as I drive my car up the gravel driveway. She is holding a toddler on her hip while two older children playfully chase one another in the yard. I step out of my car and join her on the porch where a pitcher of fresh squeezed lemonade and a tray of baked goods await us. She offers me a seat on the couch and laughs when she sees me eyeing the cookies hungrily.

"Don't worry, they're freshly made and also vegan. During our studio sessions, Noah kept ordering veggie burgers, and when we asked him about it, he explained that a woman was the inspiration for the change. We teased him about it, but I secretly thought it was cute."

"Good thing I'm vegan or else he would be in big trouble," I laugh. "Thanks for thinking of me, though. I definitely plan to eat a few of these." I reach for the tray of cookies.

"Noah and I have been friends for a few years now, and trust me when I say, I had no doubt that you were the woman he was referring to," she says, candidly.

"Good to know and thank you." I am truly appreciative of her kindness.

"You are very welcome. I figured we could talk over snacks and then I can give you a tour of the land if you'd like to see the place. We have horses, a few chickens, and a garden where we grow vegetables."

"Vegebles," The toddler repeats her mother's words excitedly. I watch her in amazement as she slides down her mother's lap and runs over to where her brothers are still playing in the yard.

"She is so adorable," I admit.

"Sarai is cute, but she is definitely a handful," Soleil laughs, "But my children are three of my greatest achievements. Them and my King of course" she blushes at the mention of her husband.

"There's a certain smile behind your eyes when you talk about them. It's as if a peacefulness washed over you when you mentioned them just now. I admire that." I admit.

"Yeah, my little tribe gives me the same feeling that music does times a thousand."

"That's deep, and I hope one day that I will be able to relate. I guess in some small ways I already can. My art as a whole brings me peace, not just my fashion line. I can't imagine waking up and not creating."

"See, your passion is exactly why I want to work with you. I heard about you through the grapevine but seeing your dress at the charity event is what convinced me that you were the real deal. I usually don't use stylists; I prefer to make all creative decisions on my own, but I've checked out your work, and I believe in your vision. Your clothes are chic but make a statement."

"You heard about me through the grapevine? I'm surprised anyone knows of me since I just started my business. You must be referring to Noah's social media post?"

"Actually, I heard about you from a good friend of mine. She led a retreat a while ago and called me to brag about a few of the young women who impressed her that weekend. She mentioned a stylist from Dallas who stole the attention during the introduction circle. She didn't mention your name or anything, but she did say that she hoped the weekend would foster a sense of confidence for you to keep going. It wasn't until Noah made the post announcing your new business venture that she finally shared your name. She knew that you lived in Dallas and suggested that I have you design a custom piece for me."

"Zane? Zane told you about me?" I am completely shocked.

"Yes ma'am, she did. I've been in this industry a long time, and I'm here to tell you that confidence and a strong work ethic will make or break you.

I was always worried about people misinterpreting my art and judging me, but after a while, I realized that I had to own it. I had to become my biggest supporter, and I hope you remember that as you move forward."

"Great advice from talented a sister." I smile, grateful for her words.

"Uh oh. It looks like the rebels are on their way over here." She nods towards her children.

"Hi," the oldest says reaching out to shake my hand, "I'm Santiago and this is my brother Shia."

"Nice to meet you, Santiago and Shia. I'm Willow."

"We saw you on TV with mommy the other night," Shia shyly responds.

"You did? Well, I was pretty nervous that night, and your mom helped me to relax. I was happy to be sitting next to her."

"Yeah, mom is cool like that," Santiago replies, causing Soleil to laugh.

"Want to see our horses?" Sarai takes my hand in hers. I look to her mother who nods in approval.

The five of us walk around the compound for nearly an hour. The kids show me their horses, their garden, and dared me to try and catch a chicken. Let's just say that I tried and failed miserably. Then, Soleil kindly invited me to stay for dinner, but I politely declined, needing to get back to the city to do some work. Before I left, she invited me to accompany her on a trip to Atlanta in a few weeks to be the lead stylist for her music video. It took me less than a minute to decide that this was an opportunity that I couldn't refuse. I'll get paid to do work that I love and also have the chance to visit my sister and her family.

50

*T*ODAY, I AM meeting Indigo Soul and his team for lunch to discuss the possibility of us working together. His schedule is completely booked over the next few weeks with label meetings and practice sessions for his upcoming tour, so he suggested that we meet while he is in town and actually has free time. I am walking into the meeting with an open mind, but I am also wary of David's words to be cautious. Noah didn't seem to be worried about Indigo's interest in working with me which came as a big shock to David. Their contrast in reactions make me wonder if Noah's brave face is a true reflection of his feelings or if he is pretending to be unbothered for my sake. I decided that the best thing for me to do is to use today's meeting as an opportunity to gauge Indigo's commitment to working with me.

I walk into the restaurant which is much fancier than I expected it to be. The place is packed with patrons drinking wine and eating small portions with expensive prices. I follow the hostess as she leads me to a more private area near the back of the restaurant which she explains has been reserved for today's meeting. Indigo and his team haven't arrived yet, so I look over some of the sketches that I have drawn out and practice my pitch in my head for the hundredth time today.

Once I realized that Indigo was serious about scheduling a meeting, I started studying his sense of style from past photoshoots and music videos as well as his day to day style from his social media posts. I then compared his style to his vision which his assistant kindly emailed over last night. It was a twelve-word email that read: *Conscious words and clothes that speak without me actually needing to talk,* followed by instructions for me to have fun and impress him. I am not sure if this is Indigo's way of challenging me or if the man is really this easygoing, but I'm up to the challenge, and I am confident in my ability to impress him.

Indigo arrives to the restaurant a few minutes later, wearing a baseball cap low on his head and a pair of sunglasses. I get the feeling that he does not want to be noticed. Lucky for him, the customers in this restaurant are mostly older people. Indigo's music is, however, on both the pop and rap charts, and he has billboards with his face plastered all over the city, so it wouldn't surprise me if he caught the attention of one or two fans.

The hostess walks him over to the table, and I stand ready to shake his hand, but he reaches in for a side hug. We both laugh at the awkward exchange, and I swear I see a flash of annoyance on the waitress' face. She informs us that our server will be with us in a few moments, and before she turns to leave, she points to the podium at the front of the restaurant and reminds Indigo that she will be there if he happens to need *anything*. Her voice is sultry and suggestive, but Indigo doesn't seem to notice her flirtation. As much as I want to giggle at her confused expression, I decide to pretend that it didn't happen.

"Is Grace on her way?" I always hated when people referred to me as "the assistant," so I made sure to memorize Grace's name after communicating with her via email.

"She had some personal things come up, so it will be the two of us today. I hope that's not a problem?" I smile and nod my head in understanding, but part of me is wondering if this is a setup. Was his assistant ever going to join us? *David definitely got inside my head.*

"No. Not a problem at all," I assure him.

The waiter walks over to take our orders, and I decide to play it safe and stick to water since this is a professional meeting and Indigo does the same. We spend the first hour of our meeting, eating and getting to know one another on a more personal level. I learned that he is born and raised in Dallas, Texas and plans to stay. He shared that his roots are important to him and that he has traveled all over the world, but Dallas is always the place he wants to return to. He is the youngest of four and was raised by a single mother.

The name Indigo is as childhood nickname which was given to him by his uncle who always told him that his skin was so dark that it resembled beautiful shades of violets and blues. Being a dark-skinned man himself, his uncle always made it his duty to affirm confidence and strength into his nephew, and as he got older, Indigo realized that his nickname could hold a much deeper meaning if he wanted it too. So, Nasir, which is Indigo's government name, decided to use his alter ego to create positive change in the world through fashion and music.

"You already have a sense of style that is different from most men in the rap game. You wear shirts that proudly display the importance of mental health, honoring and protecting women, and creating art that matters. I don't want to change your style; I do feel that I can create pieces that match your personality and your brand."

"You're confident." He sits back in his chair.

"I am." I affirm his words.

"My manager isn't going to appreciate me making last minute changes, but I would like for you to work with me on a shoot I have next week. Do you think you can bring these sketches to life by then?" He throws another challenge my way.

"Not a problem. I actually started working on one of the outfits already. I had faith that you would like my work, and I am so happy that you did." I breathe out a sigh of relief. "The other two looks will be ready next week."

"Sounds good, Miss Westbrook. See you then." He reaches across the table to shake my hand.

"You can call me Willow, and thank you for meeting with me, Indigo. I look forward to Grace's email with the details for next week's photoshoot."

"Call me Nasir. All of my friends do." His voice is straightforward and not one hint of flirtation can be found in his words.

"Are we friends?" I ask honestly; I've never been one to use the word loosely. This is business, and he is my client.

"Doing business together is the beginning of a friendship or at the very least becoming acquaintances. You don't have to call me Nasir, just know that you have the option to." His phone rings, he stands, shakes my hand again, and excuses himself from the table. Following his lead, I finish the last of my water and head home to work on the designs that I promised him.

51

I AM SITTING on the patio, looking over the sketches for Indigo's outfits when I hear a knock at my front door. I am not expecting Janae until later tonight and Noah was in the studio when we last spoke, so I grab the bat that I always have nearby in case I need to pop a burglar on the head. I realize that burglars usually don't announce themselves, so chances are that it is Janae, ready to bombard me with questions about my meeting with Indigo. My best friend is amazing, but she has no chill.

"Who is it?" I call out before reaching the door.

"It's me," Noah says, from the other side. I look out the peep hole to find him holding a bag of groceries in one hand and his guitar in the other.

"I thought you were at the studio?" I open the door. We've both been busy lately, so most of our interactions have been over the phone the past few days. I asked him to stop by if he found time, but I didn't mean for him to cut his session short.

"We finished early, and I missed you so, I figured I would come have dinner with you and stay the night if that's okay?"

"That is more than okay," I lead him into my condo.

"Alright. Let me put my stuff down, and I'll start cooking." He leans down to kiss me.

"Wait, what are we having for dinner?" I ask, between kisses.

"I was thinking tacos. I bought tortillas, cilantro, mushrooms, pinto beans, bell peppers, onions, and a whole gang of stuff. Oh, and I found this recipe for this avocado lime dressing, so I figured we could put some of that on top." He says all of that without taking a breath.

"You really missed me, didn't you?" I smile at his excitement.

"Don't even play me," he laughs. "I knew you were working and probably starving, so I came to feed you. Nothing more, nothing less."

"Oh ok. So tonight, I shouldn't expect anything *more* is what you're saying?" Catching my drift, he corrects himself.

"Wow," he laughs. "You know we both will want *more* tonight. And if not tonight then you'll definitely roll over in the morning trying to kiss all over me, so stop pretending." His logic is solid, so I quickly change the subject.

"Whatever." I roll my eyes. "You know Janae is coming over tonight, so I hope you bought enough food to feed all three of us."

"She's carrying my niece or nephew in that stomach of hers, so of course I'll make enough for her. Plus, she would try to fight me if I kept food from her."

"She will definitely attack you over food these days. Then she would blame the baby and hormones." We both laugh in agreement.

"Let me wash my hands, so I can help you." I head towards the sink.

"Nope. Go finish your work. You have a deadline to meet. Dinner will be ready in less than an hour. I'll eat and then go in the room to finish working on a song while you and Janae have sister time out here."

"You're so good to me!" I smile happily. "I might show you just how much I appreciate you later tonight." I wink before strutting onto the balcony.

◆ ◆ ◆

I hear loud laughter and what sounds like arguing coming from the kitchen, so I pause my work to go see what all the commotion is about. Janae is standing near the stove with a spatula pointed angrily in Noah's direction. He, however, does not seem to be angry and is actually laughing uncontrollably as he backs away from her with his hands in the air. Unsure of what exactly is happening, I watch their interaction for a minute longer, without announcing my presence.

"Baby, calm down and wait until the food is done." I hear David speaking, but I don't see him physically in the room.

"The tacos are finished, so please listen to your man. I'm about to plate the food now." Noah picks up his phone from the counter and hands it to Janae cautiously.

"You just had to involve David in this, didn't you?" She puts the phone up to her ear and whatever David says seems to work because she calmly hands the spatula over to Noah.

"But he told me that he only had enough for me to get one taco, and I want five tacos with extra avocado sauce," she whines into the phone. "Okay, fine. I'll take four tacos instead of five, but I want extra sauce," she says it to David but glares at Noah.

"Janae, you can have five tacos. I never said you couldn't." Noah shakes his head pretending to be annoyed, but a faint smile lingers on his lips.

"Are you two serious right now?" I laugh at their banter. I knew their argument wasn't over anything serious, but I never expected it to be about food.

"Babe, Willow is here now so don't worry. We don't need you to be our mediator anymore," she informs David.

"Alright. I love you. No more fighting over food," he warns.

"I won't have to fight over anything now that my best friend is here to keep your best friend in check," she gloats.

"I'm not here to check anybody, so stop being mean to my man, Janae. He agreed to feed you before you even got here. It was actually his idea to make us dinner in the first place."

"Oh. I didn't know that." She takes a seat at the kitchen island.

"I tried to tell you, but you wouldn't listen," Noah says, carefully placing a plate with five tacos in front of Janae. He manages to keep a straight face as he dramatically backs away from her.

"Thank you, Noah." She finally releases the laugh she'd been holding in.

"No problem," he returns her smile.

"Yeah, thanks babe." I eye the amazing food in front of me.

"You know I got you." Noah kisses me on the forehead and disappears into the room, leaving us to have girl's night in peace.

As soon as the door to my room closes, Janae digs into her food, scarfing it down like she hasn't eaten in days. She has always been greedy, but the baby is giving her an excuse to be even more extreme. Shaking my head in disbelief, I take a bite of my tacos and instantly realize that these may very well be the best tacos that I have ever eaten. Or at least the best ones that have ever been made in my kitchen.

After we finish our food, I take our plates to the sink, and we make our way over to the couch to put our feet up and relax. Janae fills me in on the things that are happening at my old company, and I finally get the chance to tell her about my meeting with Indigo and Soleil Chantae. Janae is the one person who has constantly believed in me and motivated me, so it feels good to finally have good news to share.

"So, the meeting was a success. I knew it would be. You've always been amazing at what you do," she says, with confidence.

"Janae it went so well! I'm on a tight deadline, but I have no doubt that I can have everything finished by next week."

"If I knew you had a tight deadline, I wouldn't have come by tonight. You should have told me," she reprimands.

"I had to take a break and eat dinner, so I might as well have done both with you," I explain. "Do you want some wine? I mean juice." I remember her condition.

"As much as I would love to have a glass of wine, I'll take mango juice instead," she rubs her belly, appreciatively.

"Mango juice, coming right up." I walk towards the fridge.

"Hey, someone just sent you a text. Do you want me to bring you your phone?" she kindly offers, but her feet are propped up on the couch, and it looks like getting up is the last thing she wants to do.

"Who's it from?" I fill our glasses.

"Someone named Nasir." Janae peer at my phone.

"Oh ok. I'll respond in a second." I reclaim my seat on the couch.

"Who is Nasir?" she says, observing me.

"You are so nosey!" I respond jokingly. "If you must know, it's a client."

"Do all of your clients send you heart emoji's?" she whispers, realizing that Noah is only a few feet away in the other room.

"It's just Indigo Soul, and the heart emoji was sent by accident. See?" I defuse the situation before she makes it a bigger deal than what it is. "He just texted to let me know that his assistant will be emailing me the details for a photoshoot next week. The heart emoji was quickly followed up with instructions to ignore it followed by a smiley face."

"Just be careful with him," she warns. "You have the public eye watching you now, and you don't need any attention being taken away from your business."

"Duly noted," I say, sarcastically, but I allow her words to sink in even if I don't want to admit it.

52

I STAYED UP until two in the morning the past few days making sure that I not only meet Indigo's deadline but also that I wow him and his team with my designs. Noah has been great about my being busy. In fact, he had dinner delivered to me three times this week and made sure to remind me of how much he missed me without putting pressure on me to spend time or give him all of my attention. He has a hectic schedule of his own, so naturally, he understands that my work has to be a priority. Luckily, work is important to the both of us, and it feels good to be in a relationship where neither party has to sacrifice their own dreams to be happy. We made plans for me to go to the studio tonight to check out Noah's session, but for now, my focus needs to be on this photoshoot.

I walk onto set, and I am instantly amazed by the layout. I have been on all kinds of sets over the past few years, during my time as an assistant, but it feels different to be walking in as an important member of the team rather than an employee who is overlooked by her supervisor. Indigo is in the middle of an interview with a writer from *Kindred Vibe*, one of the hottest magazines to exist, and they selected Indigo to be on the front cover. Grace sees me and wiggles her finger, signaling for me to follow her. She offers a soft smile, but I can tell that she is in assistant mode, wanting to make sure that everything runs smoothly and focused on the job at hand. This is a look that I am all too familiar with and respect.

She leads me to an area that has racks for me to set the clothes on. I take my designs out of the garment bags and carefully place each one on the rack before pulling out three pairs of men sized ten sneakers, accessories, a bag of pins, a lint brush, a hairbrush, and a portable steamer from my duffle bag. My years of working with Carter taught me to always come prepared, but my hands are shaking with nerves. I try to channel some of that nervous energy by looking over each outfit again, making sure that I have exactly what I need. A knock at the door startles me, but I relax when I see Indigo smiling back at me. He offers a quick side hug and retreats to the seat on the opposite side of the room.

"Show me what you have for me." He places his elbows on his thighs, watching me intently.

"Okay." I reach for the first outfit. "I really like this one because it ..."

"I don't mean to cut you off, but I like for the clothes to speak for themselves. If they are right for me, I will feel it. I won't need to hear a pitch or be sold on them." He stands and walks back towards me to touch the fabric. There is a flicker of challenge in his eye when he speaks, almost as if he is teasing me or challenging me, but I follow suit, holding up each outfit and staying silent while he decides. After what seems like forever, he finally says, "All of these are amazing, but I think we should shoot in this one. I want the other two for my personal collection, if that's cool. I'll pay for all of it of course." He eyes the ripped denim jacket that has the Pan African flag's colors and an inscription on the pocket of the jacket that reads: MENTAL HEALTH MATTERS.

"I dig this." He runs his fingers over the colors. "Black represents the people; red stands for what was lost, and green is for the growth and fertility of Africa."

"You shared your vision with me, and I tried my best to bring it to life." I reply, grateful for his response. "I think these flooded jeans cropped above the ankle and a pair of Nike Cortez shoes would pull it all together. It's in line with the hippie vibe people always say you give off."

"Is that what the streets are saying about me?" he laughs. "Don't let my fashion fool you. I always try to take the peaceful route, but I'm quick with these hands." He gets into a fighter stance, defending his manhood jokingly.

"Yeah, yeah. You're macho, I get it. Now, please go get ready, so the world can see you wearing my designs." I point towards the barber chair in the next room.

"Okay, but I'm only following your instructions because my fans deserve to see me in this fit." He confidently strolls away.

◆ ◆ ◆

The photoshoot is running longer than I expected or at least longer than I feel it needs to, but I was hired to bring clothes not to direct, so I am standing on the side quietly watching them work. The photographer has captured several beautiful shots of Indigo wearing my designs, and I think this outfit is going to be perfect for the magazine cover, though, I can't say that the photographer would agree. He has made several hints about Indigo's fans expecting a bit of sex appeal which is code for wanting him shirtless. We are on our way up to the top of the building to capture what I hope to be the last shot of the day, but first, I have to make what the creative directors considers to be *'a few small adjustments'* to Indigo's outfit.

Indigo was shirtless in most of the images that I saw during my research, so it doesn't surprise me that the photographer and creative director wanted him stay on brand and lose the shirt. What they fail to realize is that in addition to selling sex appeal, Indigo always uses his platform to strengthen the black community. Neither Indigo or his manager were happy with the suggested changes, but I assured them that I planned ahead and would make sure that his outfit reflected his brand and his mission. So, here I am, following him into the dressing room to make the necessary changes.

When we get inside his dressing room, Indigo quickly takes off his t-shirt and jacket. He watches me silently as I dig around my bag for the bandana that has the Pan African colors on it. The bandana is versatile, so he has the option to wear it around his head, have it hanging from his pocket, or tie it around his hand. When I try to ask which way, he would prefer to wear it, he responds with a grunt, so I decide to tie it around his forehead in hopes that it will catch the readers eye as soon as they reach for the magazine. Lucky for me, my experience as an assistant on the set of Janae's photoshoots taught me to always come prepared. Indigo looks at himself in the mirror, nods his approval, and suddenly leaves the room. I trail behind him as he walks to the roof.

"There you are, mate." The photographer walks towards Indigo.

"Here is your jacket." I hand it to Indigo. "You can place it over your shoulder like this, or you can wear it and unbutton the top buttons. Sex doesn't have to mean completely shirtless." I smile, hoping to reduce some of his stress.

"Oh, I see what you did there. Very creative. You kept the concept of the jacket but used other objects to highlight the message." The photographer says, seemingly impressed, but I can hear the disapproval behind the words.

"My client had a vision, and I had to make sure I brought it to life," I respond, sincerely. To that, the photographer rolls his eyes, but Indigo and Grace both smile which I assume means that I impressed them, and that is enough for me.

After about five or six shots, the photographer finally yells that he has all the shots he needs, and we can finally wrap up today's photoshoot. He gives a toothy smile when he says it, apparently satisfied with the way things turned out, but Indigo, on the other hand, responds with a grunt before disappearing into his dressing room. The readers will never know how frustrated he was during today's photoshoot. He transformed in front of the camera, but now that the job is done, he is sure to let everyone know how he feels.

"Do you have a minute to speak?" Grace says, pulling me to the side.

"Yes, ma'am." I place my work bag down to give her my full attention. "What's up?"

"I just wanted to let you know that I'm going to suggest that you be one of the designers for Indigo's upcoming tour. You wouldn't have to physically be on tour for each date unless you wanted to, but it is in no way required for you to do so. I don't know if you've ever seen Indigo's tour setup, but he likes to have stand out clothes to match his set design. He was impressed with you today, even if he doesn't say it. I could tell. This would be a great opportunity to get your brand more exposure."

"Are you serious?" I say in disbelief. "That would be amazing."

"Great. I will talk to Indigo and the team and get back to you with an official offer, but in the meantime, you should come out and celebrate with us tonight," Grace says, excitedly.

"I wish I could, but I already made plans. Can I take a rain check?"

"Of course, you can. And hey, take my number down in case you change your mind," she says with a hopeful tone.

"Cool." I say, handing her my phone, but I have no plans of joining them. All I want is to go to the studio with Noah and fall asleep in his arms later tonight.

53

I TIPTOE INTO the studio, careful not to interrupt the session, but the door squeaks giving notice of my presence. Noah smiles exultantly from inside the booth, and part of me is relieved because I almost expected to come in and find him surrounded by an entourage, but to my surprise, Noah and his producer Bobby are the only two people occupying the space. I shuffle past Bobby, tapping him on the shoulder in acknowledgement before making my way to the empty couch near the back of the room. Leaning forward in my seat, I gaze in Noah's direction, grateful to have the chance to experience him is his element. Watching him sing is equivalent to having hours upon hours of foreplay, and though I had a long day myself, I wouldn't mind spending my night here watching him work.

"I think we got it." Bobby approves through the intercom speaker.

"Alright. I'm on my way in there to listen and to greet my queen," Noah smiles playfully in my direction.

"I promise not to hijack your session," I say, to Bobby. "That's why I'm sitting back here so that I am out of the way."

"You can take one of the seats up here if you want. Noah is a perfectionist when it comes to his craft, so I'm definitely not worried about him getting his songs completed in time. But if I can be honest, I am curious about something." Bobby looks over his shoulder before continuing. "What are you doing to my guy? I have never seen him like this."

"What do you mean?" I am confused by his question.

"He's usually all business in the studio, but today, he stopped at least three times to remind me that you were joining us today. I started to make fun of him, but it's good to see my boy happy."

"That was sweet of you," I laugh. "Most men would have given him a hard time."

"Oh, I wanted to. Trust me," Bobby chuckles.

"What are you in here lying about, Bobby?" Noah says, knowingly.

"Nothing man. All I said is that you two make a beautiful couple."

"He also said that you were a bit of a perfectionist," I tease.

"He's the one who had me working until four in the morning last week," Noah replies jokingly.

"Speaking of 4 a.m. work sessions, I need to go call wifey and let her know that we might run late tonight." Bobby lifts his phone and heads out into the hallway.

"Is he right? Will you be here that late?" I say, repressing a yawn.

"Probably not until four but at least until midnight."

"Oh ok." I calculate the hours in my head. Midnight is only three hours away.

"So, how was your day?" Noah pulls me into his arms.

"It went really well," I say, excited. "Grace mentioned an opportunity for me to design some of the clothes for Indigo's next tour. It's not official, but I'm pretty excited about it. A few of them are going to get drinks at a bar tonight to celebrate the success of today's shoot, but I'm too tired, and I'd rather be here with you."

"As long as you didn't say no because of me. You had a long day, and my workday is just getting started. I can't expect you to be here all night."

"I choose to be here," I say, firmly. "Now kiss me before Bobby comes back in."

◆ ◆ ◆

My phone chimes for the fifth time in the past hour. I don't have to look to know that it is Grace sending yet another video of her and a few people on Indigo's creative team laughing and drinking margaritas. They went out to celebrate the success and hard work that everyone put in today, and though I wouldn't mind having a glass of wine right now, I ignore her message and focus on what Noah is saying to me.

"You didn't hear a word I said, did you?" He shakes his head at my obvious inability to focus in this moment.

"Sorry, Grace keeps sending me these stupid videos of her drinking." I hand him the phone so that he can laugh at her attempts to make me jealous.

"Do you want to go?" he asks, curiously.

"No, and I already told her that I had plans," I remind him.

"I told you we would be done by twelve, and it's already eleven. We are nowhere close to being finished for the night."

"I'm confused. Do you not want me here?" I say, annoyed with his attitude. I can tell that he is tired but that doesn't give him the right to take his frustration out on me.

"Willow, I appreciate you coming to support me, but it's obvious that you want to meet up with your friends. You accomplished something big today, so go celebrate. If I could go with you, I would but I have to finish up here."

"Are you sure you don't mind?" I study his expression to see if he is annoyed, but he seems to be sincere in what he is saying.

"Baby go enjoy yourself. I'll come to your place after I finish up here."

"Okay, fine. I might stop by to grab a drink, but I won't stay long. Grace is really the only person that I know on the team, and I've been yawning nonstop the past ten minutes. I don't want to be at a bar yawning all night," I joke, hoping to lighten the mood.

"Don't forget Indigo," he adds.

"What about him?" I say confused by his mentioning of Indigo. He hasn't showed any concern for our working together, even after David's warnings.

"You said Grace is the only person you're going to know there, but you also know Indigo."

"Oh. He hasn't been in any of the videos that Grace has sent, and she never mentioned that he would be there. I think it's mostly employees of his that wanted to go out and celebrate. Bosses usually keep work and life separate," I ramble, suddenly feeling nervous when I haven't done anything wrong. I blame David for getting into my head with his foretold warnings of trouble coming from my working with Indigo.

"You're probably right, but then again, dude isn't exactly known for being the most professional boss in the world."

"What is happening right now?" I am confused by his change in mood.

"Nothing, I'm tripping. I'm just tired is all. But hey, I have to get back in there, so I'll see you in a few hours, alright?"

"Okay," I hesitate before watching him walk back into the booth.

54

*W*HEN GRACE SENT me the address to this place, she failed to mention that it was a club, not a bar. She also failed to mention that she reserved a private section for the group and that there would be two giant bouncers guarding it to make sure that no one whose name isn't on the list gets past them. So, when I naively walked up to the guards to explain that I was an invited guest, they eagerly informed me of their "no name, no entrance" policy, and I was forced to step aside and wait around with the groupies who are lined up, waiting for a chance to get into the private section.

"You know what? Forget it. I've tried to call three times, and each time it went straight to voicemail, so if a woman named Grace comes out looking for me, *my name is Willow by the way,* can you please tell her that I went home? I don't wait around for people, especially not when I can be in the comfort of my own home drinking free wine and watching *Jason's Lyric.*"

"What about champagne? You have that at home too?" A deep voice hassles me from the VIP section above.

"Was I talking to you?" I look up to give the annoying eavesdropper a piece of my mind. I shake my head in embarrassment when I realize that the spy is actually Indigo.

"No, but you're in a club yelling, so it isn't exactly a private conversation," he smiles, reveling in my discomfort.

"Well, to answer your question I prefer wine, so no I do not have champagne at home. Now, enjoy your night." I wave him off.

"Willow, hold up. Why are you leaving?" His voice turns serious.

"As you can see these nice guards here won't let me in." I glare at the guards.

"She's cool man. Let her in." Indigo nods to the guards.

"Okay, boss man." They jump at his request.

I walk up the stairs to the private section where Indigo is waiting for me at the top. He tells a waitress to bring me any drink of my choosing and then he excuses himself, leaving me alone in a room full of strangers. I notice Grace huddled in the corner with a guy that I recognize from my research into Indigo. While my search was solely for fashion and business purposes, the internet was filled with tons of gossip about him, and If memory serves me correct, this is the friend who the media claims he fought with over a woman. I doubt Indigo would allow him to be here if the story had any truth to it, but I hope for Grace's sake that she knows what she is getting into.

"How long have you been here?" Grace saunters towards me excitedly.

"I didn't think you were going to show up."

"I called you a bunch of times, but all of my calls went unanswered. If Indigo hadn't stopped me, I would be back home in my bed by now."

"I'm so sorry." She lifts her phone for me to see. "My phone has been on silent all day, and I didn't feel it vibrate. Where is Indigo now?" She looks around the club.

"I think he left. One minute he was standing next to me, and the next thing I knew, he got a call and left."

"That doesn't surprise me. He never stays at team outings long. He stays long enough to make sure that we are all okay and then he goes home to Sophia. He's gotten worse since he found out she's pregnant." Grace slaps her hand over her mouth, realizing that she just revealed private information.

"I cannot believe I just said that!" she whimpers.

"Lucky for you I don't betray people's confidence. This conversation stays between us. In fact, I never heard a thing."

"Thank you!" she exhales heavily. "Indigo is a very private person. I could lose my job if that information got out."

"It won't get out. At least not by my doing. But you're a professional and those type of slipups cannot happen. I understand wanting to let loose and have fun, but just make sure you don't reveal that information to anyone else. People may seem drunk, but information like that will definitely sober them up enough to call the blogs. It's your job to be professional and protect his privacy."

"You're right." She nods in agreement.

"I think I'll finish this glass of wine and then go home to my man. You be safe." I nod towards the guy who hasn't stopped eyeing her since she came over to speak with me.

"Are you sure you can't stay for a few more drinks?" Grace asks.

"No, I wanted to stop by to say hi, but I didn't plan on staying long. Enjoy your night and let me know when you make it home safely."

"Will do. And Willow, thank you," she says, sincerely.

"No problem," I reply, before heading towards the exit.

I pass the bodyguards on my way out and offer them a smug grin which is progress because on my way in, all I wanted to do was offer them a four-finger salute. To say this trip was a waste of gas is an understatement, but I have to admit that I learned a lot in the thirty minutes I spent here. I learned that Indigo might not be the bad guy everyone paints him out to be, and I learned that Grace is a sweet girl, but she isn't to be trusted completely. All it took tonight was a few shots, and she let secrets slip. I cannot afford to be tied up in drama, so I will be cordial in my business dealings with Indigo and his team, but I won't be participating in anymore social outings.

55

*A*FTER I LEFT the club, I went straight home, soaked in my bathtub, and jumped in my queen size bed. I waited up for Noah, but I got a text from him around one in the morning saying that he was still working and would crash at his own place since it is closer to the studio. I have been trying to view his message as a sincere attempt to keep me updated on his whereabouts, but I would be lying if I said I wasn't wondering if his decision was some sort of passive aggressive tactic to get me to realize that he is upset about something. It could be the fact that I left the studio to be with people outside of our usual circle of friends, or it could be that he is feeling insecure about me working with Indigo.

I can't lie and say that I wasn't disappointed by his message, but I am not going to start an argument based off of assumptions. I do, however, need answers and I need them sooner rather than later. It has been two days now since we have seen each other, and our conversations have been short to say the least. Last night, he told me that he was too busy to have dinner, but Janae told me that he stopped by their place to see David. I know that I need to be upfront and ask Noah how he feels, but for now, I need to focus on my business meeting with Indigo.

"Who is your friend?" Mrs. Davis says, eyeing Indigo. We just sat down to have lunch at Vegan Tingz, and her prying eyes are exactly why I picked this location. There is just enough privacy to have a meeting but not enough to where prying eyes would assume that there was something intimate happening between the two of us.

"He's a client and a friend, Mrs. Davis," I say with a stern smile, hoping Indigo didn't notice the accusatory tone in her voice.

"Oh ok. You know I like to introduce myself to all of my customers. It's nice to meet you, young man. I'll be at the front if you need anything." She offers him a smile.

"Nice to meet you too, ma'am." He studies our awkward exchange.

"Oh, and Willow, I thought you might like to know that David usually places a to-go order on Friday's, so I expect he will be stopping in sometime today." Her tone is casual, but her eyes are warning me to be careful.

"Thank you, Mrs. Davis." I am grateful for her concern but annoyed with her delivery.

She is making me feel guilty when I have nothing to hide. Noah is fully aware that Indigo and I have scheduled a meeting today, and though I am not obligated to explain myself to him, I felt that it was best to be open and honest in order to avoid a repeat of my last relationship. Lack of trust in my partner and low self-esteem is what made me feel like I needed to always be involved in Ziggy's business, and by the end of our relationship I realized that no amount of force would have made him stay faithful.

The more he grew his business, the more he expanded outside of our relationship. People didn't see the twelve-hour days that I put in to help build his company from the ground up, and I began to resent him and feel more insignificant by the day. I don't want Noah to ever feel like I did with Ziggy. I want him to know that my growth doesn't mean that I will forget him. He is a big part of why I have clients coming through the door in the first place, and I am grateful for him. So, despite the fact that I am doing nothing wrong I feel like I need to speed this meeting up now that I know there is a chance that David will see Indigo and me.

I reach into my bag to pull out the vision board that I created for today's meeting. I could have presented him with a traditional pitch where I tell him my ideas and hope that he sees the vision, but I wanted to stand out from the other candidates by bringing my ideas for his tour outfits to life. I open my portfolio bag and search through it, but the only contents are my laptop and charger. I must have forgotten the board next to my front door where I specifically placed it so that I wouldn't forget it. The irony is all too real, but I can't let Indigo see me sweat. Luckily, I thought ahead and saved the images from the vision board to my laptop late last night. Salvaging the situation, I pull out my computer and continue the meeting as if this was my plan all along.

"Here are my ideas." I slide the laptop across the table for Indigo to see. "I wanted you to have a visual of each piece."

"I haven't even told you my vision yet," Indigo says plainly.

"I know but from our conversations I feel as though I am getting a sense of your style and the things that are important to you. For instance, if you look at the black design, I think you will be impressed. It was inspired by the way you handled yourself at the photoshoot."

"Which black piece? There are two." He turns the screen towards me.

"The one on the right." I reach across the table to point to the design.

"Wouldn't it be easier if you moved around to this side of the table and explained each piece to me?" he asks plainly.

"Umm. Sure." I slide into the booth next to him, careful to keep enough space between us.

"Plus, this angle gives you a perfect view of the door, and you will be able to see everyone who walks in," Indigo says jokingly.

"It's not like that," I lie.

"Your friend, Mrs. Davis, seems to think so, and you were nervous to sit on the same side of the table as me. But just so we're clear, this is strictly business for me. I have no other intentions."

"I understand, so let's get back to business?" I am eager to change the subject.

"Fine with me," he smirks. "Now tell me about this black design."

"Okay, so you shared the story of your uncle and how he gave you your nickname. I was so inspired by that story that I immediately started sketching ideas that I felt would represent your name and the deep history it holds. Then, at the photoshoot when the photographer kept trying to change you, I knew I had to bring this piece to life. It's trendy but also powerful. You will definitely make a statement wearing this design on tour."

"And you'll be comfortable working with me on a regular basis?" He studies me.

"This is business. You seem like a good guy to me despite what the media or anyone else says, and I would love to continue our working relationship."

"In that case, the job is yours. I'll have Grace send you over the details, so we can finalize everything."

"Are you serious?" I grin over at him. I am so engrossed in excitement that I don't notice when Noah and David walk into the restaurant.

"Pretty sure your folks just walked in." Indigo points toward David and Noah who are standing at the front talking to Mrs. Davis. I quickly readjust my body so that I am sitting further away from Indigo, but they walk around the corner too fast, and I end up looking more guilty than innocent.

"Hey, man." Indigo stands and offers his hand to Noah.

"I hope I'm not interrupting." Noah ignores his hand. "I didn't know you two were meeting here."

"We were actually just wrapping up. You two can join us if you want," Indigo offers sincerely.

"Thanks, but we're okay. I don't want to intrude on my woman's business dealings. Plus, we're just here to pick up a to-go order."

"Speaking of to-go-order. I'll go grab it. It was good seeing you, Willow." David quickly excuses his self.

"Well it was good seeing you, man. This meeting went by quicker than expected. Willow's work is different than anything I've ever seen, so the choice was easy," Indigo says, genuinely.

"Yeah, her work is definitely going to take her far. That I am sure about," Noah agrees. "But hey, I'll let you two get back to work. I came through to grab some food before I head to my mom's house. Willow, I'll see you later?" He says, placing a kiss on my cheek.

"Yeah, I'll see you later." I am not convinced by his little act at all.

"I get the feeling he doesn't like me," Indigo says once Noah is out of earshot.

"It's not that he doesn't like you. He's just heard some things, and we are packed in pretty close." I point out the small space between us.

"I told you. This is business. Nothing more. Plus, I don't mix business with pleasure."

"The blogs say different," I retort.

He straightens in his chair defensively. "If paparazzi were here right now, they would spin some tale about us dating. Tell me, Willow, are we here on a date? Are you even slightly interested in being romantic with me? No, I didn't think you were, so don't ever tell me what the blogs say. The job is yours if you want it, but if you decide to let a relationship stop your progress then more power to you. I dig your vision, but I won't force you to take the job."

"Whoa. Can we slow down for a minute?" I suddenly feel like the world's biggest idiot. "I sincerely apologize. I was out of line for the way I spoke to you, and for the record, I do want the job."

"It's okay, but don't let it happen again." He lets his guard back down.

"It won't." I promise. "Now, about this job offer... would I need to physically be on tour with you?"

"No, you don't have to be at every show, but you do realize that you would get the opportunity to travel and network, right?"

"I do." I think the offer over.

"Take advice from a man who's had to make a lot of tough decisions in life. Don't let fear stop you from living your dream. Your work ethic is the *only* reason I'm still sitting here. Give yourself the chance to be great."

"I will," I say, reclaiming my seat to finish showing him my ideas.

56

*N*OAH TEXTED TO say that he would be at his mom's house most of the day and would meet me for dinner later tonight, but I wasn't willing to wait five hours to talk, so I decided to drive to Ms. Yvette's house after my meeting with Indigo. I would never disrespect Noah's mother or her home, but this conversation is long overdue and quite frankly, I should have addressed it when I felt like Noah was mad at me for leaving the studio a few days ago. I call to let him know that I am in the driveway, and though he sounds surprised by my intrusion, he comes out and opens my door for me like the gentleman that he is.

"Do you want to come inside?" He pulls me into his arms.

"Not until we talk." I respond strongly because I know that if I walk inside the house where his mother and grandmother are, I won't have the courage to say what I came here to say.

"Okay, let's talk," he says. He leans against my car door.

"What was that about at the restaurant?" I don't want to waste any time. "Were you trying to make me look like an idiot in front of my client? No matter what you think of him, he is still *my client* who pays me pretty well might I add."

"How did I make you look like an idiot, Willow?" He shakes his head in disbelief.

"You were rude when all he did was try to be cordial. I knew David's little comments would eventually get to you."

"I am a grown man who doesn't follow anybody and that includes David," he scoffs. "And for the record, I have no issue with Indigo. You haven't heard me say anything bad about that man since you started working with him. My attitude today was based solely off of what I observed. He was sitting much closer than he needed to, and I do not appreciate him not realizing that his recent attention in the media could easily be attached to your name. You don't need any bad press - not when it comes to your personal life or your business - and neither do I. People attach your name to mine now whether you like it or not."

"So basically, what you're saying is that you are concerned with your image, and you want to make sure that I don't do anything to embarrass you?" I force out a bitter laugh.

"That is not what I said. There you go twisting my words."

"I know insecurity when I see it, Noah. Is this about me starting a career and meeting new people?"

"You can't be serious." He is obviously thrown off by my choice of words. I look to him, daring him to prove me wrong.

"You know what? You are still wearing scars from your past relationships, and I am done trying to heal them for you," he says, firmly.

"How dare you throw my past in my face? I am finally investing in myself, and you can't stand it. I don't crowd you or give any signs that I feel insecure by your prestige. In fact, I love your grind because it challenges me to work harder. You, on the other hand, blow up at the first sign of me evolving."

"You met this man at *our* spot and accuse me of feeling insecure? Ask yourself why you chose to schedule your little business meeting at our favorite restaurant. You know I eat there at least twice a week, and Indigo isn't even a vegan!" At this, he laughs which angers me even more.

"Me meeting him at our spot should prove that I wasn't hiding anything from you, and you've been a vegan for all of two months so what's your point?" I retort.

"Willow, please listen to yourself. I never asked you to prove anything to me. I am trying to look out for you because I have been in this game for a while now, and I wanted to help you avoid some of the drama that I have had to deal with. I never second guessed your ability to succeed or to be faithful. I have always supported your evolution, and I am not about to let you convince me otherwise. That's whack. This conversation is whack." The little vein in his neck starts to pop out, and I start to wonder if maybe I pushed him too far.

"What are you really trying to say Noah?" I ask for clarity.

"See, now you have my mom coming out here getting in our business. This conversation could have waited," he says. We watch as Yvette walks over to us.

"Hey, now I don't believe in getting in grown folks' business, but the two of you need to cool off before you say something you can't take back. I heard you yelling from in the house, and I can almost bet that the neighbors heard you," she warns.

"Sorry for disrespecting your home Ms. Yvette," I am embarrassed by my actions. My mother would be disappointed in me. A grown woman acting like a teenager in love for the first time.

"You aren't out here being disrespectful on your own." She looks over at Noah, "But I think it would be best if you two get some space before you say something you'll regret."

"You're right, ma," Noah says. Then, he walks back into the house.

"Yes, ma'am." I say, regretting my decision to come over and confront him. I look back to see if he will glance my way before walking into the house, but he goes in without saying another word to me.

57

I WAS HOPING to wake up this morning and find Noah lying next to me, but my bed is empty, and according to my call log, he hasn't returned any of my calls or responded to any of my messages. We promised to never leave things unresolved for more than twenty-four hours, but I have to catch a flight to Atlanta in less than three hours and I haven't even begun to pack. I could stop by his place on my way to the airport to try and talk things out, but the last thing I need is to show up there and find him drowning his sorrows in a woman.

◆ ◆ ◆

I smile at the flight attendant as she says farewell to me and the other passengers on our way off the plane. We landed earlier than expected, so I have thirty extra minutes of free time, which I plan to use to get food and get my head on straight. I spent the past two hours looking out the window, hoping that the clouds would give me clarity and help me find the right words to say to Noah, but no words came, and I feel as conflicted as I did when I boarded the plane. This business trip is a welcomed distraction because for the next two days, I will be able to throw myself into my work which is one area of my life where I thrive.

Most of my time will be spent on set with Soleil Chante and her team, but I plan to spend all of my free time with my sister and our parents. I haven't had the chance to tell Justice what has been going on with me and Noah, and I am not sure that I will have the opportunity to talk freely with my mother snooping around, but I will have to get creative and find time because I honestly feel that once I vent to my sister, I will know exactly what I need to say to Noah.

I knew that I still had issues and insecurities to work through, but last night served as proof that when I feel challenged or that there is even the slightest chance that I will get hurt, I put my guard up and hurt others before they have the chance to hurt me. That is why I accused Noah of being insecure and considered for even one second that he would jump into bed with another woman just as Ziggy did. The most contradicting part of it all is that I genuinely feel like Noah is the one for me, but how can I be in a relationship when I still have scars of my own to heal? Even more, how can I be with a man who shuts down and ignores me after one stupid argument?

Ready to get my day started, I toss my bag over my shoulder and walk towards the pickup area to wait for my ride. I originally planned to have Justice pick me up so that I could fill her in on the happenings of Noah and I, but Soleil Chante insisted on hiring a car service to drive me around all weekend, and I couldn't refuse her offer. Stepping onto the curb where the limousines and private cars are parked, I begin to scan the area for a chauffeur wearing a black suit and holding a sign with my name on it, but an older man wearing a light blue suit and a pair of white Chuck Taylors catches my eye instead. He is leaning against an old school Cadillac Eldorado, observing the people in the area, with his arms folded across his chest.

"Are you Willow?" He holds up a sign for me to see.

"Yes, sir. You must be my driver for the weekend." I notice the differences between him and the other drivers. They all seem serious, but this man seems comfortable in his skin, almost as if he refuses to blend in.

"Indeed I am. The name is Hollis, Hollis Gray, but most folks call me Gray because of my eyes." He removes his sunglasses for me to see.

"Then Mr. Gray it is," I say, admiring his confidence.

"I like your choice of shoes." He's pointing at my Chucks.

"I could say the same thing about yours," I chuckle.

"My granddaughters bought these things for my birthday. They said that seventy is the start of a new phase and that I needed to start dressing like it. I probably look silly, but I'd do just about anything for those two," he admits.

"Actually, you look stylish. I work in fashion, so trust me on this."

"Well, I'll be damned," he chuckles. "Let me take your bags and then we can be on our way."

"Sure thing." I hand him my bag. I discreetly snap a photo of him before getting into his car. He seems nice, but you can never be too careful, and if he happens to try anything, Justice will have his picture on the nine o'clock news.

"I was given the address to the house where you will be staying and the location for the video shoot, but if there is anywhere you would like to go over the next two days please let me know, and I will be glad to drive you." The words roll off his tongue naturally, and I can tell that he has said them many times before.

"Okay, thanks," is all I manage to say because I am by no means used to this lifestyle. I am not even sure if I like being chauffeured around, but Soleil went out of her way to make sure that I was comfortable, and I am grateful for it.

"So, where to Miss?" He turns to look back at me.

"Please call me Willow, and if it's okay, I would like to go grab some food before I go to work. If you know of any restaurants that offer plant-based options, that would be amazing. I have a big day ahead of me, and I had a rough night, so food is a must."

"I know just the place." He pulls the car away from the curb and onto the street.

As Hollis drives, I realize that we are moving further away from the city and deeper into the rural parts of Georgia, and though he is old enough to be my grandfather and seems harmless, I decide to share my location with Justice so that she can be aware of my every move over the next few days. Call it paranoia, but I do not know Hollis well enough to trust him blindly, and my mother taught me to always stay alert in situations like this. Despite my reservations, we arrive at a drive-in restaurant as promised with tons of plant-based options on the menu. In fact, after careful inspection I realize that the entire menu consists of vegan and vegetarian options which is surprising because we passed fields of cows and horses on the way here. This is not the type of establishment that I would have expected to find in this part of Georgia.

"Don't look so surprised." Hollis grins at me through the rearview mirror. "People drive from all over to try this place. It is one of the oldest black owned businesses in Georgia, and Mrs. Macy was serving plant-based food before it became a trend."

"Am I that obvious?" I laugh. "I'm just surprised is all. I have family from Georgia who swear they would never give up meat."

"I'm a Georgia man through and through, and though I would never give up barbecue or fried chicken, I find myself here at least once a week. The food is that good," he promises.

"Well, in that case, let's order, and please don't judge me for what I'm about to do," I say, rolling down the window.

"Okay." He watches me curiously.

I order most of the items on the menu. Partly, because I am hungry but mostly because I realize the importance of supporting black owned businesses, especially the ones that are staples in the community. Black people are said to spend more money than other groups on average and that money is seldomly reinvested back into the black community. Many of us do not realize the importance of supporting black owned businesses, and most of us are not taught about the contributions and sacrifices that our ancestor's made in order for us to succeed. This is one small way in which I purposely support the efforts of those that came before me and those that are out here hustling to be independent.

"I know you said not to judge you but that is a lot of food you just ordered young lady," Hollis says, jokingly.

"I don't know when I'll be out here again," I explain. "But I plan to share with Soleil and the rest of the crew. I also ordered enough for you."

"Oh, how nice. Thank you, young lady." He tips his hat at me.

"You are very welcome." I tip my imaginary hat to him. "But we are not waiting for the rest of the group to get their food before we eat. I have manners, but I'm also starving. Let's pull into a space and eat in the car like the rest of these people." I point to the row of cars filled with satisfied customers.

"Oh, I never eat in this car. It's a classic. But I could make an exception this one time. It will cost you though," he says, jokingly.

"Cost me, what?" I quickly reply.

"Soleil Chante already agreed to sign an autograph for my granddaughters, but it would make my day if you could sign one too. I recognize you from those blog things that my granddaughters read. You were with that singer fella that they love. But if that's too much of an ask, I understand." His grin is hopeful.

"You're the first person to ask for my autograph, but you have a deal." I am charmed by his confidence and striking gray eyes.

58

I PULL OUT my phone one last time before walking onto the set of Soleil Chantae's music video and quickly read over the text that I sent to Noah this morning before boarding the plane. Despite my better judgment, I reached out to let him know that I was headed to Atlanta but hoped that we would talk soon. It has been hours since I sent the text, and the message still shows as unread. Janae would have told me if something was wrong, so I will assume that the silence means that Noah is not ready to talk to me.

"Good luck, young lady," Gray says, pulling me from my thoughts.

I have been sure to keep my sadness away from him, but he is after all a grandfather of two teenage women, so navigating hidden emotions may be his specialty.

"Um, thank you." I wipe a tear from my left eye. "There's no need for you to wait around here all night. Go be with your family. I can have my sister pick me up when I'm finished here."

"Whatever you are going through is none of my business, but I am an excellent listener if you need to talk. And even more, I am an excellent driver whose specialty is riding in silence. Now, I'm getting paid to be on-call for the entire weekend, but if you prefer to be with your sister then do just that." He turns to look me in my eyes. "I haven't known you long, but I truly believe that you, young lady, know the best way to take care of yourself. That's what I always tell the women in my life," he says, encouragingly.

"Thanks, Mr. Gray, but there's no need to get all philosophical on me. I'm fine." I shrug off his words.

"Okay, then but the offer still stands. Now, off you go." He points towards the building.

"Mr. Gray?" I call after him.

"Oh, lord. Don't tell me you want to see my gray eyes again? My wife wouldn't approve of that, so I must insist that the shades stay on," he jokes.

"Actually, I was going to say thank you for the advice. It was exactly what I needed to hear."

"It was nothing. No need to thank me. Just call if you need a ride. Now if you don't mind, I'm going home to share this meal with my Queen, and you need to go inside and kick butt." He salutes me.

"Yes, sir." I return his salute.

◆ ◆ ◆

The video shoot went off without a hitch, and the director surprised everyone when he announced that we had all the footage we needed and would be wrapping things up on day one rather than the scheduled two. Soleil plans to use the free day as an opportunity to squeeze in a mini vacation with her husband since her kids are away with their grandmother for the weekend, so she is flying home later tonight to get what she described as some much-needed grownup time. Her assistant, Carla, also decided to return to Dallas but I plan to stay in Atlanta with my family where everything is peaceful and drama free.

I have not been able to peek at my phone for the past ten hours, so I run to it as if it is a long-lost love that I am finally able to reunite with. I scan through my messages, hoping to see a response from Noah, but the only people who have contacted me are Justice and my parents asking if I will make it to dinner and Janae wishing me luck. Deciding that I am no longer willing to wait for Noah to make the first move, I dial his number. The last time I checked, his schedule was free for the next few days which means that there is a chance that he can fly to Atlanta, and we can talk in person. I am hoping that once things are fixed between us, we can explore the city together and make new memories. He stayed in touch with Zion and Justice since they met at my place all those months ago, so maybe he could spend time with them as well. It could be good for us to spend time with a couple who has survived many ups and downs, and I am hoping that he answers so that we can finally address our fight and move past it.

I press my ear to the phone, nervous to have this conversation but ready to finally get it over with. After a few seconds, I realize that none of my theories or hopes matter because Noah obviously does not want to fix this. The call doesn't ring, instead it goes straight to voicemail and like a fool I try to come up with excuses for him. *Maybe it's going to voicemail because he is on his way to surprise me in Atlanta already. Or maybe he lost his phone charger and is looking for one so that he can call me and say that he is sorry for his part in our argument. Or what if something happened, and he needs me?* For a moment I consider calling his mom to make sure that he is okay, but I realize how dramatic and inappropriate that would be, and I am not that girl anymore, so I use my pent-up energy to take a couple of deep breaths, and I call my sister to pick me up from set.

59

JUSTICE AND I make an effort to see one another at least once a year, but with her growing family and our busy work schedules, it hasn't always been easy. When we see each other, it usually involves a family gathering or a social function involving friends, so I was ecstatic when my parents asked to meet for lunch tomorrow instead of dinner tonight, and Zion decided to stay home with my beautiful niece while Justice and I go have dinner by ourselves. Don't get me wrong, I love my niece, and I plan to spend most of tomorrow holding her in my arms, but first, I need a little grown up time with her mom for a few hours.

"Bring my wife back in one piece." Zion warns me as we walk out of the door. His words are playful, but I think he sensed my desperate need to be out of the house and far away from any resemblance of responsibility. Justice, on the other hand, has not said anything about my sudden urge to be out of the house which is strange because she can usually sense my moods long before I even speak the words. She has tried her best to be subtle in her efforts to study me, but I noticed her watching me as soon as I walked in their house. I get the feeling that she is trying to see why I'm off kilter but also wants to go with the flow because she needs an outing just as much as I do. So, tonight will include a bunch of fun with my sister while capturing it on video and possibly posting it to all of my social media accounts for Noah to see. The tactic is childish, but what else can a girl do?

◆ ◆ ◆

We decide to be responsible and have Gray drop us off at a restaurant that has bottomless mimosas, karaoke, and an incredible menu. I told him that I would order a ride to take us home, but he insisted on waiting for us in his car stating that he had crossroad puzzles and his tablet to keep him occupied. I feel bad about having a seventy-year old man out past nine o'clock, but he reminded me of the fact that he had been paid in advance, so I might as well take him up on his offer to deliver us home safely.

"I'm ordering some appetizers because that is your second mimosa, and you already have that goofy smile that you get when you're feeling the effects," Justice giggles.

"Don't judge me." I swat her leg playfully.

"No judgment. I just want to make sure that you're coherent enough to talk to me. I can tell something is up," she replies, knowingly.

"There is but we can talk about that later. Right now, all I want is to go up there and sing a song from my heart."

"Oh, lord." She shakes her head in disbelief.

"You know mommy always said that with a little vocal training I could be a pretty good singer."

"Go prove her right then." Justice points towards the stage.

"I will." I trot over to sing a rendition of RL and Deborah Cox's song "We Can't Be Friends".

"That's my sister!" Justice screams from the side of the stage giving me the courage I needed to keep going. I focus on her, not caring if the crowd is enjoying it or not, and my tactic works for the first minute of the song until she rudely takes a call in the middle of my performance, forcing me to focus on the faces in the crowd who are surprisingly enjoying the show. They have had access to bottomless mimosas all night, so I probably shouldn't pat myself on the back too hard.

I watch as Justice walks out of the restaurant with her phone still pressed to her ear. I force myself to finish the song, and as soon as it is over, I walk out to find her leaned against Gray's car, looking as though she is about to cry. I listen closely as she talks to who I assume to be Zion based on her tone of voice, hoping to hear something that will give me some understanding of what is happening. My heart starts to thump loudly in my chest as I watch her attempt to hold back emotions. After a few seconds, she finally ends the call but avoids making eye contact.

"Justice who was that? You're scaring me with the silence." I stand in front of her.

"Okay, fine. I tried to be good and mind my business, but what the hell is going on with you and Noah?" She grabs my hand and moves out of earshot of Gray and other pedestrians.

"Was that him on the phone? Did he really try to snitch on me?" I ask, playfully.

"No, that was Zion on the phone." She replies in a restrained voice.

"Wow, so he called my brother in law to snitch on me?" I roll my eyes. "I planned to tell you later, but I guess I can just tell you now. It's nothing serious but Noah and I had an argument a few days ago. He hasn't responded to my messages, but I know that we will talk soon. He just needs space." I shrug as if it's not a big deal, but, on the inside, I am freaking out.

"Are you sure that's all it was?" Justice frowns worriedly.

"You obviously know something that I don't, so just tell me," I respond, bluntly.

"Please don't freak out, but Zion sent this to me when you were on stage. He says it's all over the internet." She cautiously gives me her phone.

I zoom in on the picture of Noah walking into a restaurant with a pregnant woman. Then, I scroll down to look at the next image where she has her hand resting comfortably over his as they share a meal together. I study the photo for a full minute before deciding that it has to be some sort of mix-up. The paparazzi obviously wants the world to think that Noah is cheating, but there is no way that he would jump into another relationship without ending things with me first. Sure, we argued but this is not the kind of press that Noah likes.

"This has to be a lie." I try to convince her as well as myself.

"There are too many people around, and we've been drinking, so let's have Gray take us back to my house, and we can figure this out together."

Justice tries to comfort me, but my wall is already up, and my defenses are at all-time high.

"Gray can take you home, but I'm going back to my hotel."

"No. You can stay in the guest room at my house, or I can come with you to your hotel. Either way, you're stuck with me," Justice replies firmly.

"Everything okay, ladies?" Gray rolls the window down.

"Ask reporter Justice over here. She's the one who just showed me pictures of my so-called boyfriend who is out and about with his alleged pregnant girlfriend." I do air quotes around each word, completely misusing the gesture.

"Are you talking about Noah?" Gray's eyebrow raises in confusion.

"How do you know Noah?" I lean into the window.

"Let's talk about this inside the car. The last thing we need is someone recognizing you as the woman Noah is cheating on." Justice pleads with me.

"Fine," I hop into the passenger's seat. "Now, Mr. Gray, how do you know Noah? When you asked for my autograph this morning, you never said you knew his name."

"I swore I wouldn't tell, and though I feel like it's really not my place to say this, I feel like it would help if you knew the truth about who hired me to drive you around this weekend. And I must say that I do not think the young man would bring me out from retirement just to turn around and hurt you."

"So, Soleil didn't hire you?" My eyebrows rise in confusion. Soleil is the one who insisted that Gray be my driver.

"I've known Noah since he was a boy. His father and I grew up together, so I am somewhat of an uncle to him. When he called to tell me that he needed a favor, I didn't hesitate even when I learned that the favor would include driving around a spirited young lady such as yourself."

"And why would he do that?" My words come out daggers, laced with suspicion.

"He told me that this was your second biggest project to date, and he wanted to make sure that you felt supported this time around. I guess he felt like he let you down before, and the best way for him to ensure that didn't happen again was to get you the best chauffer to ever grace this earth." He smiles affectionately.

"I appreciate you for telling me this Mr. Gray, but none of this makes sense. He has literally ignored every single one of my calls for the past thirty-six hours, and he traveled all the way to Los Angeles without telling me, so even if he isn't involved with this woman romantically, he was still willing to risk being seen with her. He warned me about protecting his image, and here he is creating drama for the both of us."

"You heard what Gray said. Maybe you were right earlier. Maybe the paparazzi has it wrong, and there is a perfect explanation for it," Justice chimes in.

"Maybe they have it wrong, but maybe they have it right. Either way, I do not want to talk about this anymore. I can't right now." My voice breaks, and my throat starts to burn. If I talk about this now, I feel as though I will fall apart, and I refuse to give Noah that much power over me.

"Okay, we don't have to talk, but I think you should come over and spend some time with your niece." Justice pleads with me.

"She is pretty cute." I manage to smile between sniffles.

"I can return tomorrow morning to take you to the hotel to grab the rest of your belongings before driving you to the airport." Gray opens my door and grabs my hand to help me out.

"I actually packed my bags earlier because I wasn't sure if I'd be staying with my sister and her family. I think I'm in good hands now, and I can have my sister drive me to the airport. Thank you for everything, Mr. Gray."

"It was my pleasure." He pats my arm before turning to walk to his car.

"And hey, I know I'm just an old man, but I've been married for forty-three years. Some of my advice might be outdated, but here is my card if you ever want to talk. Noah is a good boy. Maybe give him a chance to explain?" I take the card and offer Gray a hug, but I do not promise to give Noah a chance to explain. The article was released eight hours ago, and he still has not attempted to contact me.

60

I USE MY TIME on the airplane to decompress and prepare for the questions to come from my parents, Omari, Janae, and the hundreds of people who do not know me personally but felt the need to pester me on social media all night. My parents were upset with me for skipping out on lunch, but I needed to come back home and clear my head. I still haven't heard from Noah, and I haven't attempted to contact him. Zion and Justice hovered over me all night, pretending to be interested in playing cards and watching movies until they fell asleep, but I know it was just their way of making sure that I was okay.

Justice talked nonstop on our way to the airport this morning, promising to be on the next flight to Dallas if I need her to be there for me. I assured her that I was fine and promised not to ignore her like I did after my breakup with Ziggy. My smiles may have been phony, but my words were true. This situation feels much different, and though I am confused and hurt, I do not feel attached to Noah in the same unhealthy manner as I did with Ziggy. I love Noah in a way that is unmatched to any man that has come before him, but if I have to walk away I will, and I won't allow myself to wallow on a couch for two weeks this time around.

◆ ◆ ◆

I walk into my apartment building to find Noah leaning against the door frame, his eyes pleading with me to let him in. I bypass him without saying a word, leaving the door open enough for him to follow me in. I walk into the kitchen, opening the refrigerator under the pretense of needing a bottle of water, but really, I am hoping to seem unbothered and as if I have everything under control. He leans against the counter and watches me as I rummage through the fridge, uncomfortably.

"I'm guessing you've seen the lies that are being spread?" he finally asks.

"No, I haven't seen any lies being spread about you. What lies are you referring to, Noah?" I respond sarcastically.

"Okay, so you want to have a repeat of our last conversation where nothing was solved because neither of us communicated like adults?" I ignore his question by walking into my room to start unpacking my clothes. He follows me and stands in the doorway, waiting to see if I will respond, and when I don't, he continues.

"I went to L.A. to see Nova because I needed perspective. She knows both of us, so I figured she would be the best person to help me sort out my feelings, and she did exactly that. She helped me see the part that I played in the argument, but I figured you needed space to focus on your work in Atlanta, so I didn't bother you or take any of your calls. I was trying to show you the trust that you deserve, but that was the wrong thing to do obviously."

"Obviously." I mimic his words. "Did that become obvious when paparazzi showed up to take pictures of you on your date, or did you realize that before then? I haven't heard from you until today, and I do not appreciate you showing up at my place without being invited."

"Willow, it is not what you think. I ran into Nina, my ex-girlfriend who I told you was pregnant and married months ago. I ran into her and her husband at a gas station, and he had no objection to two old friends meeting up for lunch because he trusts his wife. He is pissed about the situation, but he understands that it wasn't our doing. I'll call him if you don't believe me."

"No thanks," is all I manage to say.

"Can you say something else, please?" he pleads with me.

"I have work to do. Leave the key on the front table on your way out." I respond coldly.

"So that's it?" he says. He takes the key from his ring and hands it to me.

"You made the decision to give me space without consulting me, and you put me in a position to have to defend your actions when you swore, I would never have to. So, now I am telling you that I need space. I will pay you back for hiring Gray to drive me."

"I never asked you for money, and I am not about to start now. How much time do you need?" his voice cracks.

"You're a busy man. I'm a busy woman. Let's say maybe sometime in the future?" He frowns but nods his head in understanding and walks out of the front door without saying another word.

61

*I*AM CURRENTLY on a tour bus leaving from Memphis, Tennessee headed back to Dallas for Indigo's next show. So far, I have attended every date, using this tour as opportunity to challenge myself creatively while also gaining some distance from the drama back home. Being on tour has reminded me of the old adage, "Don't judge a book by its cover". Indigo and I have grown fairly close this past month, and I must say that David and the media's perception of him is way off. His work ethic is impeccable, and he spends all of his free time on the phone with his wife, Sophia and their newborn baby. She came to a few of the shows and schooled me on how to deal with dating a musician. She was honest when she revealed the bad parts which include lack of privacy and judgment from strangers but all of her concerns seemed to fade when she watched Indigo up on stage performing. She looks at him the way I used to look at Noah. After weeks of being on the road, I finally realize what it means to experience a person and truly love them without needing to possess them.

The day after I kicked Noah out of my apartment, Soleil reached out to confirm Gray's story, and Nina sent an email explaining that it was nothing more than a meal between two old friends. She even provided her husband's number for him to confirm Noah's story, but I didn't feel the need to contact him because I never truly doubted Noah's innocence. My reason for kicking him out was purely out of ego. I felt betrayed when he ignored me, and I felt that if I forgave him, I would be giving in which would somehow make me look weak. I refused to look weak in his eyes.

Noah reached out once, three weeks ago to let me know that he was proud of me for solidifying the tour deal with Indigo and wished me the best of luck on all of my future endeavors. It hurt to hear the man who penetrated my heart speak in such a careful and political manner, but I understand his reasoning for doing so. We didn't end things on the best of terms, and despite our family and friends attempts to help us fix things, we have been too stubborn to take their advice. Me more so than him.

Noah's spirit is strong, and like me, he can be stubborn and protective, and I fought him because I was afraid that he wanted to have me without actually accepting all of me. I now realize that he never wanted to tamper with my soul, all he wanted was to love me and be loved in return. He wanted to watch me evolve deeper into womanhood, and he was willing to step in the trenches with me to help me heal if that's what it took. I am ready to step in the trenches with him now. I just hope that I'm not too late because as much I enjoy traveling to different cities, I am ready to be back home in Dallas surrounded by familiar faces.

◆ ◆ ◆

David and Janae are coming to the festival this evening where Indigo is preforming and then the three of us are going out to dinner where David plans to propose. Janae thinks that we are going out to celebrate her birthday, but she is in store for a big surprise. As David's best friend and most likely his best man at the wedding, Noah will be at the restaurant along with Janae's parents and a few our closest friends. I plan to use this as an opportunity to finally speak with him, but I am terrified that he won't be in the same frame of mind as me. I thought about sending him a text to say that I would like to talk later, but I opted not to, deciding that it would be best to have the entire conversation in person. To put myself out there like he tried to a month ago.

"Long time, no see," David calls out from behind me.

"I see nothing's changed," I tease.

"And what exactly does that mean?" Janae locks arms with me.

"You two are cute is all." I admire the way David holds onto her.

"So were you and … never mind. We will get into that later. Let's go meet Indigo now," Janae squeals giddily.

"I have two backstage passes, but I'm only giving them to you if David promises to be on his best behavior." I eye him suspiciously.

"Hey, if the press lied on Noah then there's a chance that they misjudged Indigo too. So, I have no issue with the man. It's all love and respect on my end going forward unless he gives me a reason to feel otherwise."

"He won't." I assure him. "He's a married man and a father. The press never shows that side of him."

"You don't have to sell me on the man. I already promised not to be rude," David teases.

"In that case, follow me." I guide them to the VIP section.

"Oh, my goodness! There he is!" Janae blushes.

"Relax. It's just Indigo." I shake my head in disbelief.

"I was going to say the same thing," David confesses.

"Babe, don't get jealous. It's just that his music speaks to me."

"And mine doesn't?" Noah's voice catches me completely off guard, and I freeze like a statue.

"Now Noah you know I love your music." Janae's eyes widen.

"Noah? What are you doing here?" David says in a high-pitched tone, pretending to be shocked.

"Bro, I told you Soleil called me up at the last minute to ask if I'd perform the song we have together."

"You must have texted or left a voicemail because I didn't get it." David responds with a guilty expression.

"Oh, uh... yeah." Noah finally catches on.

"I'll be back. My assistant needs me." I hold up my phone for all to see.

"I'll come with you," Janae says in an apologetic tone.

"No. Stay here. I'll be back in a few minutes," I warn.

"Okay," she softly replies.

Grace's message couldn't have come at a more perfect time. She technically only needed me to tell her where my bobby pins were, but I used her message as an excuse to go into one of the dressing rooms and collect myself. Janae and David were doing a good thing in wanting me and Noah to reconnect, but it wouldn't have hurt them to give me some sort of warning. If I knew in advance, I could have prepared a speech or pretended to be cool and unaffected by him being here. Instead, he saw me go blank and run away like an immature child.

"What has you so spooked?" Grace looks worried.

"My ex is here." I reply, anxiously.

"Isn't that a good thing? You've talked my ear off about him for an entire month. Now is your chance to rekindle," she reasons.

"I know, but I just wasn't expecting to see him here," I admit.

"I understand that, but he's here now. So, go out there and be the amazing boss woman that we all know you to be."

"You're right. I got this." I tell myself in the mirror.

"Now go." She shoos me out of the room.

62

I MAKE MY way back to where I last saw David, Janae, and Noah, but they are nowhere in sight. Indigo's set starts in a few minutes, so I wouldn't be surprised if David and Janae already made their way to their seats to watch the show. I passed Soleil's dressing room on the way to meet Grace, so I decide to walk back in that direction in hopes that Noah will be around, preparing for his performance. I reach the door to Soleil's dressing room and hear voices filled with laughter. For a second, I wonder if I should wait to talk to Noah at the dinner tonight when we can be alone, but I channel my inner boss that Grace so kindly reminded me I had and lift my hand to knock on the door.

"Hey, are you looking for Soleil?" Noah's voice catches me off guard once again.

"No, I was actually looking for you," I admit.

"Oh ok. Well, just so you know, I didn't mean to ambush you earlier. I told Janae and David to tell you I was performing so that things wouldn't be awkward, but you know how they are. They don't listen." He chuckles softly.

"Yeah, you would have been better off sending me a text personally."

"I thought about it, but you said you needed space, and I wanted to give you room to grow," he admits.

"I appreciate that," I say softly. "You probably couldn't tell by my reaction to your being here, but I really have grown."

"I know," he says, straightforwardly.

"How do you know?" I am intrigued by his confidence in me.

"Can I tell you later tonight at the dinner? I have to go in here for a quick interview with Soleil." He looks over his shoulder at the reporter waiting on the couch.

"Sure." I feel slightly disappointed.

"Don't do that. If I see you frowning, I might be tempted to skip the interview and our performance." He smiles.

"Your fans would never forgive me, and I need to find our crazy friends anyways." I grin playfully.

"I'll see you at the restaurant, and don't run away this time," he teases.

"Last time I checked, running was something we both did...except I go to dressing rooms while you catch flights to L.A." I smile wide before sauntering away.

"That's cold, woman," I hear him say when I reach the end of the hall.

◆ ◆ ◆

With the show being in Dallas, Indigo, Soleil, and Noah received a lot of hometown love and support. I have Noah's entire album on my music playlist, and I have listened to each of his songs over a hundred times, but it felt amazing to see him on stage performing in front of thousands of screaming fans. I used to be worried about sharing him with the world but seeing him in his element assures me that this is what he was destined to do. Despite Janae's growing belly, she managed to stay on her feet during Indigo's entire set. At first, I was mad at her and David, but I realize that they were trying to help their best friends find their way back to one another. So even though I was tempted to give them a hard time, I took the high road and enjoyed being in the moment with my friends.

After the show, we each hopped in our cars and head to the restaurant where David has reserved a private section under the guise of a birthday celebration. I just arrived, and my heart is thumping loudly in my chest at the thought of sitting a few feet away from Noah. I would not be surprised if everyone inside the restaurant could hear it. I take my key out of the ignition, step out of my car, and nervously hand the valet driver my keys. I know what I have to say to Noah, but I just hope it isn't too late. I haven't heard anything about his love life since the incident a few weeks ago, but that doesn't mean he isn't seeing someone. Honestly, I wouldn't care if he was because I know that the two of us are meant to be.

When I reach the back of the restaurant, I see Noah standing in all of his six-foot-tall, beautiful browned skinned glory. He seems to be just as nervous as me when he comes over to say hi, and our exchange ends up being part handshake part hug which makes both of us laugh. Following the place cards, we take our seats which are directly across from each other. As much as I would like to blame Janae, I have a feeling that this was David's doing.

"You just missed the waitress. She already took our drink orders, but I can go to the bar and get you something if you want," Noah offers.

"No, I should probably be of sober mind tonight," I admit.

"I had the same idea." He lifts his glass of water.

"Can you believe our friends are getting engaged? Well if Janae says yes, they will be," I whisper, jokingly.

"I knew it would happen but not this soon. It's funny because Lotus actually predicted our engagement when we first started dating."

"I wonder why she didn't tell me."

"You serious?" He is shocked by my confusion. "She knew you couldn't handle it. You would have run if she put something that heavy on you."

"Yeah, I guess you're right," I admit.

"You still feel that way?" he asks.

"I told you I've grown. I realize my part in our issues, and I could have handled things much differently."

"Yeah, me too. Moms and Nova still haven't forgiven me for that L.A. trip."

"Yeah, Nova told me she beat you up like she used to when you were kids," I laugh.

"Man, Nova talks too much," he laughs. "She ignored me for two weeks, but there was no fighting."

"And I ignored you for an entire month," I say, shaking my head.

"Yeah, but I deserved it," he admits. "I'm sorry for that by the way. I didn't mean for things to turn out the way they did."

"I know, and I forgave you weeks ago honestly."

"So why didn't you reach out?" he asks.

"Sorry to interrupt" David says, clinking a fork against his glass. He is totally oblivious to the intense conversation that was brewing between Noah and me. "If I could just have your attention for a few minutes to toast the birthday girl, I would appreciate it." The room goes quiet.

"As you all know, we are here to celebrate Janae's birthday, but we are also here because I couldn't let her go another day without knowing how much she means to me. So, I have to do this now because I can't waste another minute holding this ring in my pocket." He drops to one knee, and the room fills with gasps of excitement.

"Um. What are you doing?" Janae has tears in her eyes.

"I knew I was going to marry you that day in the woods when you accidentally told me you loved me, and I have been trying to catch my balance ever since. We may have done things backwards in our parents' eyes, but I wouldn't have it any other way. You are love in its purest form, and I thank God that you are the woman who will bring my child into this world. So, Janae Omoye Hill, will you accept this ring and become my wife?"

"Fuck yes, I will!" Janae says, releasing the ugliest cry I have ever seen.

She is going to be mad once she plays the recording back and sees herself, but these are her true emotions, and I would be a bad friend if I didn't capture it.

She says yes a million more times before pulling David to stand. I watch them in awe until she decides to stick her tongue down his throat. Noah walks over to congratulate his best friend and pulls Janae in for a hug with a wide gap between them, careful not to bump her belly. It is funny to see him behave so cautious and loving towards her especially when they argue as much as they do, and it makes me wonder what he would be like as a father, but I quickly shake the thought from my head when his phone rings.

"Hey, ma." He smiles happily, but his smile quickly disappears, and it is obvious that whatever news he is getting is not good. He slides his chair away from the table seemingly lost or unsure of what to do next, so I place my hand inside of his, willing him to focus on me.

"What's wrong Noah?" I ask, hoping that he will let me support him in whatever this is.

"They just rushed my uncle to the hospital. I need to go be there with him. They said he was having trouble breathing or something like that. I'm not really sure. I think I blanked out for a second."

"Can I drive you?" I ask, sincerely. He looks as though he is about to object but nods his head in agreement.

"I'm coming with you." David grabs his keys.

"No, bro. Stay here with Janae and your family. I promise to keep you posted as soon as I know more," Noah promises.

"Okay, but please don't forget to keep me posted, and please, be careful." He pulls Noah in for a two-handed hug.

63

Ms. Yvette's eyes go wide like saucers when she sees me walking towards her with Noah. He has one arm wrapped tightly around my waist as if he is promising to never let me out of his sight again. She taps Lotus, who is kneeled down in the chair beside her, praying. The two of them exchange a knowing glance that says they knew this moment was coming, and they are happy to finally see us back together. I, however, am not confusing this moment for anything other than what it is. Noah needed me to comfort him, but that doesn't mean that he wants anything more. We can have that conversation at a later time when he is ready, but right now is not the time to hash things out.

"Have you seen him?" Noah is on the verge of tears.

"Everything is going to be fine, baby. Take a seat." Yvette pats the chair next to her.

"He was exercising and started complaining of chest pains, so we brought him to the hospital. They are doing a few tests to make sure it wasn't a heart attack." Her and Lotus share another telling look, but Noah doesn't notice, so I decide to keep it myself. I do not want to stress him out any more than he already is.

"Mrs. Lewis?" The doctor says, looking at Lotus.

"Oh, I'm not his wife. I'm just a friend of the family who happened to be there when he started having trouble. This is his sister and his nephew." She points to Yvette and Noah.

"Oh, I apologize. I just assumed ..." He smiles at Lotus awkwardly and then shifts his body to face Noah and Yvette.

"Well, I am happy to let you know that Mr. Lewis did not have a heart attack. He had a little too much excitement and indigestion is all."

"Indigestion?" Lotus is surprised by the news.

"Too much excitement?" Noah and Yvette blurt out at the same time. I giggle inwardly at the revelation. I hope what I think happened didn't happen, but if my suspicions are correct, Lotus and Buzzard were being intimate when he started having chest pains.

"You can go back to see him now. He is in room 111." The doctor says before walking over to another family in the waiting room. Lotus and Yvette make a beeline towards Buzzard's room.

"I know it was just a false alarm, but I should really be there for him. Mom and Lotus will definitely be making fun of him all night, and I need to be here to defend him," Noah laughs.

"I understand. Go handle your business."

"Can we continue our conversation soon?" he asks, nervously.

"Yeah, I would like that." I respond genuinely. He reaches down to hug me, and we go our separate ways. This is not how I expected my night to end, but I am glad that he let me be here for him.

"Hey" - I say turning back to face him - "I haven't had the chance to tell you, but I'm doing a pop-up store in a few days, and I would love for you to be there."

"I wouldn't miss it." He disappears behind the door.

64

I CANNOT TELL if I am more nervous because I am about to see Noah for the first time since the hospital or because we are moments away from the grand opening of my very first pop up store. What I do know is that I am sure of two things. The first is that this pop-up store has to be a success. The second thing is that I want Noah back in my life on a permanent basis. The lease for the store is for thirty days, and I am praying that my clothing line is well received because I literally put my all into this project, and it has to pay off. There will be a lot of high-profile people in attendance tonight along with a few reporters, so word should definitely be spread about the store, but those things do not guarantee success. I also have several people who are near and dear to my heart coming out to support me. My family will of course be here along with Lotus, Zane, Yvette, Janae, David, Indigo Soul, Sophia, Soleil Chantae, and a few of the women from the retreat.

"I think we're ready to open," Grace says. She gives the store one last once-over before switching the sign from closed to open.

The two of us have grown closer the past two months, and she assists me with my projects from time to time. After that night at the club all those months ago, I was suspicious of her, so I ignored her as much as I could on tour, but the close quarters made it nearly impossible to avoid one another. Then one day, I was talking to Indigo, and he told me that Grace admitted her mistake the night after it happened, and I decided that if she was willing to risk her job to protect his image then maybe she wasn't so bad after all, and it turns out that she is genuinely a good person.

"Yeah, it's time." I give her the go ahead.

The neon sign lights up and, *This Is What You've Been Looking For,* blinks in all of its neon glory. With happy tears in my eyes, I take a deep breath and twist the knob to open the door. People start to pile in, and I instantly realize that Noah is not amongst them, but the night is still young, and he said he would not miss this for anything, and I believe him.

My parents are the first to make their way over to me, each holding one of the complimentary freshly squeezed juices that the staff are serving. Anyone who knows me knows that I love fresh juices, so it made sense to serve it at the grand opening of my store. So, we have a selection of watermelon and mango juice being served alongside the champagne. My dad is somehow managing to carry six outfits with his free hand, and my mom looks as though she is about to add two more to the pile. I laugh as I watch them exchange silent looks, and after a sixty-second stare down, she puts the three of the outfits back on the rack where she found them.

I smile as I watch David and Janae walk in with Omari, Justice, and my brother-in-law Zion. They are all whispering and smiling about something, and if I didn't have to give this speech right now, I would totally be in the middle of the conversation, but duty calls, so I grab one of the champagne flutes and watch as the servers offer one to each of my guests. I notice a few of the women from the retreat, and I tip my cup to them in gratitude, promising to make my way over to them after my speech. Lotus and Yvette must have come when my head was down because I spot them standing near my family towards the back of the room. Justice or Janae had to have introduced them to my parents because they haven't met before today, but they are laughing and talking like people who have known each other for years.

"Excuse me everybody, if I can please have your attention for a few moments. I would like to say thank you for coming out to the Grand opening of *For the Love of Fashion*." Cheers and whistles ring out giving me an extra boost of confidence.

"I never expected to be standing is this crowd surrounded by beautiful people such as yourselves, but here I am, and I am so excited to introduce you to my clothing line. Please, use tonight as an opportunity to laugh, have fun, do a little networking and for the love of God spend some money to let me know that you enjoyed the fashion." I raise my glass, and everyone joins me in toasting to the success of my new business venture.

After about an hour, I finally make my way over to a few of the women from the retreat. They laugh as I hand them my business card which they waited over a year to receive. We make plans to meet up in California in the next few months as sort of a group reunion and celebration for all our growth, and I pull each of them into an embrace before making my way over to my family.

"Did you see how many items mama had in her hand?" Justice laughs.

"Yeah, and daddy looked like he was about to throw a fit," I giggle.

"The two of them are a mess but not as big of a mess as you," she accuses.

"What did I do?" I am confused by her change of tone.

"You've been looking around the room every few seconds, and I can only imagine who you are searching for," Omari blurts out.

"Am not." I revert to my childhood years.

"Are too," he rebuts.

"Am not," I say more firmly.

"Okay, well in that case, it shouldn't be a big deal that he is on his way over here at this very second?" Justice says, sporting a grin.

"Lies." I am determined not to fall for her trick.

"No, she's serious," Omari says.

"Like I would believe you?" I reply, blowing him off.

"Hey, sorry, I'm late." Noah's voice stuns me into silence.

"We're just glad you could make it." Omari answers for me.

"Yeah, we're happy to see you," Justice adds.

"Would you mind if I steal your sister away for a few minutes?" He acknowledges both Omari and Justice.

"Take her," Omari says, sarcastically.

"It's cool with me if it's cool with her." Justice studies me.

"Yea, we can go talk in my office, but only if you let me talk first." I suddenly feel bold.

"Whatever you want." He follows my lead.

"Okay, so this is the thing." I turn to him. "This apology is long over-due, but I need you to know that I regret shutting you out when what I should have done is communicated with you. I am so sorry for starting a relationship with you when I obviously had issues that needed to be sorted out first, and I apologize for overlooking your attempts to love and nur-ture me. I want you to know that I believed you when you said that you and Nina were meeting for lunch as friends, and as angry as I was, I can honestly say that I forgive you. You never needed my permission to spend time with a friend, that isn't where my upset came from. I was just hurt that you hopped on a plane and ignored me for days, but I also understand that I have done the same thing to you many times except in different ways. Like being awkward with Indigo and accusing you of being jealous, for example, but I want you to know that he is a good friend and nothing more. I should have said that two months ago."

"Do me a favor and take a deep breath," he chuckles. "Me and Indigo squashed our beef a while ago, but thank you for your apology. It only makes sense that I follow your lead and apologize for my part. Is that cool with you?" he asks.

"Of course." I feel relieved.

"First, I have to apologize for being impatient when I knew you still needed time. I never wanted to consume or control you, I just wanted to be with you. I apologize for asking you to trust me to lead you and then screwing things up when you finally began to trust me. I led you without a clear understanding of where I wanted to go, and most importantly, I didn't give you the chance to understand that it is also your job to lead me and allow me to learn from you."

"Can you say that whole speech again in front of David?" I say, jokingly.

"I'll say it in front of the entire party if that's what it takes." He pulls me closer and hugs me. "I missed you. I missed us."

"Did you, now?" I look into his eyes.

"Don't laugh at me for saying this, but I think you're imprinted on my soul." He shakes his head in embarrassment. "And I could walk away if I thought that's what you really wanted, but I'd be walking around feeling like part of me is missing."

"I'm so sorry!" Grace says, knocking on the door. Fate seems to have a way of interrupting us every time we get closer to resolving our issues. "I hate to disturb you, but some very important people just came through the door, and I don't think you should let them leave without introducing yourself."

"Okay. I'll be right out." I pull away from Noah.

"Duty calls." He releases me from his grasp. "I should be heading out anyways. I have to pick up Nova and my niece from the airport. They were sad they couldn't make it to the opening, but I'm sure they will in here tomorrow buying up the whole store."

"Yeah, I actually invited her to have brunch with me and the family tomorrow. You are more than welcome to join if that isn't too soon for you." We've been broken up for a while, and I don't want to force him to jump back in if he isn't ready.

"I made plans already, but I'll get back to you with a for sure answer in the morning if that's cool?"

"Yep, no problem." I smile, but all I really want to do is tell him to cancel whatever plans he's made to be with me.

65

I WAKE UP feeling ecstatic at how well last night went. Not only was my grand opening a success, but I also made up with Noah which in itself is a huge accomplishment. A few of us went out to celebrate last night which is why it is eleven o'clock, and I am still lying in bed, but I have guests meeting me for brunch, so I need to get up and ready. I hear Omari rustling around in the living room, attempting to be quiet, but the sounds coming from the television and loud whispering between my parents are enough to pull me from underneath the covers. I pull my phone from the charger to see if Noah texted me, but I have zero messages and zero missed calls. Disappointed, I walk into the living room to see what all of the commotion is about.

"Good morning, sleepy head. We were trying not to wake you, but some of us are loud and have no etiquette." My mom grins at Omari.

"That was you and your husband doing all the loud talking, but she needed to wake up, anyways. We have to leave for brunch in thirty minutes, and I am starving, so go shower and brush your teeth. Run a comb through your hair if you're feeling up to it." I roll my eyes at Omari's snide comment. If mommy wasn't in front of me, I would give him the finger.

"Ouch." He grabs his ear. Mommy gave him an old-fashioned thump which is so satisfying that I take his advice and head in the bathroom to shower.

◆ ◆ ◆

All of my invited guests arrive to the restaurant on time which almost never happens. I usually have to lie and say an event is starting an hour earlier for people to show up on time, but I guess they decided to be on their best behavior and arrive on time since my parents planned today's outing. I smile as we follow the hostess to a more private section of the restaurant that has outdoor seating and tables for big groups such as this one. It is a perfect seventy-degree day and the venue couldn't be more perfect.

"There's an empty seat by me if anyone wants it." I notice that no one seems interested in taking the seat to the left of me.

"Oh, we left that seat open in case Noah could make it," Nova says, apprehensively.

"Oh ok. I haven't heard from him, so I just assumed he wasn't coming."

"He had an errand to run, but I'm sure he will be here." She offers a hopeful smile.

"Hey, Willow. Will you come with me to the restroom?" Justice interrupts my conversation with Nova.

"Sure." I am not really interested in hearing her lecture me on how well I have done without Noah, but still, I follow my sister into the restroom.

"Everything okay?" She freshens up her lipstick.

"Yes, everything is great, and I do not need a lecture."

"I wasn't going to lecture you. I just wanted to make sure that you were okay. You looked disappointed when Nova mentioned that Noah was coming. I thought you would be happy about that."

"I am, but I haven't heard from him since last night. He told me that he would text me today to let me know if he was coming, but I understand if he can't make it. I'm here to have a good time, and I don't want to make tonight all about me and Noah's relationship," I say, honestly.

"Okay, well I will let it go, but I'm here if you need to talk. Now, let's go celebrate your successes because my baby sister is a boss!" She shouts proudly before putting her arm over my shoulder and leading me back to the table.

My smile widens when I see Noah sitting in the chair next to mine. I also notice his father, Elgin, sitting at the end of the table between Lotus and Yvette. I assume that he snuck in with Noah when I was in the restroom because he wasn't here a second ago.

"Hey." Noah stands to hug me. He places a soft kiss on my forehead and then he timidly kisses me on my lips. Everyone awes in approval except for Omari who makes a gagging sound. We laugh at his silliness and kiss one more time before taking our seats.

"Thanks for ordering me a drink." I am grateful for the orange pineapple mimosa sitting in front of me. The waiter must have taken drink orders when I was in the restroom because everyone has a drink sitting in front of them including me. I take a sip of the orange pineapple mixture and smile giddily when everyone lifts theirs in salute to me.

"No problem. The waitress should be back in a second to take your food order." He looks around for her.

"There she is now." Nova gives the waitress the thumbs up from across the room.

"I'll be right there." The lady replies before dashing off.

"That was weird." I laugh. "She must be super busy or starstruck." I smile over at Noah.

"Chill out," he laughs. "I am sure she probably went to grab a menu or something."

"Twenty bucks says she comes back without menus."

"I'll take that bet." He holds his hand out for me to shake.

"Here she comes now." Nova is intrigued by our bet.

I look over my shoulder to find her walking towards us with a guitar in her hand.

My heart races as Noah stands from his seat and takes the guitar from her hands and places the strap over his shoulder. Our table is secluded from the rest of the restaurant, but I have no doubt that people are going to walk our way once they hear his beautiful and probably familiar voice. I smile nervously as Noah starts to sing "Ready for Love" by India Arie. The song we danced to over a year ago in a record store.

"What are you doing?" I watch him slowly remove the guitar from his chest and drop down on one knee. I look around the table, and it is obvious that everyone knew this was about to happen because Justice, Nova, and Janae have their phones out, recording the entire interaction.

"Willow, the past month has been one of the toughest times in my life but also one of the most profound. I learned what it felt like to be without you, but I also got to watch you flourish in ways that I always knew you would. I've been holding onto this ring for six months now, and I don't want to wait another second to see it on your finger. I know things won't always be easy, but I want you by my side. I know this may seem random and reckless, but will you marry me?"

"Yes!" I pull him up to me and crash my mouth onto his. He moans when my tongue reaches out to greet his.

"Oops. Sorry." I break our kiss to apologize to my parents and soon to be in laws. They all laugh and clap in approval.

Epilogue

I am sitting on the front porch watching my three-year-old son laugh hysterically as his cousin chases after him in a game of tag. If my belly wasn't so big, I would be out there with my feet in the grass chasing both of them, but Noah made me promise to relax until his baby girl arrives, and that is exactly what I am doing. My feet are up, and I am reading old journal entries from five years ago when I had no clue how life would turn out, but I dared to dream anyways. I smile as I watch Hendrix run up the porch steps frantically, deciding to make me base and keep him safe from Dallas, his cousin who is only a year and a half older but swears that she is so much bigger than him. We agreed to babysit for a few days, knowing that Janae and David will return the favor once our baby girl is born, but a newborn will probably put up less of a fit than Dallas does. She truly has her mama's fierceness.

"I'm thirsty mama." My son rubs his tired eyes. It is his naptime, but he is fighting to stay awake.

"Your daddy just made a fresh pitcher of watermelon juice, so let's go inside and drink some. Then, we will have naptime because daddy is working on a song and needs to focus."

"Only babies take naps," Dallas protests.

"Oh yeah?" I challenge her. "Your mom told me your naptime was at two o'clock. I guess I will have to call her to see if I heard wrong."

"No auntie Lo', do not call my mom." She sticks her bottom lip out.

"Fine, but both of you need to go wash your hands, and I will have some snacks ready when you get back. *Then* it's naptime." I give them both a stern look and they sprint towards the bathroom, turning handwashing into yet another one of their competitions. I laugh at their silliness as I pull two cookies from the jar and pour them each a glass of juice. This isn't the healthiest snack, but I can't make them eat healthy when I plan to devour a cookie in front of them.

Just as I stuff two cookies into my mouth, I feel Noah's arms wrap around my waist. The water is still running in the bathroom which means we have exactly thirty seconds before the kids are back demanding their snack. Noah presses a kiss against the side of my neck and moves his hands up higher to rub my belly. He turns me around and kneels so that he is eye level with my stomach. He does this at least twice a day, and I can't say that I mind it at all. He did the same when I was pregnant with Hendrix and the two of them are as thick as thieves.

"Are you talking to Lyric, daddy?" Hendrix says, kneeling beside his father.

"Yeah, and she said to tell you that she can't wait to meet you. She already thinks you're the coolest big brother." Hendrix's eyes go wide with pride, and my heart melts into a thousand pieces.

"Did she say anything about having an awesome cousin?" Dallas places her hand on my belly.

"She sure did. She told me to tell Dallas that she can't wait to be big enough to play tag with her."

Dallas laughs, "She did not say that Uncle Noah."

"Yes, she did." He picks her up and tickles her until she screams in surrender.

"Babe, it's time for these two to eat their snacks and take a nap. Mommy needs a nap too." I finally release the yawn that I've been holding in all afternoon.

"Let me handle snack time and I'll come find you when I put them down for their nap." Noah places a soft kiss to my lips and shoos me out of the kitchen.

◆ ◆ ◆

I can hear the kids attempting to negotiate their naptime, but Noah stands firm in his decision. After spending several minutes debating on which sound to listen to on the sound machine, the kids finally agree on rain sounds, and Noah puts them to bed. A few moments later, I hear his footsteps coming down the hall, and I quickly close my eyes and pretend to be asleep. I clamp my lips shut, desperate to avoid laughing and giving myself away. He starts to tickle the bottom of my feet, getting the exact reaction he hoped for.

"Fine. I'm awake." I squeal with laughter.

"I can go do some work if you really want to take a nap, babe. I know you've been up with the kids all morning, and I know it's not easy carrying baby girl in there." He moves higher onto the bed and places a kiss on my stomach. He spoils me in more ways than I can count, but he is definitely going to give his daughter the royal treatment.

"I could definitely use a nap, but I want to show you something first. Hand me that journal." I point to the gold embossed manifestation journal that Lotus bought me as a wedding present five years ago.

"Read here." I point to the paragraph written in green ink.

"Okay." He reads the passage aloud.

I have finally learned what it means to be impeccable with my word, and I communicate so much better now that I have released the pain that I was holding onto from past relationships. I also learned to forgive myself for the role that I played in the demise of my own happiness. I am a mother now to two healthy, beautiful, intelligent children. I have a career that allows me flexibility and provides so much purpose and joy. My husband loves himself and understands the importance of self-care. He did his work prior to our marriage (as did I), so when we joined together, our union was sacred, and we put sincere effort into learning what it means to love and honor one another. I realize now that we will continue to change and grow as individuals and that it is important to support one another on our personal and collective journeys. I could not have chosen a better life partner, and I am excited to spend the rest of my life with him by my side.
Ase. So it is. Amen.

Tears gleam in Noah's eyes when he finishes reading. He places the journal back on the nightstand and walks over to lock the door. Hendrix loves to bust in our room, and apparently, my husband does not want to be interrupted for whatever he is about to do to me. He takes his rightful place on the bed and lifts my chin so that our mouths are aligned. He slides his tongue into my mouth and kisses me hungrily. I lift up to remove his shirt from his body and trail kisses down his neck. He reaches down to remove my clothes, but I feel a sudden gush of water.

"Babe, I think my water just broke," I say, frantically. I've given birth before, but it's been three years, and I am not due for another week.

"Okay, umm. I'll call the midwife and the doula and your doctor and our parents and your siblings and my sister and who else? Who else needs to be here?" he asks, frantically.

"Our parents can come watch the kids, but I only want the two of us to be in the room during the birth. We can update everyone else once the baby is here, but for now, we need to call our doctor so that he knows it's happening, then call Lotus since she is our doula, and of course call our midwife." Noah grabs his cellphone to update the entire team of birthing experts and our family, and three hours later, Lyric Marie Daniels is born.

The End

Acknowledgements

There are so many people that I must thank but I can't start without saying thank you to the *readers* first. So, dear readers, thank you for going on this journey with me. I believe that this book will be the first of many and your support is truly appreciated.

Thank you to my mother. You are my biggest cheerleader and I love you so much! No words could ever truly explain how grateful I am.

Thank you to my father. You speak excellence and boldness over my life daily and because of you I know that I have to keep going even when I'm afraid.

Thank you to my best friend Jelisa Lynn for putting in hours of your time helping me edit as well as coaching me through doubt on many occasions. I am beyond grateful.

Thank you to my sisters Taray and Tye for always being so honest while also being supportive. Thank you for believing in me and my journey.

To my brother Terrell and my sister Parnaessa. I love you both. P, thank you for always supporting me.

Thank you to DJ Norman for your support and constant encouragement. I appreciate you.

Thank you to Alessandra, my spiritual homie. Thank you for your continuous words of encouragement and for being a huge book nerd like me.

Thank you to Eddy for this amazing author's photo. Much gratitude.

Thank you to Buzzard who I met only once years ago. Though the actions of the character, Uncle Buzzard, who was mentioned in this book were completely made up. The real Buzzard was a grandfather to a friend of mine. As I mentioned, we only met once but during that meeting he lectured me on love and told me to remember to choose myself over any man. His words stuck with me and once I learned of his passing, I knew that I wanted to honor him in some way, and I was able to with this book.

Thank you to Tia Cole at The Cole Lab LLC for being an editing genius.

Thank you to Jessie York, Graphics Specialist, at Ngenius Mindz Design for this amazing book cover.

Thank you to Sarah Blondin who will probably never see this but your meditations on Insight Timer continue to inspire me.

Thank you to Jalisa, Chris, Jarika, and Mrs. Brad for your support.

Talisha Renee believes that self-care and healing can be achieved through the power of word. At a time where she felt lost, writing was her return to freedom. She feels that the power of word is her mother, father, and ancestor's way of reminding her that she has a voice that needs to be heard. She lives in Texas with her family.

Made in the USA
Coppell, TX
14 January 2021